LEGO DC UNIVERSE SUPER HEROES

LAST LAUGH!

STORY BY TREY KING
ILLUSTRATED BY
KENNY KIERNAN

SCHOLASTIC INC.

ISBN 978-0-545-48029-1

12 11 10 9 8 7 6 5 4 3 2 13 14 15 16 17 18/0
PRINTED IN THE U.S.A. 40
FIRST PRINTING, AUGUST 2013

FLYING OVER METROPOLIS IS A HERO WHO CAN LEAP BUILDINGS IN A SINGLE BOUND, LIFT CARS ABOVE HIS HEAD, FREEZE CROOKS WITH HIS BREATH, AND HEAR THINGS MILES AWAY.
THIS IS THE WORLD'S PROTECTOR. THIS IS SUPERMAN!
HELP!
SOUNDS LIKE SOMEONE NEEDS MY HELP.

THE VILLAINS BANE AND MR. FREEZE ARE ROBBING METROPOLIS BANK. WONDER WOMAN IS TRYING TO STOP THEM, BUT MR. FREEZE'S FREEZE GUN IS KEEPING HER AT A DISTANCE.
METRO BANK
100
STOP IN THE NAME OF JUSTICE, CRIMINALS!
ZAP!
ZAP!
DON'T YOU MEAN, "FREEZE"?!

SUPERMAN SWOOPS ONTO THE SCENE TO HELP HIS FRIEND.
PUT THE MONEY BACK WHERE IT BELONGS.
OR ELSE.
OR ELSE WHAT?
POW!!!
WITH ONE PUNCH, SUPER-STRONG BANE KNOCKS SUPERMAN THROUGH A WALL.
CRASH!!
OUCH!

SUPERMAN IS QUICK TO GET BACK IN THE BATTLE. BUT IT SEEMS MR. FREEZE HAS A DARING TRICK IN STORE FOR SUPERMAN . . .
. . . HIS GUN IS LOADED WITH SUPERMAN'S ONE WEAKNESS: KRYPTONITE!
ZZZZAP!
SUPERMAN, ARE YOU OKAY?
I DON'T FEEL SO WELL.

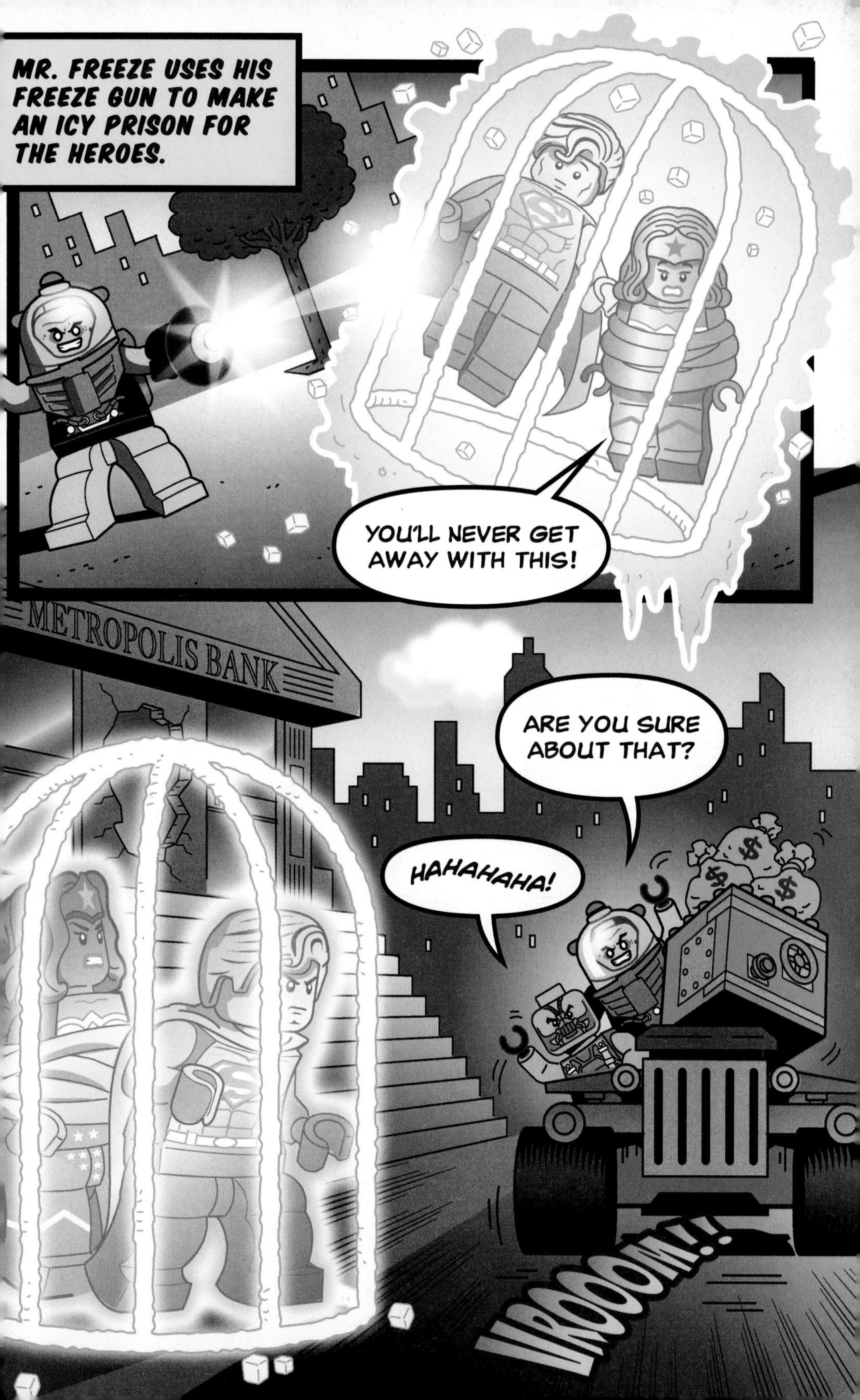
MR. FREEZE USES HIS FREEZE GUN TO MAKE AN ICY PRISON FOR THE HEROES.
YOU'LL NEVER GET AWAY WITH THIS!
METROPOLIS BANK
ARE YOU SURE ABOUT THAT?
HAHAHAHA!
VROOOM!!

WHAT ARE WE GOING TO DO?
WE'LL CALL A FRIEND FOR HELP.
WHO?
BATMAN!
SUPERMAN USES HIS WALKIE-TALKIE TO CALL BATMAN! WITHIN MINUTES, GOTHAM CITY'S DARK KNIGHT ARRIVES TO HELP!
WHERE DO YOU TWO THINK YOU ARE GOING?
THAT MONEY DOESN'T BELONG TO YOU!
KABOOM!
SCREEECHHH!!

AFTER WRECKING BANE'S TUMBLER, BATMAN SWOOPS IN TO STOP THE COLD CRIMINALS.
WHAP!
YOU'RE RUINING ALL OF OUR FUN!
YOU SHOULD HAVE THOUGHT OF THAT BEFORE YOU MESSED WITH MY FRIENDS.
OH, AND STEALING MONEY IS BAD, TOO!

BATMAN CATCHES THE CRIMINALS QUICKLY AND NOW HE HAS QUESTIONS FOR THEM.
WHO HELPED YOU ESCAPE FROM ARKHAM ASYLUM?
AND WHO HIRED YOU TO ROB A BANK IN METROPOLIS?
WE'LL NEVER TELL!
THEN I GUESS I'LL HAVE TO TELL YOUR *MOMS*.
NO, PLEASE DON'T! WE'LL GET GROUNDED!
IT WAS LEX LUTHOR! HE MADE US!

ONCE THE CROOKS ARE SAFELY BEHIND BARS, BATMAN RETURNS TO HELP HIS FRIENDS.
THANKS, BATMAN.
WHAT CAN I SAY? I'M THE BEST.
SO ARE WE!
YEAH, BUT YOU CALLED *ME* TO SAVE YOU.
THERE'S NOTHING WRONG WITH ASKING YOUR FRIENDS FOR A HELPING HAND.
ONLY BABIES NEED HELP.

YOU'LL NEVER CATCH ME ASKING FOR HELP.
EVERYONE NEEDS AID SOMETIMES.
NOT ME.
GOTHAM CITY IS ALWAYS IN TROUBLE, SO BATMAN FLIES AWAY IN A HURRY.
HE CAN BE SO STUBBORN!
ONE DAY, HE'LL LEARN. . . .

A FEW DAYS LATER, BATMAN IS IN GOTHAM CITY. HE IS DRIVING AFTER THE VILLAINOUS TWO-FACE IN A DANGEROUS STREET CHASE.
WHY DO VILLAINS ROB BANKS SO OFTEN?!
I HAVE A VERY EXPENSIVE VIDEO GAME HABIT.

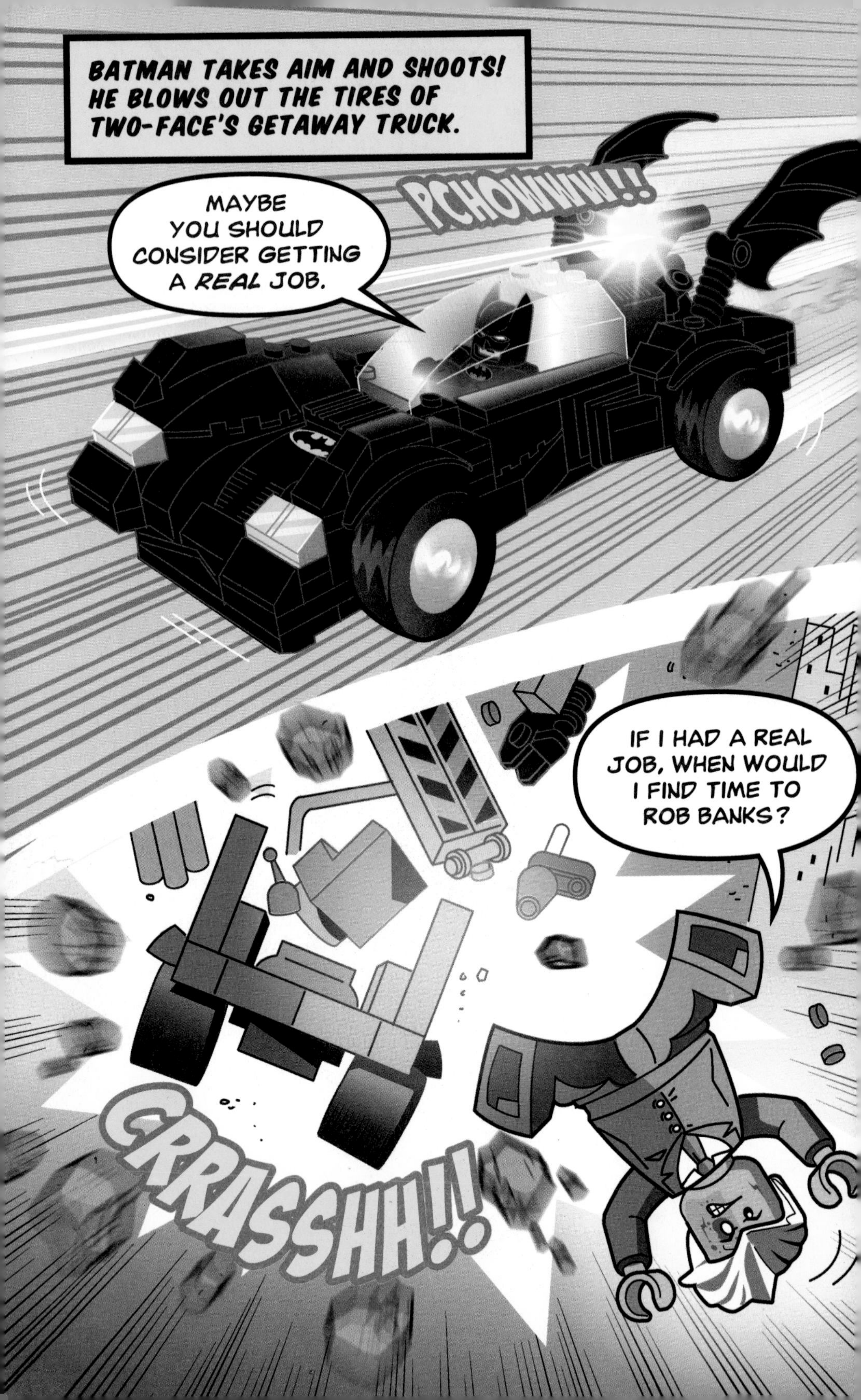
BATMAN TAKES AIM AND SHOOTS! HE BLOWS OUT THE TIRES OF TWO-FACE'S GETAWAY TRUCK.
PCHOWWW!!
MAYBE YOU SHOULD CONSIDER GETTING A *REAL* JOB.
IF I HAD A REAL JOB, WHEN WOULD I FIND TIME TO ROB BANKS?
CRRASSHH!!

I GUESS YOU'LL HAVE PLENTY OF TIME TO THINK ABOUT YOUR CAREER BEHIND BARS, TWO-FACE.
BATMAN!
SWAT
BUT BATMAN'S WORK IS NEVER DONE. COMMISSIONER GORDON, HEAD OF GOTHAM CITY'S POLICE, NEEDS BATMAN'S HELP.
GOTHAM CITY IS IN TROUBLE.
THERE'S AN ARMY OF VILLAINS IN POWER ARMOR ROBBING THE BIGGEST BANK IN TOWN!
SWAT
I'M ON MY WAY!

BATMAN'S WORST ENEMIES HAVE COME TOGETHER TO ROB GOTHAM CITY'S BIGGEST BANK. THE RIDDLER, POISON IVY, THE PENGUIN, AND HARLEY QUINN ARE ALL ON A RAMPAGE. HOW CAN BATMAN FIGHT SO MANY ON HIS OWN?
HERE'S A RIDDLE— WHAT LIKES TO BE STOLEN, THEN SPENT? MONEY!
CRASHH!
I CAN'T WAIT TO BUY MORE CLOWN SUITS!
SMASHH!
CRUSHH!
MY FAVORITE COLOR IS GREEN – THE COLOR OF PLANTS AND CASH!
ACK, ACK. THE ONLY THING BETTER THAN CHICKEN NUGGETS IS GOLD NUGGETS!

MEANWHILE, ON A NEARBY ROOFTOP, THE JOKER AND LEX LUTHOR ARE WATCHING THE MAYHEM!
EVERYTHING IS GOING ACCORDING TO MY PLAN.
DON'T YOU MEAN *OUR* PLAN, LEXY?
DON'T CALL ME THAT!
WHEN BATMAN COMES O SAVE THE DAY, WE'LL AP HIM AND I'LL FINALLY HAVE THE LAST LAUGH.
WHAT ARE YOU GOING TO *DO*?
I AM GOING TO DO SOMETHING *TERRIBLE* TO HIM. . . .

FIRST, I'LL TIE HIM UP...
THEN I'LL UNMASK HIM...
HA! HA! HO HO HO HO! HA HEE HEE HO HA HA HA!!
THEN I'M GOING TO PAINT HIS FACE WHITE AND HIS LIPS RED, AND THEN I'LL GIVE HIM GREEN HAIR, THEN I'LL GIVE HIM A *FUNNY MOUSTACHE*!
HO HO! HA! HA HA!! HO HO! HEE HEE! HA! HARDY-HAR-HAR!! HA!
SO BASICALLY YOU'RE JUST GOING TO MAKE HIM LOOK LIKE YOU, BUT WITH A *MOUSTACHE*?
MOUSTACHES ARE *FUNNY*!

WHILE THE JOKER AND LEX LUTHOR DISCUSS THEIR PLANS, BATMAN SWINGS INTO ACTION. FIRST, HE TAKES DOWN THE PENGUIN.
WAP!!
WHY ME FIRST? ACK, ACK!
YEAH, BATMAN. DON'T YOU KNOW?
LADIES FIRST.

BATMAN JUMPS BETWEEN HARLEY QUINN AND POISON IVY, TRICKING THEM INTO BLASTING EACH OTHER.
AGH! NO FAIR.
KAPOW!!
YOU MESSED UP MY HAIR!
SMASH!
WHERE'D THE FOURTH ONE GO? DID I ALREADY WIN?

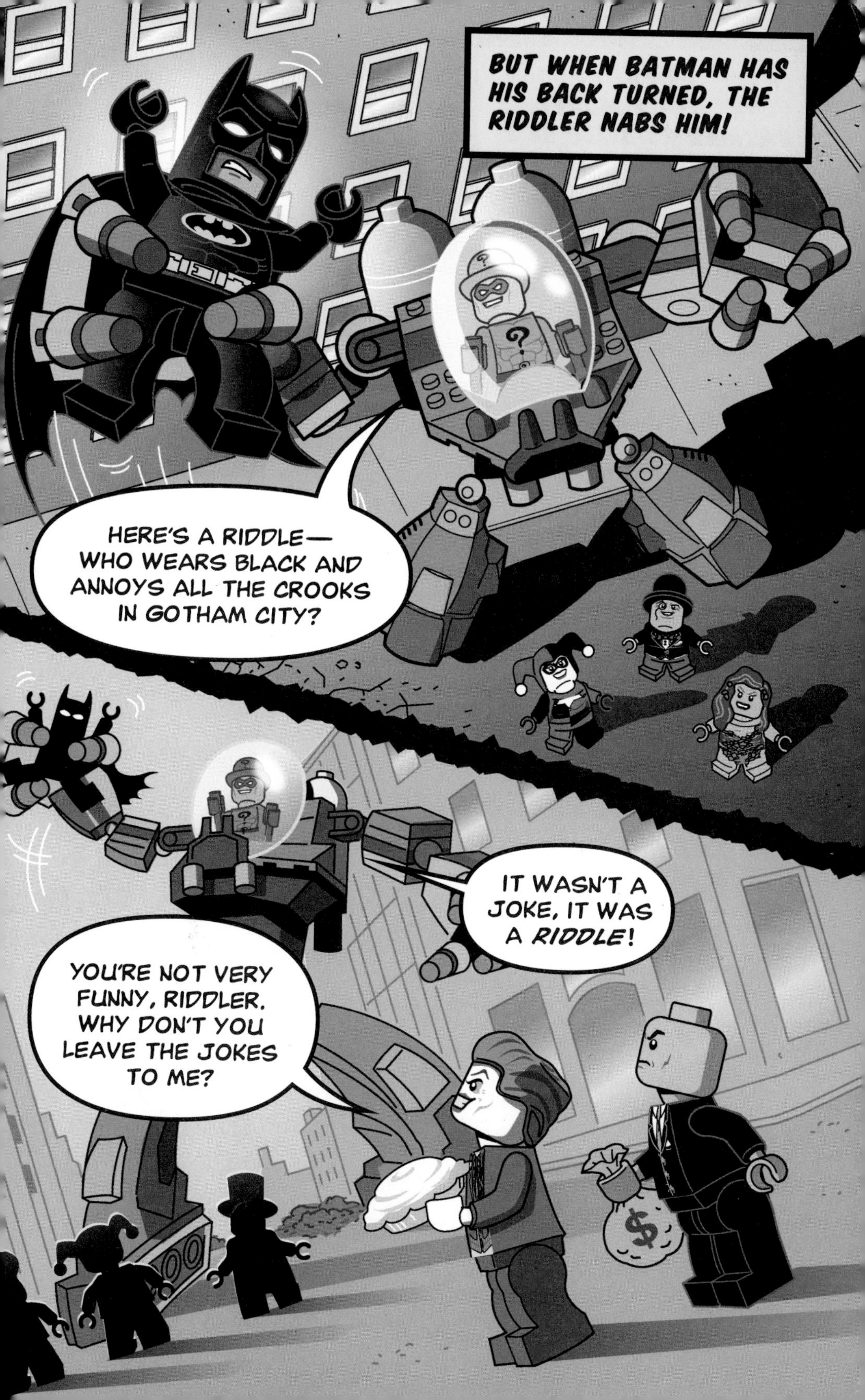
BUT WHEN BATMAN HAS HIS BACK TURNED, THE RIDDLER NABS HIM!
HERE'S A RIDDLE— WHO WEARS BLACK AND ANNOYS ALL THE CROOKS IN GOTHAM CITY?
YOU'RE NOT VERY FUNNY, RIDDLER. WHY DON'T YOU LEAVE THE JOKES TO ME?
IT WASN'T A JOKE, IT WAS A *RIDDLE*!

LATER, AS THE CROOKS COUNT THEIR MONEY, BATMAN REALIZES HE'S IN REAL TROUBLE. HE NEEDS HELP.
WHERE'S MY FACE PAINT?!
BATMAN NEEDS A *MOUSTACHE MAKEOVER*!
BATMAN REMEMBERS WHAT SUPERMAN SAID ABOUT ASKING FRIENDS FOR HELP.
UH. . . SUPERMAN. I THINK I OWE YOU AN *APOLOGY*. . . .

JUST A FEW MINUTES LATER, BATMAN WONDERS IF IT'S TOO LATE FOR HIM.
...IT'S TIME TO TEACH BATMAN A LESSON ABOUT MESSING WITH THE VILLAINS OF GOTHAM CITY AND METROPOLIS.
MAKEUP KIT
YOU'RE ABOUT TO GET A *MOUSTACHE* YOU WON'T SOON FORGET—
THE JOKE'S ON *YOU*, JOKER...

JUST AS JOKER AND LEX LUTHOR ARE ABOUT TO UNMASK BATMAN, SUPERMAN SHOWS UP, AND HE ISN'T ALONE. HE BROUGHT HELP!
WONDER WOMAN!
GREEN LANTERN!
THE FLASH!
...NO ONE MESSES WITH ONE OF OUR FRIENDS!
...AND AQUAMAN!

THE RIDDLER MAY BE SMART, BUT THE FLASH IS THE FASTEST MAN ALIVE!
I HAVE A RIDDLE FOR YOU—
NO, THANKS, I'M ALREADY BORED!
POISON IVY CAN CONTROL ALL LIVING PLANTS, BUT SHE CAN'T CONTROL THE WILLPOWER OF A GREEN LANTERN!
HEY, WHAT'RE YOU—?
HEY! GREEN IS SUPPOSED TO BE MY THING.

THE PENGUIN MAY BE GOOD WITH BIRDS, BUT AQUAMAN IS EVEN BETTER WITH SEA LIFE!
ACK, ACK, BIRDS EAT FISH!
SMASH!
NOT *THIS* TIME, BIRD.
CRRASSHHH!!!

AND HARLEY QUINN MAY BE THE BADDEST GIRL IN TOWN, BUT SHE'S NO MATCH FOR THE MIGHT OF WONDER WOMAN!
YOU'LL NEVER CATCH ME, TOOTS!
WANNA BET?
KLONK!

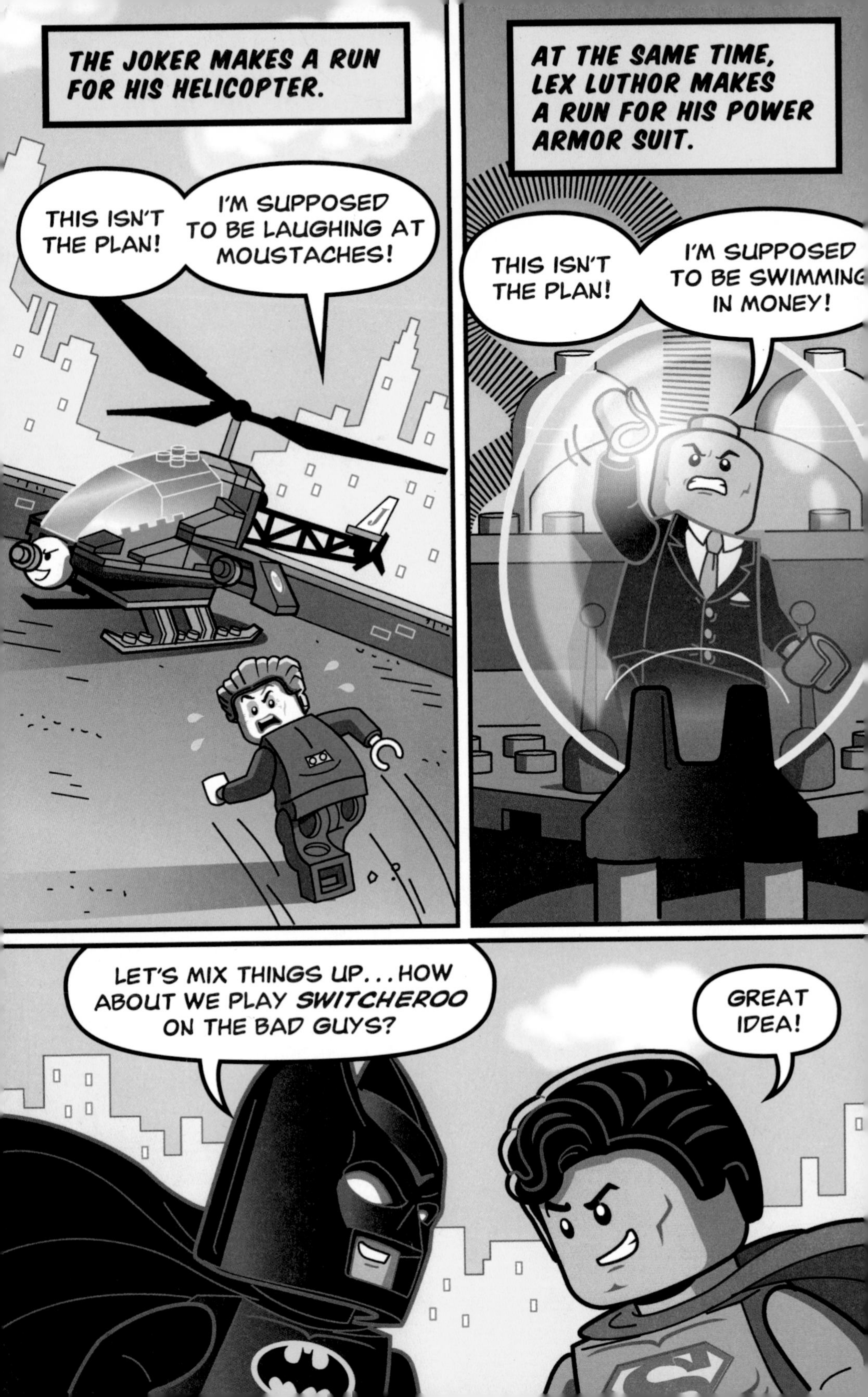
THE JOKER MAKES A RUN FOR HIS HELICOPTER.
THIS ISN'T THE PLAN!
I'M SUPPOSED TO BE LAUGHING AT MOUSTACHES!
AT THE SAME TIME, LEX LUTHOR MAKES A RUN FOR HIS POWER ARMOR SUIT.
THIS ISN'T THE PLAN!
I'M SUPPOSED TO BE SWIMMING IN MONEY!
LET'S MIX THINGS UP... HOW ABOUT WE PLAY *SWITCHEROO* ON THE BAD GUYS?
GREAT IDEA!

WHILE SUPERMAN CAPTURES THE JOKER...
CHUG-A
CHUG-A
WHY ISN'T THIS BUCKET OF BOLTS MOVING?
CHUG-A
CHUG-A
CHUG-A
WHHHIRRRIIRRR-
CHUG-A
CHUG-A
TEE-HEE.
...BATMAN TAKES CARE OF LEX LUTHOR.
THUNK!
HEY, STOP THAT!!
THUNK!
THUNK!
THUNK!
NO WAY.

USING TEAMWORK, BATMAN, SUPERMAN, AND THE REST OF THEIR FRIENDS CAPTURE THE VILLAINS AND CLEAN UP THE CITY. WHILE THEY WAIT FOR THE POLICE TO PICK UP THE CRIMINALS, THEY TAKE TIME FOR A PICNIC.
WHO MADE THESE PEANUT BUTTER AND JELLY SANDWICHES?
THEY'RE AMAZING!
I DID!
I'M HUNGRY, TOO!!
NONE FOR VILLAINS!

SO, DID YOU LEARN YOUR LESSON?
THAT PB&J MAKES THE BEST PICNIC SANDWICH EVER?
HE'LL NEVER LEARN.
LEARN WHAT?

LATER, IN PRISON, LEX LUTHOR REALIZES THAT CRIME DOESN'T PAY. ESPECIALLY WHEN THE JOKER IS YOUR CELL MATE . . .
...HEYA, LEXY, HOW ABOUT NEXT TIME, WE USE GIANT ROBOT CLOWNS INSTEAD?
OOH, AND WE'LL GIVE THEM MOUSTACHES... THEN I'LL HAVE THE LAST LAUGH FOR SURE...
...OH, AND, LEX, DID I TELL YOU THE ONE ABOUT THE CHICKEN THAT WANTED TO CROSS THE ROAD?
...LEXY, I HAVE A JOKE. READY? KNOCK, KNOCK...
GUARDS! MOVE ME TO A DIFFERENT CELL. THE JOKER WON'T STOP TELLING BAD JOKES. HE'S NOT EVEN FUNNY!
WHAT?!
I'M HILARIOUS!
END!

LITERATURE

A Collection of Mythology and Folklore, Short Stories, Poetry, Drama, and Literary Criticism

9.50

James Burl Hogins

25 matching authors of stories
2 essays

SRA
SCIENCE RESEARCH ASSOCIATES, INC.
Chicago, Palo Alto, Toronto, Henley-on-Thames, Sydney, Paris
A Subsidiary of IBM

The text of this book was set by computer in Palatino, a modern typeface designed by Herman Zapf. Palatino was named for a famous sixteenth-century penman and is strongly calligraphic in style. Display type is Americana.

Composition: Black Dot, Inc., Crystal Lake, Illinois, with special attention from Richard Haefele
Sponsoring editor: Frank B. Geddes
Designer: Judy Olson; assistant: Naomi Takigawa
Artists: Bonnie Brown, Patty Dwyer, Nancy Freeman, Nancy Golub (cover), Katsumi Omura, Barbara Ravizza, Jack Tom, Dennis Ziemienski
Editors and assistants: Richard Carter, Jean Erickson, Carol Harris, Kay Nerode, Lynn Peacock

Printed in the United States of America.

Library of Congress Catalog Card Number: 73-76241

Table of Contents

Drama

Literary Criticism

Thematic Table of Contents

ILLUMINATING MAN'S FOIBLES: IRONY, COMEDY, SATIRE

Poetry:

The Nymph's Reply to the Shepherd
To Julia, Under Lock and Key
Song (Herford)
Ozymandias
The Latest Decalogue
#1207 (He preached upon "Breadth")
The Man He Killed
from A Shropshire Lad (On Moonlight Heath)
Mr. Flood's Party
Richard Cory
the Cambridge ladies who live in furnished souls
The Naked and the Nude
Litany for Dictatorships
The Rehearsal
Reflections on Ice Breaking
Inter-Office Memorandum
I, Too, Sing America
The Day After Sunday
Twelve Songs, VIII
Museums
Lessons of the War: Naming of Parts
Lessons of the War: Judging Distances
Life, Friends, is Boring
Award
Suburban Homecoming
To David, About His Education
Life Cycle of the Common Man
Santa Claus
Mind
Formal Application
April Inventory

Short Stories:

The Pins
Mr. Preble Gets Rid of His Wife
Mule in the Yard
After You, My Dear Alphonse
The Condor and the Guests
Dotson Gerber Resurrected
Saul Bird Says: Relate! Communicate! Liberate!

Drama:

Sganarelle
How He Lied to Her Husband
The Electronic Nigger
Picnic on the Battlefield

MAN IN CONFLICT WITH NATURE (MAN VERSUS A HOSTILE ENVIRONMENT)

Poetry:

Lines Written in Early Spring
Work Without Hope
Dover Beach
from War Is Kind, III and XXI
Patterns
Secretary

Short Stories:

The Man Who Saw the Flood
The Adulterous Woman
The Swimmer

Drama:

Macbeth
Oedipus

MAN IN HARMONY WITH NATURE AND HIS ENVIRONMENT

Poetry:

Sonnet 18 (Shall I compare thee)
Sonnet 97 (How like a winter)
Sonnet 98 (From you have I been absent)
Composed Upon Westminster Bridge
The Solitary Reaper
When Lilacs Last in the Dooryard Bloomed
#328 (A Bird came down the Walk)

#441 (This is my Letter to the World)
#986 (A narrow Fellow in the Grass)
Dust of Snow
Birches
The West Wind
God's World
May All Earth Be Clothed in Light

Short Stories:

The Revolt of Mother
Flight
The Circular Ruins
Love
Chee's Daughter
The Lion

Man and His Myths

Poetry:

To Lesbia
Hymn to Diana
Ulysses
The Wild Swans at Coole
The Second Coming
Leda and the Swan
Peter Quince at the Clavier
Santa Claus
Onan

Short Stories:

The Lion
The Swimmer
A Fable

Drama:

Oedipus
A View from the Bridge

Youth and Age

Poetry:

Crabbed Age and Youth
To the Virgins, to Make Much of Time
Ulysses
Rabbi Ben Ezra
Spring and Fall
The Wild Swans at Coole
Mr. Flood's Party
Blue Girls
Fern Hill
To David, About his Education
April Inventory

Short Stories:

Chee's Daughter
After You, My Dear Alphonse
The Use of Force

Drama:

A View from the Bridge

Man and the Laws of Men: Morality

Poetry:

Sir Patrick Spens
Song: To Celia
On the Late Massacre in Piedmont
The Chimney Sweep
Song to the Men of England
The Man He Killed
from A Shropshire Lad (On Moonlight Heath)
Patterns
Grass
Shine, Perishing Republic
Dulce Et Decorum Est
Arms and the Boy
Litany for Dictatorships
The Rehearsal
Ode to the Confederate Dead
Inter-Office Memorandum
I, Too, Sing America
John Doe, Jr.

The Family: Brothers, Parents, Mothers and Daughters, Fathers and Sons, Etc.

Poetry:

Edward
my father moved through dooms of love
The Bad Children
Do Not Go Gentle Into That Good Night
The Children of the Poor
The Bee
Abraham's Madness
Daddy
The Disquieting Muses
Photograph of My Father in His Twenty-Second Year

Short Stories:

My Kinsman, Major Molineux
The Death of Ivan Ilych
The Revolt of Mother
Enemies
The Judgment
The Use of Force
The Man Who Saw the Flood
Flight
Love
After You, My Dear Alphonse
Chee's Daughter

Drama:

Oedipus
Macbeth
A View from the Bridge
Picnic on the Battlefield

The Myth of Manhood: Initiation, Coming of Age

Poetry:

Indian Summer
Poem in October
Black Jackets

Short Stories:

My Kinsman, Major Molineux
The Judgment
Flight
The Lion
A Fable

Drama:

A View from the Bridge
Picnic on the Battlefield

The Social Contract: Man Versus Institutions, Traditions, Customs

Poetry:

The Passionate Shepherd
The Constant Lover
Say, But Did You Love So Long
The Chimney Sweep
Richard Cory
Sympathy
Prayers of Steel
Grass
Shine, Republic
Shine, Perishing Republic
The Love Song of J. Alfred Prufrock
The Hollow Men
Dulce et Decorum Est
Arms and the Boy
next to of course god
Southern Mansion
John Doe, Jr.
Come Live With Me and Be My Love
The Unknown Citizen
Museums
The Conscientious Objector
The Death of the Ball Turret Gunner
Suburban Homecoming

Structure and Shaping Elements of Poetry, Short Stories, and Drama

SATIRE, IRONY

Poetry:

They Flee From Me
Since There's No Help
The Nymph's Reply to the Shepherd
The Constant Lover
When I Heard the Learned Astronomer
#1207 (He preached upon "Breadth")
The Man He Killed
Richard Cory
Arms and the Boy
the Cambridge ladies who live in furnished souls
Incident
The Unknown Citizen
Life, Friends, Is Boring
Dilemma
To David, About His Education
Santa Claus

Short Stories:

The Pins
A Dill Pickle
After You, My Dear Alphonse
Saul Bird Says: Relate! Communicate! Liberate!
Dotson Gerber Resurrected

Drama:

How He Lied to Her Husband
Picnic on the Battlefield
The Electronic Nigger

COMEDY, HUMOR

Poetry:

To Julia, Under Lock and Key
Song (Herford)
#61 (Papa above!)
#324 (Some keep the Sabbath going to Church)
Indian Summer
Resumé
Inter-Office Memorandum

Short Stories:

Mr. Preble Gets Rid of His Wife
Mule in the Yard

Drama:

Sganarelle
How He Lied to Her Husband

IMAGERY, METAPHOR, SIMILE

Poetry:

Sonnet 18 (Shall I compare thee)
Sonnet 97 (How like a winter hath my absence been)
The Good-Morrow
The Ecstasy
A Red, Red Rose
The Solitary Reaper
O Lovely Fishermaiden

To the Reader
Dover Beach
When It Is Given to You to Find a Smile
The Taxi
Birches
The Red Wheelbarrow
The Mind Is an Enchanting Thing
The Love Song of J. Alfred Prufrock
Lady Love
Ode to the Confederate Dead
Elegy for Jane
Auto Wreck
Buick
Reading Time: 1 Minute 26 Seconds
Love Poem
Do Not Go Gentle Into That Good Night
Mind
Joy
Mad Girl's Love Song
The Pill Versus the Springhill Mind Disaster
Today is a Day of Great Joy

Short Stories:

Flight
Hills Like White Elephants
The Adulterous Woman
The Condor and the Guests
The Swimmer

Drama:

Macbeth

Rhythm and Meter

Poetry:

Edward
Lines Written in Early Spring
Battle Hymn of the Republic
Spring and Fall
After Apple-Picking
Prayers of Steel
Domination of Black
in just
Snake (Roethke)
Fern Hill
Poem in October
The Bee
A Poem for Black Hearts
Goodbye and Hello
I Would not be Here

Short Stories:

Flight
The Judgment
Saul Bird Says: Relate! Communicate! Liberate!

Drama:

Oedipus
Sganarelle
How He Lied to Her Husband

Sound—Rhyme, Lyricism, Alliteration and Assonance

Poetry:

Sir Patrick Spens
Sonnet 30 (When to the sessions of sweet silent thought)
Upon Julia's Clothes
On the Late Massacre in Piedmont
Song to the Men of England
Cavalry Crossing a Ford
#1463 (A route of evanescence)
Pied Beauty
The West Wind
Study of Two Pears
Snake (Lawrence)
"Dover Beach": A Note to that Poem
my father moved through dooms of love
A Simile for Her Smile

Diction

Poetry:

To His Coy Mistress
Kubla Khan
When Lilacs Last in the Dooryard Bloomed
#328 (A Bird came down the Walk)
from War is Kind, III and XXI
This Is Just to Say
Roses Only
Poetry
Bells for John Whiteside's Daughter
Lessons of the War: Naming of Parts
Lessons of the War: Judging Distances
The Children of the Poor
Dancing in the Street

Short Stories:

The Lion
The Condor and the Guests
The Judgment

Plot

Poetry:

The Twa Corbies

Short Stories:

The Pins

Drama:

Oedipus

Character

Poetry:

To a Common Prostitute
Curiosity
Black Jackets

Short Stories:

The Revolt of Mother

Drama:

A View from the Bridge

Sense and Meaning

Poetry:

#1755 (To make a prairie it takes a clover and one bee)
Study of Two Pears
A Virginal
Underwear
As By Water

Short Stories:

My Kinsman, Major Molineux
The Judgment
Hills Like White Elephants
The Use of Force
The Adulterous Woman

Drama:

Picnic on the Battlefield

Description

Poetry:

Describes Rationally the Irrational Effects of Love
Composed Upon Westminster Bridge
The Eagle
May All Earth Be Clothed in Light
A Blessing
Secretary
Corner
Photograph of my Father in His Twenty-Second Year

Short Stories:

The Use of Force
Flight

Drama:

Macbeth

Point of View

Poetry:

My Last Duchess
#465 (I heard a Fly buzz—when I died)
#712 (Because I could not stop for Death)
Next to of course god
The Death of the Ball Turret Gunner
Formal Application
When In Rome

Short Stories:

My Kinsman, Major Molineux
Hills Like White Elephants
The Revolt of Mother

Drama:

The Electronic Nigger
Picnic on the Battlefield

Tone

Poetry:

When We Two Parted
The Latest Decalogue
Terence, This Is Stupid Stuff
Mr. Flood's Party
Patterns
The Emperor of Ice-Cream
Dulce et Decorum Est
Come Live with Me and Be My Love
Award
Suburban Homecoming
April Inventory
The Disquieting Muses

Short Stories:

Hills Like White Elephants
The Man Who Saw the Flood
Dotson Gerber Resurrected

Drama:

Sganarelle
How He Lied to Her Husband
The Electronic Nigger

Theme

Poetry:

The Passionate Shepherd to His Love
To the Virgins, to Make Much of Time
La Belle Dame sans Merci
Sonnet 14 *from* Sonnets from the Portuguese
Ulysses
Sympathy
Peter Quince at the Clavier
Blue Girls
Dr. Sigmund Freud Discovers the Sea Shell
Litany for Dictatorships
I, Too, Sing America
from Macchu Picchu, III, IV, V
English A
Lies

Short Stories:

The Death of Ivan Ilych
Enemies
A Painful Case
Flight
Chee's Daughter

Drama:

Picnic on the Battlefield

SYMBOLISM, ALLEGORY

Poetry:

The Chimney Sweep
The Tiger
Ozymandias
Ode to a Nightingale
The Second Coming
The Wild Swans at Coole
Leda and the Swan
from The Black Riders II, XXIV, XLVII
Journey of the Magi
The Hollow Men
Truth
Dream Deferred
Nice Day for a Lynching
The Heavy Bear
Game Called on Account of Darkness
In the Night Fields
Daddy
A Hell of a Day

Short Stories:

My Kinsman, Major Molineux
The Judgment
Love
The Condor and the Guests
The Lion
The Swimmer
A Fable

Drama:

The Electronic Nigger
Picnic on the Battlefield

General Introduction

The impulse to tell stories, sing songs, and act out dramas seems to be spontaneous in mankind. "Tell me a story about when you were little," begs the child, delighted to hear how different, and yet how similar, life was before he came along. "In the beginning God created Heaven and Earth," intones the churchman, and he explains to his congregation how their problems can be solved in the light of what happened long ago in Israel. A parable or a story can be more palatable and powerful than any sermon.

The roots of the oral tradition are primitive and obscure, but that tradition carried civilization well past the time when writing became established. Part of it remains viable to this day, having been preserved in literary creations such as Mother Goose rhymes, fairy tales, the Norse tales, the Greek myths, *The Iliad,* and *The Odyssey.* In most countries at most times in history a relatively small percentage of the public has been literate. This does not mean, however, that most people have been unable to appreciate or contribute to the culture in other ways, such as continuing the oral tradition. The fact that our knowledge of Greek drama came to us through fragments of written versions does not mean that writing was the only—or even the major—way in which contemporaries of the classic dramatists knew these works.

It is hard to say why man has always been drawn to such imaginative creations. Perhaps it began as a way of finding answers to apparently unanswerable questions about the universe and mankind, or perhaps it began as one way in which to alleviate boredom. Whatever the reason, the attraction has lasted for a long time.

Today we are trying to recover from having had our wings clipped. The last few generations have looked to synthetic means or technological means for rising above their troubles. We now buy more nonfiction than fiction because we're sure that another book by an economist, an historian, or a politician will add to our knowledge and somehow improve our minds. Religion has gone the way of myth and folklore. Without even knowing it, we have robbed ourselves of a birthright that has always belonged to people everywhere. Because of this loss we now suffer from timidity of reach.

Of course, the appreciation of literature does require one thing of the reader: the willing suspension of disbelief. Unlike the economist, the historian, the politician, or the newspaper reporter, the author does not pretend that what he is presenting is factually true. Literature does not offer mere facts, but let's look at what it does offer.

Literature offers you a way to escape. Through literature you are released from the bounds of self. You are able to experience what it is to be a poor Italian peasant, to endure the Napoleonic war, or to be an unwanted child.

Literature offers you affiliation. We are all really alone. Perhaps no man is an island in John Donne's sense, but in another sense each of us is made up of our own particular experience. We used to feel closer to others through affiliations with family, institutions, and the traditions of our particular culture; slowly, however, these bonds have been eroded. Though we try fitfully to replace them in various ways, more and more we feel alone, alienated, unable to perceive any order or point to the chaos in which we find ourselves.

But if you have had an experience it sometimes makes you feel less lonely and strange to know that others—in other times and other places—have had a similar experience. Maybe you feel that your relatives, your neighbors, and your friends do not understand you; but somewhere, someplace, there is an author who can put into words what you feel—and even justify those feelings. Our response on such occasions—regardless of the work's merit by some abstract method of measurement—is to feel warm and relieved. We may even say to someone else, "Read this and you will see what I mean."

Literature offers truth and order. Many nonfiction books and articles claim to be more factual and more complete than they really are. If their authors were honest, they would all have to say, "We really don't know everything that went into these events; we really don't know all the reasons; we really don't know all of the consequences." Their air of authority and dogmatism is assumed because the authors know that people like to believe they have found out "what really happened" at the Bay of Pigs, in the last election, in the unhappy life and death of a movie star.

But science and art have this in common: given the exact dimensions of the laboratory experiment or of the mathematical universe, what happens is exact, totally describable, and true; given the universe of a particular book, story, play, set of poems, picture, or piece of music, what happens to those particular characters or in that particular setting is exact, totally describable, and true. The artist, of course, has the additional burden of making what happens seem believable and realistic, because it is hard for the reader to resist comparing the reality of the work with the reality he lives in. The reader may say, "But I don't believe there are any people like that." However, if the author has done his work well, he will have laid foundations that make his characters and their actions credible. (Of course, our tendency to compare the artist's universe to our own may work in his favor. He can add verisimilitude to an otherwise unconvincing narrative merely by including details that we are familiar with in one way or another.)

Literature offers you insight. Literature, perhaps more than any other art form, offers an opportunity for enlightenment and enjoyment. Sometimes literature describes, organizes, and helps us understand feelings and situations. Literature helps us discover ourselves and identify who we are. When we read how characters work out problems or conflicts, it says something to us about the way *we* approach life's complexities. And yet, after all is said and done, a piece of literature has an existence in and of itself; it can offer us ways in which to search, but we must do the searching for ourselves.

Literature is relatively inexpensive, it encompasses so much, and you can pick it up and put it down at will. It would seem that only a fool would allow himself to remain cut off from something that has so many advantages and almost no drawbacks. So while you have probably already come in contact with literature—if not in your private life, then in textbooks at school—this book is intended to make the introduction formal.

In all of our extolling of literature thus far, we have not really defined it. The fact is that there are very few good definitions. Literature has been equated with "imaginative or creative writing," but good nonfiction would fit the same description. If this book were being written long ago, it would be easier to establish fairly definite boundaries in respect to the scope of our concern. We could restrict the term to the traditional three genres and consider fiction, drama, and poetry, and, we would know what we meant by these terms. But over the years the lines of distinction have become more and more vague. As authors experiment in form and subject, definitions of literature change. If we define *fiction* as "prose literary work whose content is produced by the imagination and is not necessarily based on fact," does this mean that the works of Tom Wolfe are not fiction? If we define *poetry* as "composition designed to convey a vivid and imaginative sense of experience, characterized by the use of condensed language chosen for its sound and suggestive power as well as its meaning and by the use of such literary techniques as structured meter, natural cadences, rhyme, and metaphor," can we include Mari Evans' "When in Rome"? If *drama* is defined as "prose or verse written to be performed by actors on a stage," does it include Beckett's extended stage directions? And do any of these descriptions fit the worst stories in women's magazines or light verse? (In the introductions to the genres you will find more extensive discussions of the merits of these definitions.)

Literature is writing that is regarded as having an intrinsic worth beyond its immediate appeal. Literature is the creative expression of individual experiences that, nevertheless, have universal appeal. Literature has form, beauty of expression, and intellectual as well as emotional appeal. Further, we can look at the substance of literature and find a number of characteristics that are common to all works:

- Each work uses or builds on certain conventions of the particular genre it represents. These conventions are somewhat artificial, but custom has made them acceptable. Examples include an operatic star singing two arias after having been fatally stabbed, a poem describing a state of mind in perfect iambic pentameter, and the division of a story into chapters or a play into acts. Even character types, themes, or motifs can become a matter of convention.

- All works use conflict, either overt or implicit, as an organizing principle. The conflict may be between one's view of oneself and one's view of others, between what is and what was, between tradition and change, between what is said and what is not said, between innocence and maturity, or between any of the countless other contrasts that make the human condition both happy and sad.

- Literature usually moves from the specific to the general, though the generalization may only be implied. One character or incident should represent all such people or incidents.

- All works offer a certain richness of ambiguity that encourages enjoyment and interpretation at different levels of complexity. If the work is a classic, it has become one because its ambiguities can be reinterpreted with application to each succeeding generation of readers.

- Literature usually deals with experience. Philosophical ideas may be discussed, but they are presented in terms of personal experience.

- Literary works of high quality offer a story, a situation, an image, or a metaphor rather than a direct statement of what the author wishes to communicate. Instead of simply describing an emotion or an experience, an author endeavors to recreate it for the reader.

- Literature is usually the product of a mysterious inner compulsion combined with a fully conscious discipline. While a student essay on the feeling of loneliness after the death of one's mother or on the social stigma attached to an unwanted pregnancy may carry conviction, it is not necessarily (or usually) art. Art is also form. On the other hand, an artist may modify his own deeply felt experience—frequently in order to make it more universal—but unless we can sense the feeling behind it, it seems artificial. When both form and feeling are present, the reader is likely to experience the work in terms of Emily Dickinson's definition of poetry—as something that makes one feel as though the top of his head had been blown off.

- All well-written works have unity. After reading a work, the reader should feel that each part contributed to the whole, that things were there for a reason, and that the ending or outcome was an inevitable outgrowth of what came before.
- All works take advantage of literary elements such as plot, characterization, imagery, diction, tone, style, and pace that are appropriate to that particular piece.

Most of these characteristics will become apparent in anything more than a superficial reading of a literary work. Admittedly, studying a work in order to find them is not prerequisite to enjoying the piece itself. In fact, people who have learned to enjoy literature often resist analyzing it. To them paraphrase is deadly and analyzing a poem is analogous to dissecting it. Why not then just offer an anthology of prose, poetry, and drama, and let the student make what he will of it?

Analysis forces the reader to interact with a work and thereby helps him get more out of it. Analysis not only contributes to a better understanding of individual works, but it also enables one to develop some procedures for approaching new pieces and some criteria for judging them. In analyzing a particular piece, however, it is impossible to make absolute judgments. Overall trends can be pointed out and comparisons can be made. But there is no way to support flat statements of worth.

This book deals with only a few of the mechanics of literature. In a sense, to say that one has to understand the mechanics before he can enjoy literature is like saying that one must know the technical aspects of anatomy before he can appreciate the beauty of the human body, or that one must understand all of the mechanics of a car in order to drive it well. However, the more interested one gets in a subject, the more details he wants to know about it. Since the mechanics contribute to the overall effect of the work, understanding them will facilitate a better understanding of the work as a whole. As long as the mechanics do not get in the way of the substance, studying them can make for a more meaningful and more pleasurable experience.

The selections in this book begin with the area of mythology because this is where literature began. The other genres are arranged in the time-honored order—fiction, poetry, and plays—from the most familiar to the reader to the least. The final section deals with literary criticism. Having had your own chance at grappling with literature, you may enjoy seeing how others approach the problem.

The selections in this book are meant to present a variety of works, themes, viewpoints, stances, and techniques. The preponderance of them are pieces written in the twentieth century because these are more obviously applicable to our times; they require less historical background on the part of the reader, and they will be the basis for new works that will be written in the twenty-first century. The selections are arranged chronologically within genre so that you can see how the passage of time has changed both what is considered appropriate subject matter and how a subject is handled. Of course, there are always some mavericks, some writers who demonstrate that genius recognizes no restrictions as to subject or technique.

Some observers have been surprised at the revived interest in folklore and mythology among today's youth and scoffingly pass it off by saying, "They're searching for something." Since the day man crawled in out of the cold, he has been searching for something, for answers, and his search has been catalogued in the long pages of philosophy and literature. When we read literature, we are being given the opportunity to learn the history, the successes and failures, of that search.

This anthology does not purport to be a definitive collection of the best or most representative or most useful works of Western civilization. These works are, however, ones that have survived years—or centuries—of changing standards of literary excellence, and they will give you a fairly complete notion of the character of the new creature to whom you are being introduced.

FOLKLORE, MYTHS, AND RELIGIOUS MOTIFS

Introduction to Folklore, Myths, Religious Motifs

Because of the apparent discontinuity between the oral and the literate traditions, what was long ago familiar to everyone is now known and appreciated by very few. If it had not been for the academicians who demand that candidates for degrees know something about Greek and Roman mythology, the devoted folklorists who delight in tracking aged backwoodsmen to their hilltop cabins, and a sporadic interest in ethnic histories, folk literature might well have become an extinct genre.

Folk tales, legends, myths, and fables transmitted through the oral tradition are part of the earliest and most delightful evidence of human creative genius. Later writers may have turned out more sophisticated pieces, but most of their stories and dramas are merely some type of folk tale parading in modern dress.

Where did these stories originate? Most of them were created by the common people themselves or by religious leaders to answer basic questions such as: Where did man come from? What determines man's fate? What happens to a person after death? Who or what controls the weather? Some of these questions are the same ones science tries to answer; some have become the province of formal religion or philosophy. But given the extent of primitive man's observations of natural phenomena and the inexplicable order of the universe, his answers are not without merit.

According to Carl Jung, Maude Bodkin, and other philosophers and psychologists, these stories are the end product of a process in which man tried to resolve the tensions resulting from conflicts in his inner life, first by means of ritual, then through art. Art, like ritual, provided a way for the individual to deal on another plane with those matters he found frustrating in real life. He could identify with priests, heroes, or kings with power; he could feel exalted through their victories and absolved through their sufferings.

Since these tales grew out of the typical experiences of our ancestors, their specific content might vary from one culture group to another. For instance, there were a number of different names for malevolent supernatural creatures—witches, goblins, trolls. Some issues concerned all groups everywhere: the conflict between fathers and sons, an interest in the origin of the world, the establishment of an ethic, and the fear of death. Other subjects seem to have been limited to a particular civilization (the Greeks, for example, had no stories about astrology).

These stories can be classified in terms of their subject matter. There are *myths,* which attempt to explain the workings of the universe in terms of the supernatural. The familiar European *fairy tales* appear to be a fairly recent version of older folk literature; the supernatural heroes of the myths have become in the fairy tales virtuous, good-hearted humans. In myths, the outcome is only occasionally satisfactory from the human standpoint, since the gods play by different rules. In fairy tales, the good characters are always rewarded and the evil ones are always punished.

Another group of tales falls under the heading of *allegory.* These stories may almost be considered extended analogies. They express abstract meanings in terms of concrete illustrations, each element in the allegory standing for some idea or characteristic. When the purpose of the tale is to exemplify a moral, it may be called a *parable* or a *fable.* If the characters in such a tale are animals, it is called a *beast fable* or *beast epic.* As a method of teaching, this type of story is almost unexcelled.

The *dilemma tale* is one in which both sides of a problem are presented to the reader without a solution being proposed.

While stories in the foregoing classifications are almost wholly the product of the imagination, another group of folk tales has more of a basis in fact. These are semihistorical accounts, or *legends,* connected with historical persons. Both Charlemagne and Johnny Appleseed did exist and did perform at least some of the deeds attributed to them. There is even a suspicion that King Arthur and the Round Table were not completely fictitious creations.

Perhaps the most American type of folk tale is the *tall tale,* in which the hero accomplishes almost superhuman feats. The German Baron Munchhausen is almost the only foreign rival to Paul Bunyan, John Henry, Stormalong, Pecos Bill, and the countless other inventions of the frontier mind who are palely shadowed in some of the works of Mark Twain and in Liar's Clubs today.

Remember that most of the stories you are about to read in the following section are only one version of a particular folk tale. When the tale was still alive orally, it was changed and embroidered by each storyteller's art. He added to it or substracted details from it; he acted out parts or sang them. He did whatever he felt necessary to hold the audience's interest. Each story represents one storyteller's formulation that passed from the oral tradition into the written one and thus became a permanent form.

The selections include some that are connected with Western literature and some that reflect the way in which people around the world have a commonality of interest even when they have no means of communication with each other.

One question you might consider while reading these stories is: Is our highly advanced civilization capable of producing anything as intellectually powerful as these simple tales? And if Jung was right about their therapeutic nature, what kind of condition does their passing leave us in?

The Indians and Death

In those days long ago neither the Indians nor the animals were subject to Death. They all lived for ever, and there was yet enough room for everyone. Only the coyote, discontented grumbler that he was, went about grousing: "Why do we have to be squashed here like this? If only the old were to die, we'd be far better off." And he ran all over the prairie, shouting so loudly that he could be heard in both forest and desert. But no one paid any heed to his talk, for it was well-known that the coyote was a scoundrel who always tried to make trouble for everything and everybody.

This time, however, it soon became apparent that he would not so easily give up the idea that had lodged firmly in his crooked, dishevelled head. And when the snow remained lying on the ground especially long that year and famine threatened, he again started to shout:

"There, you see? I told you! There are too many of us, and that's why we are hungry. If only the old were to die, there would be plenty to eat for all of us."

In the end the Great Shaman heard of the coyote's suggestions. The wise old man became very angry and wanted to punish the evil-minded ruffian, but then he thought better of it and decided to call a meeting, which he hoped would prove to the coyote how repugnant his suggestion really was to one and all. Perhaps, thought the Great Shaman, the coyote may yet mend his ways.

And thus the Indians and the animals assembled at the foot of the Sacred Rock, with the Great Shaman sitting on a tree-stump on top of the cliff; his head-dress touched the sky when he raised his head to address them in the following words:

"My children! I could no longer bear to listen to the yelping of your brother coyote, who keeps proposing that we bring Death into the world. That is why I have now called you together. Tell the coyote what you think of his idea, so that he may be taught a lesson."

The animals conferred together quietly, while the coyote sat alone, scratching behind his ears with his paw and getting up every now and again to trot from one to the other, pricking up his ears to hear what they were saying.

All of a sudden he called out:

"O Great Shaman, I never intended to harm anyone! But there isn't enough food to go round, and we can't all survive." His cunning eyes were narrowed into mere slits. "It was never my intention that those who die should not return to this world."

"What is it you suggest, then?" asked the squirrel.

"I would tell you, only . . . I don't know, nobody trusts me, that's the trouble."

"Go on, tell us!" the Indians urged him, and the Great Shaman leaned forward in order to hear him better.

"Very well, then," said the coyote. "I suggest we make a hole in heaven, and all the dead can move there for a time. Then, when there is again enough food for all, we'll simply call them back."

"But there isn't a tree so high," murmured the bear.

"I have thought it all out," replied the coyote smugly. "An Indian arrow will reach the sky. Then a second arrow can be shot to join up with the first, then a third and a fourth, until they link heaven and earth. Anyone can climb up then, and it will be even easier to get down again."

The coyote's proposal seemed sensible enough. A little too pat, the Great Shaman said to himself; but think as he might, he could find no objection. Even the most sceptical among them approved of the idea. The coyote was smiling benevolently. If only they knew!

In the meantime the Indians had run off to fetch their bows and arrows, bringing as many as they could carry. Then the best marksmen prepared to shoot.

Whizz! the first arrow whistled over their heads and pierced a low cloud. It was immediately followed by another, which split the first arrow all the way up to its feather ornament and stuck fast.

The animals looked on in admiration as the Indians displayed their marksmanship. Not a single arrow went astray. The coyote ran about under the bowmen's legs, getting in the way and giving advice as if it had been he who had taught them to shoot.

Now the long line of arrows reached down as far as the Sacred Rock. The Great Shaman rose from his tree-stump, and he pulled at the arrows to test their strength. They held firm, strong enough to take even a bear's weight.

By this time dusk had set in, and the Great Shaman motioned with his hand for the crowd to disperse and go home.

"Go to sleep now, but as from this day, Death will be here with us; it is you who have decided so. I shall now open a door in the Sacred Rock for Death to come through, and those whom it chooses will climb up to heaven to stay there for a certain time. . . . "

Night settled over the countryside—the first night in which Death walked the Indian country, the first night during which an old badger died in his den, a lonely hunter in his cabin, and an eagle in his eyrie high up among the rocks.

The dead walked in the dark to the Sacred Rock, and before dawn the last of them had vanished inside the hole in the star-filled sky.

Time passed. Soon the weeping of the bereaved could be heard everywhere, and many went to the Great Shaman for advice. But even he was powerless to help for the time being.

"We must wait for the stars to sink a little lower," he told all comers. "As they are now, they cannot hear us calling."

Night after night, therefore, people as well as animals fixed their eyes on the sky, waiting for the return of those who had left them.

Only the coyote was nowhere to be seen. He had taken to his lair, and those who passed by it heard strange grating noises coming from inside. They wondered what the old rascal might be doing, but mostly they were convinced that he was afraid to come out in case they wanted to punish him for his little prank that had caused all the trouble.

However, a new and even more dastardly plan had taken shape in that crooked skull of his. The coyote had brought sharp-edged stones to his lair and now spent long days sharpening his teeth on them, making his fangs sharper than the Indian tomahawk. It was this that produced those strange sounds that could be heard coming from his lair.

When at last he all but cut his own tongue on his teeth, the coyote decided he had done all he could to prepare himself for the task in hand, and he went out quietly into the night.

It was the last hour before dawn, and everything was absolutely still. The coyote crept stealthily up to the Sacred Rock, putting his paws down cautiously so as not to give himself away by as much as a disturbed blade of grass.

He stopped at the foot of the cliff and listened. There was complete silence everywhere, only the night wind could be heard whistling in the rock crevices. There was thus nothing to prevent him from carrying out his evil intent. Standing up on his hind legs, he caught hold of the last arrow with his teeth and began to gnaw at it. The soft wood soon gave way, but the remaining arrows were still firmly attached to the sky. This infuriated the coyote—in his rage he shook the line of arrows furiously, hoping to pry the first one loose from the cloud above.

He succeeded only too well; with a resounding crash, the arrows came tumbling down about his ears. Some landed on his back with a thump, and the coyote squealed with pain: "Wowww! Wowww!"

Bruised and battered, he crept back to his lair. Pandemonium broke out. The noise had awakened the bear and he, discovering what had happened, quickly roused the others, as well as the Great Shaman.

But there was nothing to be done—the dead could now never return to the land of the living again.

The Great Shaman was very angry. Without a moment's hesitation he pronounced judgment over the culprit:

"You must leave our midst as punishment. We were long patient with you, hoping that you might mend your ways, but all to no avail. Now go out into the prairie, where you will henceforth live alone, so that you should not do any more mischief."

The coyote heard the verdict and, seeing that there was no other way, trotted off humbly, his tail between his legs.

He wandered a whole day long and perhaps even longer, finally settling down in a lonely spot where there was no other living creature for miles around—so afraid was he of the wise magician.

Now at last he began to regret his evil ways, and ever since then he has been wailing and begging to be allowed to return. But though his pleas are often to be heard, no one takes pity on him and calls him back, just as Death, whom he so carelessly brought into the world, will never go back to its abode in the Sacred Rock.

Considerations

1. In such a pictorial tale it seems odd that the figure of Death is not clearly defined, not fully personified. Why do you suppose this the case?
2. Are the motives of the coyote explained in the legend? What are his motives? Why is the coyote, instead of another animal, chosen to depict the bringer of Death?
3. What relationships between the Indians and animals are depicted in this tale?
4. Is the character of the Great Shaman clearly presented? How does he differ from god figures in other myths?

The Numbakulla and the First Aborigines

The myths of the central Australian Aranda tribe describing the creation of the first aborigines differ markedly from those of other Australian peoples.

The Aranda myth tells how, at one time in the dim and ghostly past, two great beings called the Numbakulla brothers, who lived in the western sky, saw a number of embryonic creatures, the Inapatua, whom it was the duty of those two creators to make into aboriginal men and women.

These Inapatua were crouched under low boulders on the shores of the salt lakes; the outlines of the different parts of their bodies could be vaguely seen in the rounded masses of which their forms consisted. They had no powers of sight or hearing, or even of movement.

Coming to earth with their stone knives, the Numbakulla took the incomplete bodies of the Inapatua, and began to make them into human beings. Using their knives, they first released the arms and legs of each body; then, by making four cuts at the end of the extremities, made the fingers and toes. The newly created people could now stand upright. With knives, the Numbakulla opened the eyes and the mouth of each one, and with their fingers formed the nose and the ears. The Inapatua then became fully developed men and women.

Gradually these newly formed people increased in numbers and spread over the land, gathering their food and obeying the complex laws of tribal behaviour that belong only to the men and women of the Aranda tribe.

Considerations

1. Why might the Aranda tribesmen attribute plurality to their creators, the Numbakulla brothers?
2. In what way could the sea location of the Aranda tribe have influenced their interpretation of the creation of mankind? In comparison to widely accepted theories of evolution, does this interpretation seem more or less sophisticated than Christianity's?

How the Earth Was Peopled

In the beginning there were no men on earth. The people lived in the sky with Akongo and they were happy. But there was a woman named Mbokomu who bothered everybody.

One day Akongo put the woman in a basket with her son and her daughter, some cassava, maize, and sugarcane and lowered the basket down to the earth.

The family planted a garden on earth and the garden flourished through their care.

One day the mother said to her son: "When we die there will be no one left to tend the garden."

"That can't be helped," the son replied.

"You must have children," the mother said.

"How?" asked the son. "We are the only people here. Where shall I find a wife?"

"Your sister is a woman," his mother replied. "Take her and have children by her." But the son recoiled from his mother's suggestion. The mother insisted, however. "That, or die childless, with nobody to continue our work. You can only get children by your sister so go and take her."

In the end the son gave in and went to his sister. The sister yielded to him quite willingly and became pregnant.

One day the sister met a creature who looked like a man except that he was completely covered by hair. She was afraid but the creature spoke so kindly to her that after a while they became friends. One day the sister took her husband's razor and went out to look for the hairy man. When she found him she made him lie down and shaved him. Now he looked like a man.[1] His name was Ebenga, meaning the beginner.

Ebenga bewitched the woman, so that when her child was born it brought witchcraft into the world. The child grew up under the spell of Ebenga. He practiced witchcraft and brought evil and sorrow to men.

In the course of time the brother and sister had other children. So the earth was peopled. But evil and witchcraft continued to the present.

The sky is supported by two creatures, Libanja and Songo. Libanja holds up the sky in the east by an enormous pole, and Songo in the west. When they grow tired the sky will fall down and men will turn into lizards.

1. A hairy body is an abomination to the Ngombe; it is the wife's duty to keep her husband's body shaved.

Considerations

1. What is the significance of the garden in this tale?
2. Why is the tale not explicit about the ways in which evil and witchcraft are manifest among mankind? Is incest likely to be an evil among these tribesmen?
3. Is it important to know where Ebenga came from or to know any other details of his relationship with the child? Who is the comparable figure to Ebenga in Christian mythology? How might he have bewitched the woman?

The Perverted Message

The Moon, it is said, once sent an insect to men, saying, "Go to men and tell them, 'As I die, and dying live; so you shall also die, and dying live.'"

The insect started with the message but while on his way was overtaken by the hare, who asked, "On what errand are you bound?" The insect answered, "I am sent by the Moon to men, to tell them that as she dies and dying lives, so shall they also die and dying live."

The hare said, "As you are an awkward runner, let me go." With these words he ran off, and when he reached men, he said, "I am sent by the Moon to tell you, 'As I die and dying perish, in the same manner you also shall die and come wholly to an end.'"

The hare then returned to the Moon and told her what he had said to men. The Moon reproached him angrily, saying, "Do you dare tell the people a thing which I have not said?"

With these words the Moon took up a piece of wood and struck the hare on the nose. Since that day the hare's nose has been slit, but men believe what Hare had told them.

Considerations

1. Why is the Moon a good spokesman for a theory of life in death?
2. What is the impact of the perverted version of the Moon's message?

The Leftover Eye

Pay heed to this tale. This is a tale of things that have never happened. But we will suppose these things did happen for certainly there are such things possible.

This is a tale of a man who was blind. His mother, too, was blind. His wife and his wife's mother were also blind. They dwelt together in a wretched condition; their farm was poor and their house was badly built. They consulted together and decided to go away. They would journey until they came to some place where their lot would be better.

They set out and traveled along the road. As they walked, the man stumbled over something. He picked it up and felt it, and then knew he had come upon seven eyes. He immediately gave two eyes to his wife, and then took two for himself. Of the three eyes remaining to him, he gave one to his mother and another to his wife's mother. He was left with one eye in his hand. Kai, this was a startling thing. Here was his mother with her one eye looking at him hopefully. There was his wife's mother with her one eye looking at him hopefully. To whom should he give the leftover eye?

If he gives the eye to his mother he will forever be ashamed before his wife and her mother. If he gives it to his wife's mother, he will fear the angry and disappointed heart of his own mother. A mother, know you, is not something to be played with.

This is difficult indeed. Here is the sweetness of his wife. She is good and loving. How can he hurt her? Yet his mother, too, is a good mother and loving. Can he thus injure her? Which would be easier, and which would be the right way to do this thing?

If this thing would come to you, which would you choose?

Considerations

1. What are the ironies of this tale?
2. What might give impetus for such a tale to be written?
3. Is this a perfect dilemma? Is it solvable?
4. Are the eyes symbolic?

Daniel, Bel, and the Snake

A Detective Story

When King Astyages was gathered to his fathers he was succeeded on the throne by Cyrus the Persian. Daniel was a confidant of the king, the most honoured of all the King's Friends.

Now the Babylonians had an idol called Bel, for which they provided every day twelve bushels of fine flour, forty sheep, and fifty gallons of wine. The king held it to be divine and went daily to worship it, but Daniel worshipped his God. So the king said to him, "Why do you not worship Bel?" He replied, "Because I do not believe in man-made idols, but in the living God who created heaven and earth and is sovereign over all mankind." The king said, "Do you think that Bel is not a living god? Do you not see how much he eats and drinks each day?" Daniel laughed and said, "Do not be deceived, your majesty; this Bel of yours is only clay inside and bronze outside, and has never eaten anything."

Then the king was angry, and summoned the priests of Bel and said to them, "If you cannot tell me who it is that eats up all these provisions, you shall die; but if you can show that it is Bel that eats them, then Daniel shall die for blasphemy against Bel." Daniel said to the king, "Let it be as you command." (There were seventy priests of Bel, not counting their wives and children.) Then the king went with Daniel into the temple of Bel. The priests said, "We are now going outside; set out the food yourself, your majesty, and mix the wine; then shut the door and seal it with your signet. When you come back in the morning, if you do not find that Bel has eaten it all, let us be put to death; but if Daniel's charges against us turn out to be false, then he shall die." They treated the whole affair with contempt, because they had made a hidden entrance under the table, and they regularly went in by it and ate everything up.

So when the priests had gone, the king set out the food for Bel; and Daniel ordered his servants to bring ashes and sift them over the whole temple in the presence of the king alone. Then they left the temple, closed the door, sealed it with the king's signet, and went away. During the night the priests, with their wives and children, came as usual and ate and drank everything. Early in the morning the king came, and Daniel with him. The king said, "Are the seals intact, Daniel?" He answered, "They are intact, your majesty." As soon as he opened the door, the king looked at the table and cried aloud, "Great art thou, O Bel! In thee there is no deceit at all." But Daniel laughed and held back the king from going in. "Just look at the floor," he said, "and judge whose footprints these are." The king said, "I see the footprints of men, women, and children." In a rage he put the priests under arrest, with their wives and children. Then they showed him the secret doors through which they used to go in and consume what was on the table. So the king put them to death, and handed Bel over to Daniel, who destroyed the idol and its temple.

Considerations

1. What attributes in Daniel's character are particularly striking? Why is he a fit hero for this tale?
2. From this account of Daniel can you make inferences about the "living God" he worshipped? What is the relation of that God to mankind?

Northern Mythology

The stories which have engaged our attention thus far relate to the mythology of southern regions. But there is another branch of ancient superstitions which ought not to be entirely overlooked. It belongs to the nations from which some of us, through our English ancestors, derive our origin. It is that of the northern nations, called Scandinavians, who inhabited the countries now known as Sweden, Denmark, Norway, and Iceland. These mythological records are contained in two collections called the Eddas, of which the oldest is in poetry and dates back to the year 1056, the more modern or prose Edda being of the date of 1640.

According to the Eddas there was once no heaven above nor earth beneath, but only a bottomless deep, and a world of mist in which flowed a fountain. Twelve rivers issued from this fountain, and when they had flowed far from their source, they froze into ice, and one layer accumulating over another, the great deep was filled up.

Southward from the world of mist was the world of light. From this flowed a warm wind upon the ice and melted it. The vapours rose in the air and formed clouds, from which sprang Ymir, the Frost giant and his progeny, and the cow Audhumbla, whose milk afforded nourishment and food to the giant. The cow got nourishment by licking the hoar frost and salt from the ice. While she was one day licking the salt stones there appeared at first the hair of a man, on the second day the whole head, and on the third the entire form endowed with beauty, agility, and power. This new being was a god, from whom and his wife, a daughter of the giant race, sprang the three brothers Odin, Vili, and Ve. They slew the giant Ymir, and out of his body formed the earth, of his blood the seas, of his bones the mountains, of his hair the trees, of his skull the heavens, and of his brain clouds, charged with hail and snow. Of Ymir's eyebrows the gods formed Midgard (mid earth), destined to become the abode of man.

Odin then regulated the periods of day and night and the seasons by placing in the heavens the sun and moon, and appointing to them their respective courses. As soon as the sun began to shed its rays upon the earth, it caused the vegetable world to bud and sprout. Shortly after the gods had created the world they walked by the side of the sea, pleased with their new work, but found that it was still incomplete, for it was without human beings. They therefore took an ash tree and made a man out of it, and they made a woman out of an alder, and called the man Aske and the woman Embla. Odin then gave them life and soul, Vili reason and motion, and Ve bestowed upon them the senses, expressive features, and speech. Midgard was then given them as their residence, and they became the progenitors of the human race.

The mighty ash tree Ygdrasill was supposed to support the whole universe. It sprang from the body of Ymir, and had three immense roots, extending one into Asgard (the dwelling of the gods), the other into Jotunheim (the abode of the giants), and the third to Niffleheim (the regions of darkness and cold). By the side of each of these roots is a spring, from which it is watered. The root that extends into Asgard is carefully tended by the three Norns, goddesses, who are regarded as the dispensers of fate. They are Urdur (the past), Verdandi (the present), Skuld (the future). The spring at the Jotunheim side is Ymir's well, in which wisdom and wit lie hidden, but that of Niffleheim feeds the adder Nidhogge (darkness), which perpetually gnaws at the root. Four harts run across the branches of the tree and bite the buds; they represent the four winds. Under the tree lies Ymir, and when he tries to shake off its weight the earth quakes.

Asgard is the name of the abode of the gods, access to which is only gained by crossing the bridge Bifrost (the rainbow). Asgard consists of golden and silver palaces, the dwellings of the gods, but the most beautiful of these is Valhalla, the residence of Odin. When seated on his throne he overlooks all heaven and earth. Upon his shoulders are the ravens Hugin and Munin, who fly every day over the whole world, and on their return report to him all they have seen and heard. At his feet lie his two wolves, Geri and Freki, to whom Odin gives all the meat that is set before him, for he himself stands in no need of food. Mead is for him both food and drink. He invented the Runic characters, and it is the business of the Norns to engrave the runes of fate upon a metal shield. From Odin's name, spelt Woden, as it sometimes is, came Wednesday, the name of the fourth day of the week.

Odin is frequently called Alfdaur (All-father), but this name is sometimes used in a way that shows that the Scandinavians had an idea of a deity superior to Odin, uncreated and eternal.

Of the Joys of Valhalla

Valhalla is the great hall of Odin, wherein he feasts with his chosen heroes, all those who have fallen bravely in battle, for all who die a peaceful death are excluded. The flesh of the boar Schrimnir is served up to them, and is abundant for all. For although this boar is cooked every morning, he becomes whole again every night. For drink the heroes are supplied abundantly with mead from the she-goat Heidrum. When the heroes are not feasting they amuse themselves with fighting. Every day they ride out into the court or field and fight until they cut each other in pieces. This is their pastime; but when meal time comes they recover from their wounds and return to feast in Valhalla.

The Valkyrior

The Valkyrior are warlike virgins, mounted upon horses and armed with helmets and spears. Odin, who is desirous to collect a great many heroes in Valhalla, to be able to meet the giants in a day when the final contest must come, sends down to every battlefield to make choice of those who shall be slain. The Valkyrior are his messengers, and their name means "Choosers of the slain." When they ride forth on their errand, their armour sheds a strange flickering light, which flashes up over the northern skies, making what men call the "Aurora Borealis," or "Northern Lights."[1]

OF THOR AND THE OTHER GODS

Thor, the thunderer, Odin's eldest son, is the strongest of gods and men, and possesses three very precious things. The first is a hammer, which both the Frost and the Mountain giants know to their cost, when they see it hurled against them in the air, for it has split many a skull of their fathers and kindred. When thrown, it returns to his hand of its own accord. The second rare thing he possesses is called the belt of strength. When he girds it about him his divine might is doubled. The third, also very precious, is his iron gloves, which he puts on whenever he would use his mallet efficiently. From Thor's name is derived our word Thursday.

Frey is one of the most celebrated of the gods. He presides over rain and sunshine and all the fruits of the earth. His sister Freya is the most propitious of the goddesses. She loves music, spring, and flowers, and is particularly fond of the Elves (fairies). She is very fond of love ditties, and all lovers would do well to invoke her.

Bragi is the god of poetry, and his song records the deeds of warriors. His wife, Iduna, keeps in a box the apples which the gods, when they feel old age approaching, have only to taste of to become young again.

Heimdall is the watchman of the gods, and is therefore placed on the borders of heaven to prevent the giants from forcing their way over the bridge Bifrost (the rainbow). He requires less sleep than a bird, and sees by night as well as by day a hundred miles around him. So acute is his ear that no sound escapes him, for he can even hear the grass grow and the wool on a sheep's back.

Considerations

1. In what ways is Odin similar to or different from creative gods of other mythologies?
2. In Valhalla the heroes cut each other into pieces but are made whole again at the end of the day; the boar Schrimnir is reborn each day. What are the implications of and possible reasons for these phenomena?
3. Does Norse mythology seem to cover all fields of man's activities? Why do you suppose there is a heavy emphasis on the warlike endeavors of man?

1. Gray's ode, "The Fatal Sisters," is founded on this superstition.

The Gods, the Creation, and the Earliest Heroes

EDITH HAMILTON

1 THE GODS

Strange clouded fragments of an ancient glory,
Late lingerers of the company divine,
They breathe of that far world where from they come,
Lost halls of heaven and Olympian air.

The Greeks did not believe that gods created the universe. It was the other way about: the universe created the gods. Before there were gods heaven and earth had been formed. They were the first parents. The Titans were their children, and the gods were their grandchildren.

THE TITANS AND THE TWELVE GREAT OLYMPIANS

The Titans, often called the Elder Gods, were for untold ages supreme in the universe. They were of enormous size and of incredible strength. There were many of them, but only a few appear in the stories of mythology. The most important was CRONUS, in Latin SATURN. He ruled over the other Titans until his son Zeus dethroned him and seized the power for himself. The Romans said that when Jupiter, their name for Zeus, ascended the throne, Saturn fled to Italy and brought in the Golden Age, a time of perfect peace and happiness, which lasted as long as he reigned.

The other notable Titans were OCEAN, the river that was supposed to encircle the earth; his wife TETHYS; HYPERION, the father of the sun, the moon and the dawn; MNEMOSYNE, which means Memory; THEMIS, usually translated by Justice; and LAPETUS, important because of his sons, ATLAS, who bore the world on his shoulders, and PROMETHEUS, who was the savior of mankind. These alone among the older gods were not banished with the coming of Zeus, but they took a lower place.

The twelve great Olympians were supreme among the gods who succeeded to the Titans. They were called the Olympians because Olympus was their home. What Olympus was, however, is not easy to say. There is no doubt that at first it was held to be a mountain top, and generally identified with Greece's highest mountain, Mt. Olympus in Thessaly, in the northeast of Greece. But even in the earliest Greek poem the *Iliad,* this idea is beginning to give way to the idea of an Olympus in some mysterious region far above all the mountains of the earth. In one passage of the *Iliad* Zeus talks to the gods from "the topmost peak of many-ridged

Olympus," clearly a mountain. But only a little further on he says that if he willed he could hang earth and sea from a pinnacle of Olympus, clearly no longer a mountain. Even so, it is not heaven. Homer makes Poseidon say that he rules the sea, Hades the dead, Zeus the heavens, but Olympus is common to all three.

Wherever it was, the entrance to it was a great gate of clouds kept by the Seasons. Within were the gods' dwellings, where they lived and slept and feasted on ambrosia and nectar and listened to Apollo's lyre. It was an abode of perfect blessedness. No wind, Homer says, ever shakes the untroubled peace of Olympus; no rain ever falls there or snow; but the cloudless firmament stretches around it on all sides and the white glory of sunshine is diffused upon its walls.

The twelve Olympians made up a divine family:—

(1) ZEUS (JUPITER), the chief; his two brothers next, (2) POSEIDON (NEPTUNE), and (3) HADES, also called PLUTO: (4) HESTIA (VESTA), their sister; (5) HERA (JUNO), Zeus's wife, and (6) ARES (MARS), their son; Zeus's children: (7) ATHENA (MINERVA), (8) APOLLO, (9) APHRODITE (VENUS), (10) HERMES (MERCURY), and (11) ARTEMIS (DIANA; and Hera's son (12) HEPHAESTUS (VULCAN), sometimes said to be the son of Zeus too.

ZEUS (JUPITER)

Zeus and his brothers drew lots for their share of the universe. The sea fell to Poseidon, and the underworld to Hades. Zeus became the supreme ruler. He was Lord of the Sky, the Rain-god and the Cloud-gatherer, who wielded the awful thunderbolt. His power was greater than that of all the other divinities together. In the *Iliad* he tells his family, "I am mightiest of all. Make trial that you may know. Fasten a rope of gold to heaven and lay hold, every god and goddess. You could not drag down Zeus. But if I wished to drag you down, then I would. The rope I would bind to a pinnacle of Olympus and all would hang in air, yes, the very earth and the sea too."

Nevertheless he was not omnipotent or omniscient, either. He could be opposed and deceived. Poseidon dupes him in the *Iliad* and so does Hera. Sometimes, too, the mysterious power, Fate, is spoken of as stronger than he. Homer makes Hera ask him scornfully if he proposes to deliver from death a man Fate has doomed.

He is represented as falling in love with one woman after another and descending to all manner of tricks to hide his infidelity from his wife. The explanation why such actions were ascribed to the most majestic of the gods is, the scholars say, that the Zeus of song and story has been made by combining many gods. When his worship spread to a town where there was already a divine ruler the two were slowly fused into one. The wife of the early god was then transferred to Zeus. The result, however, was unfortunate and the later Greeks did not like these endless love affairs.

Still, even in the earliest records Zeus had grandeur. In the *Iliad* Agamemnon prays: "Zeus, most glorious, most great, God of the storm-cloud, thou that dwellest in the heavens." He demanded, too, not only sacrifices from men, but right action. The Greek Army at Troy is told "Father Zeus never helps liars or those who break their oaths." The two ideas of him, the low and the high, persisted side by side for a long time.

His breastplate was the aegis, awful to behold; his bird was the eagle, his tree the oak. His oracle was Dodona in the land of oak trees. The god's will was revealed by the rustling of the oak leaves which the priests interpreted.

Hera (Juno)

She was Zeus's wife and sister. The Titans Ocean and Tethys brought her up. She was the protector of marriage, and married women were her peculiar care. There is very little that is attractive in the portrait the poets draw of her. She is called, indeed, in an early poem,

Golden-throned Hera, among immortals the queen.
Chief among them in beauty, the glorious lady
All the blessed in high Olympus revere,
Honor even as Zeus, the lord of the thunder.

But when any account of her gets down to details, it shows her chiefly engaged in punishing the many women Zeus fell in love with, even when they yielded only because he coerced or tricked them. It made no difference to Hera how reluctant any of them were or how innocent; the goddess treated them all alike. Her implacable anger followed them and their children too. She never forgot an injury. The Trojan War would have ended in an honorable peace, leaving both sides unconquered, if it had not been for her hatred of a Trojan who had judged another goddess lovelier than she. The wrong of her slighted beauty remained with her until Troy fell in ruins.

In one important story, the Quest of the Golden Fleece, she is the gracious protector of heroes and the inspirer of heroic deeds, but not in any other. Nevertheless she was venerated in every home. She was the goddess married women turned to for help. Ilithyia (or Eileithyia), who helped women in childbirth, was her daughter.

The cow and the peacock were sacred to her. Argos was her favorite city.

Poseidon (Neptune)

He was the ruler of the sea, Zeus's brother and second only to him in eminence. The Greeks on both sides of the Aegean were seamen and the God of the Sea was all-important to them. His wife was Amphitrite, a granddaughter of the Titan, Ocean. Poseidon had a splendid palace beneath the sea, but he was oftener to be found in Olympus.

Besides being Lord of the Sea he gave the first horse to man, and he was honored as much for the one as for the other.

Lord Poseidon, from you this pride is ours,
The strong horses, the young horses, and also the rule of the deep.

Storm and calm were under his control:—

He commanded and the storm wind rose
And the surges of the sea.

But when he drove in his golden car over the waters, the thunder of the waves sank into stillness, and tranquil peace followed his smooth-rolling wheels.

He was commonly called "Earth-shaker" and was always shown carrying his trident, a three-pronged spear, with which he would shake and shatter whatever he pleased.

He had some connection with bulls as well as with horses, but the bull was connected with many other gods too.

HADES (PLUTO)

He was the third brother among the Olympians, who drew for his share the underworld and the rule over the dead. He was also called Pluto, the God of Wealth, of the precious metals hidden in the earth. The Romans as well as the Greeks called him by this name, but often they translated it into *Dis,* the Latin word for rich. He had a far-famed cap or helmet which made whoever wore it invisible. It was rare that he left his dark realm to visit Olympus or the earth, nor was he urged to do so. He was not a welcome visitor. He was unpitying, inexorable, but just; a terrible, not an evil god.

His wife was Persephone (Proserpine) whom he carried away from the earth and made Queen of the Lower World.

He was King of the Dead—not Death himself, whom the Greeks called Thanatos and the Romans, Orcus.

PALLAS ATHENA (MINERVA)

She was the daughter of Zeus alone. No mother bore her. Full-grown and in full armor, she sprang from his head. In the earliest account of her, the *Iliad,* she is a fierce and ruthless battle-goddess, but elsewhere she is warlike only to defend the State and the home from outside enemies. She was pre-eminently the Goddess of the City, the protector of civilized life, of handicrafts and agriculture; the inventor of the bridle, who first tamed horses for men to use.

She was Zeus's favorite child. He trusted her to carry the awful aegis, his buckler, and his devastating weapon, the thunderbolt.

The word oftenest used to describe her is "gray-eyed," or, as it is sometimes translated, "flashing-eyed." Of the three virgin goddesses she was the chief and was called the Maiden,

Parthenos, and her temple the Parthenon. In later poetry she is the embodiment of wisdom, reason, purity.

Athens was her special city; the olive created by her was her tree; the owl her bird.

Phoebus Apollo

The son of Zeus and Leto (Latona), born in the little island of Delos. He has been called "the most Greek of all the gods." He is a beautiful figure in Greek poetry, the master musician who delights Olympus as he plays on his golden lyre; the lord too of the silver bow, the Archer-god, far-shooting; the Healer, as well, who first taught men the healing art. Even more than of these good and lovely endowments, he is the God of Light, in whom is no darkness at all, and so he is the God of Truth. No false word ever falls from his lips.

O Phoebus, from your throne of truth,
From your dwelling-place at the heart of the world,
You speak to men.
By Zeus's decree no lie comes there.
No shadow to darken the word of truth.
Zeus sealed by an everlasting right
Apollo's honour, that all may trust
With unshaken faith when he speaks.

Delphi under towering Parnassus, where Apollo's oracle was, plays an important part in mythology. Castalia was its sacred spring; Cephissus its river. It was held to be the center of the world, so many pilgrims came to it, from foreign countries as well as Greece. No other shrine rivaled it. The answers to the questions asked by the anxious seekers for Truth were delivered by a priestess who went into a trance before she spoke. The trance was supposed to be caused by a vapor rising from a deep cleft in the rock over which her seat was placed, a three-legged stool, the tripod.

Apollo was called Delian from Delos, the island of his birth, and Pythian from his killing of a serpent, Python, which once lived in the caves of Parnassus. It was a frightful monster and the contest was severe, but in the end the god's unerring arrows won the victory. Another name often given him was "the Lycian," variously explained as meaning Wolf-god, God of Light, and God of Lycia. In the *Iliad* he is called "the Sminthian," the Mouse-god, but whether because he protected mice or destroyed them no one knows. Often he was the Sun-god too. His name Phoebus means "brilliant" or "shining." Accurately, however, the Sun-god was Helios, child of the Titan Hyperion.

Apollo at Delphi was a purely beneficent power, a direct link between gods and men, guiding men to know the divine will, showing them how to make peace with the gods; the purifier, too, able to cleanse even those stained with the blood of their kindred. Nevertheless, there are a few tales told of him which show him pitiless and cruel. Two ideas were fighting in him as in all the gods: a primitive, crude idea and one that was beautiful and poetic. In him only a little of the primitive is left.

The laurel was his tree. Many creatures were sacred to him, chief among them the dolphin and the crow.

ARTEMIS (DIANA)

Also called Cynthis, from her birthplace, Mount Cynthus in Delos.

Apollo's twin sister, daughter of Zeus and Leto. She was one of the three maiden goddesses of Olympus:—

Golden Aphrodite who stirs with love all creation,
Cannot bend nor ensnare three hearts: the pure maiden Vesta,
Gray-eyed Athena who cares but for war and the arts of the craftsmen,
Artemis, lover of woods and the wild chase over the mountain.

She was the Lady of Wild Things, Huntsman-in-chief to the gods, an odd office for a woman. Like a good hunstman, she was careful to preserve the young; she was "the protectress of dewy youth" everywhere. Nevertheless, with one of those startling contradictions so common in mythology, she kept the Greek Fleet from sailing to Troy until they sacrificed a maiden to her. In many another story, too, she is fierce and revengeful. On the other hand, when women died a swift and painless death, they were held to have been slain by her silver arrows.

As Phoebus was the Sun, she was the Moon, called Phoebe and Selene (Luna in Latin). Neither name originally belonged to her. Phoebe was a Titan, one of the older gods. So too was Selene—a moon-goddess, indeed, but not connected with Apollo. She was the sister of Helios, the sun-god with whom Apollo was confused.

In the later poets, Artemis is identified with Hecate. She is "the goddess with three forms," Selene in the sky, Artemis on earth, Hecate in the lower world and in the world above when it is wrapped in darkness. Hecate was the Goddess of the Dark of the Moon, the black nights when the moon is hidden. She was associated with deeds of darkness, the Goddess of the Crossways, which were held to be ghostly places of evil magic. An awful divinity,

Hecate of hell,
Mighty to shatter every stubborn thing.
Hark! Hark! her hounds are baying through the town.
Where three roads meet, there she is standing.

It is a strange transformation from the lovely Huntress flashing through the forest, from the Moon making all beautiful with her light, from the pure Maiden-Goddess for whom

Whoso is chaste of spirit utterly
May gather leaves and fruits and flowers.
The unchaste never.

In her is shown most vividly the uncertainty between good and evil which is apparent in every one of the divinities.

The cypress was sacred to her; and all wild animals, but especially the deer.

APHRODITE (VENUS)

The Goddess of Love and Beauty, who beguiled all, gods and men alike; the laughter-loving goddess, who laughed sweetly or mockingly at those her wiles had conquered; the irresistible goddess who stole away even the wits of the wise.

She is the daughter of Zeus and

Dione in the *Iliad,* but in the later poems she is said to have sprung from the foam of the sea, and her name was explained as meaning "the foam-risen." *Aphros* is foam in Greek. This sea-birth took place near Cythera, from where she was wafted to Cyprus. Both islands were ever after sacred to her, and she was called Cytherea or the Cyprian as often as by her proper name.

One of the Homeric Hymns, calling her "Beautiful, golden goddess," says of her:—

The breath of the west wind bore her
Over the sounding sea,
Up from the delicate foam,
To wave-ringed Cyprus, her isle.
And the Hours golden-wreathed
Welcomed her joyously.
They clad her in raiment immortal,
And brought her to the gods.
Wonder seized them all as they saw
Violet-crowned Cytherea.

The Romans wrote of her in the same way. With her, beauty comes. The winds flee before her and the storm clouds; sweet flowers embroider the earth; the waves of the sea laugh; she moves in radiant light. Without her there is no joy nor loveliness anywhere. This is the picture the poets like best to paint of her.

But she had another side too. It was natural that she should cut a poor figure in the *Iliad,* where the battle of heroes is the theme. She is a soft, weak creature there, whom a mortal need not fear to attack. In later poems she is usually shown as treacherous and malicious, exerting a deadly and destructive power over men.

In most of the stories she is the wife of Hephaestus (Vulcan), the lame and ugly god of the forge.

The myrtle was her tree; the dove her bird—sometimes, too, the sparrow and the swan.

Hermes (Mercury)

Zeus was his father and Maia, daughter of Atlas, his mother. Because of a very popular statue his appearance is more familiar to us than that of any other god. He was graceful and swift of motion. On his feet were winged sandals; wings were on his low-crowned hat, too, and on his magic wand, the Caduceus. He was Zeus's Messenger, who "flies as fleet as thought to do his bidding."

Of all the gods he was the shrewdest and most cunning; in fact he was the Master Thief, who started upon his career before he was a day old.

The babe was born at the break of day,
And ere the night fell he had stolen away
Apollo's herds.

Zeus made him give them back, and he won Apollo's forgiveness by presenting him with the lyre which he had just invented, making it out of a tortoise's shell. Perhaps there was some connection between that very early story of him and the fact that he was God of Commerce and the Market, protector of traders.

In odd contrast to this idea of him, he was also the solemn guide of the dead, the Divine Herald who led the souls down to their last home.

He appears oftener in the tales of mythology than any other god.

Ares (Mars)

The God of War, son of Zeus and Hera, both of whom, Homer says, detested him. Indeed, he is hateful throughout the *Iliad,* poem of war though it is. Occasionally the heroes "rejoice in the delight of Ares' battle," but far oftener in having escaped "the fury of the ruthless god." Homer calls him murderous, bloodstained, the incarnate curse of mortals; and, strangely, a coward, too, who bellows with pain and runs away when he is wounded. Yet he has a train of attendants on the battlefield which should inspire anyone with confidence. His sister is there, Eris, which means Discord, and Strife, her son. The Goddess of War, Enyo,—in Latin Bellona,—walks beside him, and with her are Terror and Trembling and Panic. As they move, the voice of groaning arises behind them and the earth streams with blood.

The Romans liked Mars better than the Greeks liked Ares. He never was to them the mean whining deity of the *Iliad,* but magnificent in shining armor, redoubtable, invincible. The warriors of the great Latin heroic poem, the *Aeneid,* far from rejoicing to escape from him, rejoice when they see that they are to fall "on Mars' field of renown." They "rush on glorious death" and find it "sweet to die in battle."

Ares figures little in mythology. In one story he is the lover of Aphrodite and held up to the contempt of the Olympians by Aphrodite's husband, Hephaestus: but for the most part he is little more than a symbol of war. He is not a distinct personality, like Hermes of Hera or Apollo.

He had no cities where he was worshiped. The Greeks said vaguely that he came from Thrace, home of a rude, fierce people in the northeast of Greece.

Appropriately, his bird was the vulture. The dog was wronged by being chosen as his animal.

Hephaestus (Vulcan and Mulciber)

The God of Fire, sometimes said to be the son of Zeus and Hera, sometimes of Hera alone, who bore him in retaliation for Zeus's having brought forth Athena. Among the perfectly beautiful immortals he only was ugly. He was lame as well. In one place in the *Iliad* he says that his shameless mother, when she saw that he was born deformed, cast him out of heaven; in another place he declares that Zeus did this, angry with him for trying to defend Hera. This second story is the better known, because of Milton's familiar lines: Mulciber was

Thrown by angry Jove
Sheer o'er the crystal battlements: from morn
To noon he fell, from noon to dewy eve,
A summer's day, and with the setting sun
Dropt from the zenith like a falling star,
On Lemnos, the Aegean isle.

These events, however, were supposed to have taken place in the far-distant past. In Homer he is in no danger of being driven from Olympus; he is highly honored there, the workman of the immortals, their

armorer and smith, who makes their dwellings and their furnishings as well as their weapons. In his workshop he has handmaidens he has forged out of gold who can move and who help him in his work.

In the later poets his forge is often said to be under this or that volcano, and to cause eruptions.

His wife is one of the three Graces in the *Iliad,* called Aglaia in Hesiod; in the *Odyssey* she is Aphrodite.

He was a kindly, peace-loving god, popular on earth as in heaven. With Athena, he was important in the life of the city. The two were the patrons of handicrafts, the arts which along with agriculture are the support of civilization; he the protector of the smiths as she of the weavers. When children were formally admitted to the city organization, the god of the ceremony was Hephaestus.

Hestia (Vesta)

She was Zeus's sister, and like Athena and Artemis a virgin goddess. She has no distinct personality and she plays no part in the myths. She was the Goddess of the Hearth, the symbol of the home, around which the newborn child must be carried before it could be received into the family. Every meal began and ended with an offering to her.

Hestia, in all dwellings of men and immortals
Yours is the highest honor, the sweet wine offered
First and last at the feast, poured out to you duly.
Never without you can gods or mortals hold banquet.

Each city too had a public hearth sacred to Hestia, where the fire was never allowed to go out. If a colony was to be founded, the colonists carried with them coals from the hearth of the mother-city with which to kindle the fire on the new city's hearth.

In Rome her fire was cared for by six virgin priestesses, called Vestals.

Concept: Oedipus

A TERRIFYING MYTH HAS REVERBERATED THROUGH 27 CENTURIES AND WILL NEVER LEAVE US

There is no more powerful and terrible legend than that of Oedipus, king of Thebes, a foundling fated to kill his father, marry his mother and, in the agony of revelation, blind himself. Sophocles made the legend of Oedipus, first king, then eyeless wanderer into ultimate art, and in doing so made us understand tragedy. No one will ever do it better, but the legend lives on into its third millenium through others who have made their own truths out of indestructible myth.

Homer's Oedipus

I saw the mother of Oidipous, Epikaste, whose great unwitting deed it was to marry her own son. He took that prize from a slain father; presently the gods brought all to light that made the famous story. But by their fearsome wills he kept his throne in dearest Thebes, all through his evil days, while she descended to the place of Death, god of the locked and iron door. Steep down from a high rafter, throttled in her noose, she swung, carried away by pain, and left him endless agony from a mother's Furies.

From *The Odyssey*
Translated by Robert Fitzgerald

Sophocles' Oedipus

JOCASTA: He shall come, but I too have a right to know what lies so heavy upon your heart, my King.

OEDIPUS: Yes: and it shall not be kept from you now that my fear has grown so heavy. Nobody is more to me than you, nobody has the same right to learn my good or evil luck. My father was Polybus of Corinth, my mother the Dorian Merope, and I was held the foremost man in all that town until a thing happened—a thing to startle a man, though not to make him angry as it made me. We were sitting at the table, and a man who had drunk too much cried out that I was not my father's son—and I, though angry, restrained my anger for that day; but the next day went to my father and my mother and questioned them. They were indignant at the taunt and that comforted me—and yet the man's words rankled, for they had spread a rumor through the town. Without consulting my father or my mother I went to Delphi, but Phoebus told me nothing of the thing for which I came, but much of other things—things of sorrow and of terror: that I should live in incest with my mother, and beget a brood that men would shudder to look upon; that I should be my father's murderer. Hearing those words I fled out of Corinth, and from that day have but known where it lies when I have found its direction by the stars. I sought where I might escape those infamous things—the doom that was laid upon me. I came in my flight to that very spot where you tell me this king perished. Now, lady, I will tell you the truth. When I had come close up to those three roads, I came upon a herald, and a man like him you have described seated in a carriage. The man who held the rein and the old man himself would not give me room, but thought to force me from the path, and I struck the driver in my anger. The old man, seeing what I had done, waited till I was passing him and then struck me upon the head. I paid him back in full, for I knocked him out of the carriage with a blow of my stick. He rolled on his back, and after that I killed them all. If this stranger were indeed Laius, is there a more miserable man in the world than the man before you? Is there a man more hated of Heaven? No stranger, no citizen, may receive him into his house, not a soul may speak to him, and no mouth but my own mouth has laid this curse upon me. Am I not wretched? May I be swept from this world before I have endured this doom! . . .

Second Messenger: A short tale in the telling: Jocasta, our Queen, is dead.

Chorus: Alas, miserable woman, how did she die?

Second Messenger: By her own hand. It cannot be as terrible to you as to one that saw it with his eyes, yet so far as words can serve, you shall see it. When she had come into the vestibule, she ran half crazed toward her marriage bed, clutching at her hair with the fingers of both hands, and once within the chamber dashed the doors together behind her. Then called upon the name of Laius, long since dead, remembering that son who killed the father and upon the mother begot an accursed race. And wailed because of that marriage wherein she had borne a two-fold race-husband by husband, children by her child. Then Oedipus with a shriek burst in and running here and there asked for a sword, asked where he would find the wife that was no wife but a mother who had borne his children and himself. Nobody answered him, we all stood dumb; but supernatural power helped him, for, with a dreadful shriek, as though beckoned, he sprang at the double doors, drove them in, burst the bolts out of their sockets, and ran into the room. There we saw the woman hanging in a swinging halter, and with a terrible cry he loosened the halter from her neck. When that unhappiest woman lay stretched upon the ground, we saw another dreadful sight. He dragged the golden brooches from her dress and lifting them stuck them upon his eyeballs, crying out, "You have looked enough upon those you ought never to have looked upon, failed long enough to know those that you should have known; henceforth you shall be dark." He struck his eyes, not once, but many times, lifting his hands and speaking such or like words. The blood poured down and not with a few slow drops, but all at once over his beard in a dark shower as it were hail.

Translated by William Butler Yeats

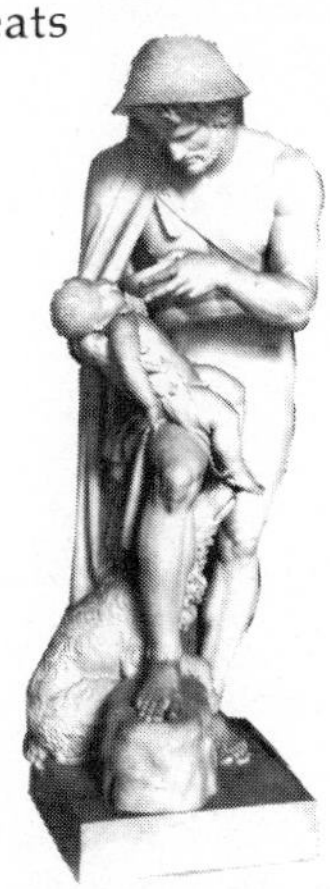

Culver Pictures

Through the ages, the Oedipus story has haunted artists and players. Above, Le Berger Phorbas et Oedipe by sculptor Antoine Chaudet (1763–1810).

Bettmann Archive

J. A. Ingres' nineteenth century painting Oedipus Consulting the Sphinx (above) in the Louvre.

Photo by Fred Fehl

Above, John Kerr and Joan McCracken starred in the 1958 Phoenix Theatre production of Jean Cocteau's *The Infernal Machine.* The play, written in 1934, recreated the ancient Oedipus legend in surrealistic form.

Seneca's Oedipus

This Roman version of the myth does not achieve the starkness of the Greek. In this scene Oedipus unroots his past from an unwilling shepherd.

OEDIPUS: Yet I must find the truth, though it be shameful,
About my parentage—and search I will. . .
An aged man approaches; it is Phorbas,
He that was master of the royal shepherds.
Do you recall his name or know his face?

OLD MAN: His looks awake a memory; that face
Is one I know, yet do not know for certain. . .
When Laius was king, were you a shepherd
Tending his prime flock on Cithaeron's slopes?

PHORBAS: Ay, there was always fine fresh pasturage
In summer on Cithaeron, where I worked.

OLD MAN: Have you seen me before?

PHORBAS: Not to remember—

OEDIPUS: Do you remember giving him a child,
A boy? Speak out. Why does your face turn pale?
You are not sure? You need not choose your words.
Truth won't be hidden by procrastination.

PHORBAS: You delve into the long-forgotten past.

OEDIPUS: Speak, or else torture must fetch out the truth.

PHORBAS: 'Tis true, I gave an infant to this man—
A useless gift, it never could have grown
To enjoy the light of day.

OLD MAN: Say no such thing!
He is alive, and may his life be long.

OEDIPUS: Why do you think the infant must have died?

PHORBAS: An iron bolt was driven through the feet
To pin the legs together; swelling sores
Had festered and inflamed the whole small body.

OEDIPUS: Need you ask more! Fate stands beside you now.
Tell me what child it was.

PHORBAS: Duty forbids—

OEDIPUS: Let fire be brought! Hot coals will burn out duty!

PHORBAS: Must truth be sought by such inhuman means?
Have pity!

OEDIPUS: If you think me harsh and ruthless,
Yours is the power to punish that offense,
By telling me the truth. Who was the child?
What father's and what mother's son was he?

PHORBAS: Your wife was that child's mother.

OEDIPUS: Earth, be opened!
Ruler of darkness, hide in deepest hell
This monstrous travesty of pro-

creation!
Thebans, heap stones upon this cursed head,
Strike me to death with weapons! Let all sons,
All fathers, draw their swords upon me; husbands,
Brothers take arms against me; let my people,
Stricken by pestilence, seize brands from pyres
To hurl at me! Here walks this age's sin,
Here walks the abomination of the gods,
The death of sacred law—from his first day
Of innocent life deserving only death. . .
Now be your courage keen; now dare a deed
To match your sins! Into the palace, go,
Go quickly, give your mother joyful greeting,
Blest in the increase of her happy home! . . .

Translated by E. F. Watling

Dryden's Oedipus

John Dryden and Nathaniel Lee, Restoration playwrights, made Oedipus into a charged, highly emotional collaborative work. Here Haemon describes what happened to "the desperate king."

Haemon: Thrice he struck,
With all his force, his hollow groaning breast,
And thus, with out-cries, to himself complain'd.
But thou canst weep then, and thou think'st 'tis well,
These bubbles of the shallowest emptiest sorrow,
Which Children vent for toys, and Women rain
For any Trifle their fond hearts are set on;
Yet these thou think'st are ample satisfaction
For bloodiest Murder, and for burning Lust:
No, Parricide; if thou must weep, weep blood;
Weep Eyes, instead of Tears: O, by the Gods,
'Tis greatly thought, he cry'd, and fits my woes.
Which said, he smil'd revengefully, and leapt
Upon the floor; thence gazing at the Skies,
His Eye-balls fiery Red, and glowing vengeance;
Gods, I accuse you not, tho'I no more
Will view your Heav'n, till with more durable glasses,
The mighty Souls immortal Perspectives,
I find your dazling Beings: Take, he cry'd,
Take, Eyes, your last, your fatal farewell-view.
When with a groan, that seem'd the call of Death,
With horrid force lifting his impious hands,
He snatch'd, he tore, from forth their bloody Orbs,
The Balls of sight, and dash'd 'em on the ground.

Corneille's Oedipus

Corneille's Oedipe is jammed with preciousness and subplots. The hero, more French than mortal, finally acknowledges his fate in a monologue, translated by Richard Howard.

OEDIPE: Aux crimes malgré moi l'ordre du ciel m'attache;
Pour m'y faire tomber à moi-même il me cache;
Il offre, en m'aveuglant sur ce qui'il a prédit,
Mon père à mon épée, et ma mère á mon lit.
Helas! qui'il est bien vrai qu'en vain on s'imagine
Dérober notre vie à ce qui'il nous destine!
Les soins de l'éviter font courir audevant,
Et l'adresse à le fuir y plonge plus avant.
Mais si les dieux m'ont fait la vie abominable,
Ils m'en font par pitié la sortie honorable,
Puisque enfin leur faveur mêlée à leur courroux
Me condamne à mourir pour le salut de tous,
Et qu'en ce même temps qu'il faudrait que ma vie
Des crimes qu'ils m'ont faits traînât l'ignominie,
L'éclat de ces vertus que je ne tiens pas d'eux
Reçoit pour récompense un trépas glorieux.

OEDIPUS: The commands of the gods constrain me to these crimes,
And I have become the ignorant victim of myself:
Deluded by their blinding oracles, I put
My father to my sword, my mother in my bed.
How mad our faith, how vain our enterprise
To divert our life from what is preordained!
Trying to avoid fate casts us in its path,
And all our skill in evasion leads us farther on.
Yet if the gods have made my life anathema,
They have mercifully bestowed an honorable escape,
Since now their favor, united with their frown,
Dooms me to die for the common good of all,
So that even as my life must demonstrate
The ignominy of their crimes committed upon me,
The light of virtues I never had from them
Receives, in recompense, a glorious downfall.

Freud's Oedipus

It was Sigmund Freud in The Interpretation of Dreams *who took the legend and made us understand our desires.*

According to my already extensive experience, parents play a leading part in the infantile psychology of all persons who subsequently become psychoneurotics. Falling in love with one parent and hating the other forms part of the permanent stock of the psychic impulses that arise in early childhood, and are of such importance as the material of the subsequent neurosis. But I do not believe that psychoneurotics are to be sharply distinguished in this respect from other persons who remain normal—that is, I do not believe that they are capable of creating something absolutely new and peculiar to themselves. It is far more probable—and this is confirmed by incidental observations of normal children—that in their amorous or hostile attitude toward their parents, psychoneurotics do no more than reveal to us, by magnification, something that occurs less markedly and intensively in the minds of the majority of children. Antiquity has furnished us with legendary matter that corroborates this belief, and the profound and universal validity of the old legends is explicable only by an equally universal validity of the above-mentioned hypothesis of infant psychology.

I am referring to the legend of King Oedipus and the Oedipus Rex of Sophocles. . . .

If the Oedipus Rex is capable of moving a modern reader or playgoer no less powerfully than it moved the contemporary Greeks, the only possible explanation is that the effect of the Greek tragedy does not depend upon the conflict between fate and human will, but upon the peculiar nature of the material by which this conflict is revealed. There must be a voice within us that is prepared to

The Bettmann Archive

In the engraving above, Oedipus has just discovered that his wife is his mother.

acknowledge the compelling power of fate in Oedipus, while we are able to condemn the situations occurring in Die Ahnfrau or other tragedies of fate as arbitrary inventions. And there actually is a motive in the story of King Oedipus that explains the verdict of this inner voice. His fate moves us only because it might have been our own, because the oracle laid upon us before our birth the very curse that rested upon him. It may be that we were all destined to direct our first sexual impulses toward our mothers, and our first impulses of hatred and violence toward our fathers; our dreams convince us that we were. King Oedipus, who slew his father Laius and wedded his mother

Jocasta, is nothing more or less than a wish fulfillment—the fulfillment of the wish of our childhood. But we, more fortunate than he, insofar as we have not become psychoneurotics, have since our childhood succeeded in withdrawing our sexual impulses from our mothers and in forgetting our jealousy of our fathers. We recoil from the person for whom this primitive wish of our childhood has been fulfilled with all the force of the repression that these wishes have undergone in our minds since childhood. As the poet brings the guilt of Oedipus to light by his investigation, he forces us to become aware of our own inner selves, in which the same impulses are still extant, even though they are suppressed. The antithesis with which the chorus departs—

. . . Behold, this is Oedipus,
Who unraveled the great riddle, and was first in power,
Whose fortune all the townsmen praised and envied;
See in what dread adversity he sank!

—this admonition touches us and our own pride, us who since the years of our childhood have grown so wise and so powerful in our own estimation. Like Oedipus, we live in ignorance of the desires that offend morality, the desires that nature has forced upon us and after their unveiling we may well prefer to avert our gaze from the scenes of our childhood.

In the very text of Sophocles' tragedy there is an unmistakable reference to the fact that the Oedipus legend had its source in dream material of immemorial antiquity, the content of which was the painful disturbance of the child's relations to its parents caused by the first impulses of sexuality. Jocasta comforts Oedipus—who is not yet enlightened, but is troubled by the recollection of the oracle—by an allusion to a dream that is often dreamed, though it cannot, in her opinion, mean anything:

For many a man hath seen himself in dreams
His mother's mate, but he who gives no heed
To suchlike matters bears the easier life.

The dream of having sexual intercourse with one's mother was as common then as it is today with many people, who tell it with indignation and astonishment. As may well be imagined, it is the key to the tragedy and the complement to the dream of the death of his father. The Oedipus fable is the reaction of fantasy to these two typical dreams, and just as such a dream, when occurring to an adult, is experienced with feelings of aversion, so the content of the fable must include terror and self-chastisement. The form that it subsequently assumed was the result of an uncomprehending secondary elaboration of the material, which sought to make it serve a theological intention. The attempt to reconcile divine omnipotence with human responsibility must, of course, fail with this material as with any other.

Gide's Oedipus

Andre Gide, who had made a play out of the Oedipus myth in 1931, returned to the legend in Theseus, *excerpted here.*

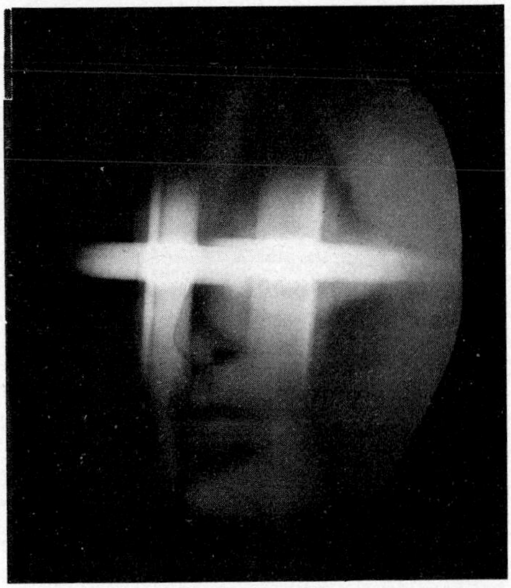
Norm Schaefer/Intellectual Digest

Oedipus, when I (Theseus) welcomed him at Colonus, had been driven from Thebes, his fatherland; without eyes, dishonored and wretched as he was, he at least had his two daughters with him, and in their constant tenderness he found relief from his sufferings. He had failed in every part of what he had undertaken. I have succeeded. Even the enduring blessing that his ashes are to confer upon the country where they are laid—even this will rest, not upon his ungrateful Thebes, but upon Athens.

I am surprised that so little should have been said about this meeting of our destinies at Colonus, this moment at the crossroads when our two careers confronted each other. I take it to have been the summit and the crown of my glory. Till then I had forced all life to do obeisance to me. . . . In Oedipus alone did I recognize a nobility equal to my own. His misfortunes could only enhance his grandeur in my eyes. No doubt I had triumphed everywhere and always; but on a level that, in comparison with Oedipus, seemed to me merely human—inferior, I might say, He had held his own with the Sphinx; had stood man upright before the riddle of life and dared to oppose him to the gods. How then, and why, had he accepted defeat? By putting out his eyes, had he not even contributed to it? There was something, in this dreadful act of violence against himself, that I could not contrive to understand. I must admit it hardly satisfied me—or else I did not fully understand it.

"True," he said, "I yielded to an impulse of rage—one that could only be directed against myself; against whom else could I have turned? In face of the immeasurable horror of the accusations I had just discovered, I felt an overwhelming desire to make a protest. And besides, what I wanted to destroy was not so much my eyes as the canvas they held before me; the scenery before which I was struggling, the falsehood in which I no longer believed; and this so as to break through to reality.

"And yet, no! I was not really thinking of anything very clearly; I acted rather by instinct. I put out my eyes to punish them for having failed to see the evidence that had, as people say, been staring me in the face. But, to speak the truth—ah, how can I put it to you? . . . Nobody understood me when I suddenly cried: 'O darkness, my light!' And you also, you don't understand it—I feel that distinctly. People heard it as a cry of grief; it was a statement of fact. . . . I meant: 'Darkness, thou are henceforth my light'. And at the moment when the blue of the sky went black before me, my inward firmament became bright with stars."

He was silent and for some moments remained deep in meditation. Then he went on:

"As a young man, I passed for one who could see the future. I believed it myself, too. Was I not the first, the only man, to solve the riddle of the Sphinx? Only since my eyes of flesh were torn with my own hand from the world of appearances have I begun, it seems to me, to see truly. Yes; at the moment when the outer world was hidden forever from the eyes of my body, a kind of new eyesight opened out within myself upon the infinite perspectives of an inner world, which the world of appearances (the only one that had existed for me until that time) had led me to disdain. And this imperceptible world (inaccessible, I mean, to our senses) is, I now know, the only true one. All the rest is an illusion, a deception, moreover, that disturbs our contemplation of what is divine. Tiresias, the blind sage, once said to me: 'Who wishes to see God must first cease to see the world'; and I didn't understand him then; just as you, yourself, O Theseus, do not understand me now."

"I shall not attempt to deny," I replied, "the importance of this world beyond temporal things of which your blindness has made you aware; but what I still cannot understand is why you oppose it to the outer world in which we live and act."

"Because," said Oedipus, "for the first time, when with my inward eye I perceived what was formerly hidden from me, I suddenly became aware of this fact: that I had based my earthly sovereignty upon a crime, and that everything which followed from this

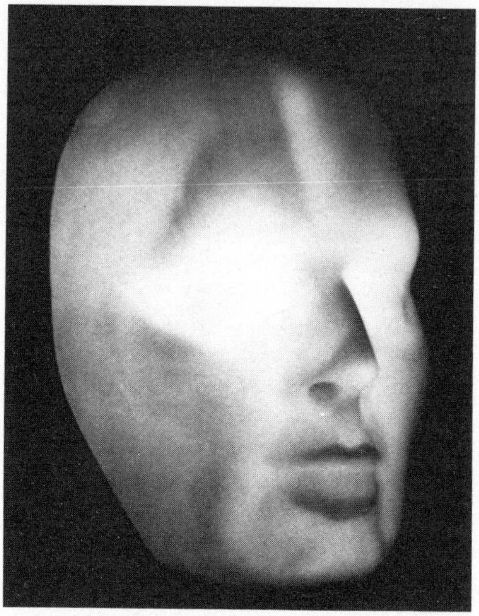

Norm Schaefer/Intellectual Digest

was in consequence tainted; not merely all my personal decisions, but even those of the two sons to whom I had abandoned my crown—for I at once stepped down from the slippery eminence to which my crime had raised me. . . . "

He was silent again for a few moments, as if preparing to plunge still deeper, and then went on:

"You are astonished that I should have put out my eyes. I am astonished myself. But in this gesture, inconsidered and cruel as it was, there may yet be something else: an indefinable secret longing to follow my fortunes to their farthest limit, to give the final turn of the screw to my anguish, and to bring to a close the destiny of a hero."

The Quest of the Golden Fleece

Edith Hamilton

This is the title of a long poem, very popular in classical days, by the third-century poet Apollonius of Rhodes. He tells the whole story of the Quest except the part about Jason and Pelias which I have taken from Pindar. It is the subject of one of his most famous odes, written in the first half of the fifth century. Apollonius ends his poem with the return of the heroes to Greece. I have added the account of what Jason and Medea did there, taking it from the fifth-century tragic poet Euripides, who made it the subject of one of his best plays.

These three writers are very unlike each other. No prose paraphrase can give any idea of Pindar, except, perhaps, something of his singular power for vivid and minutely detailed description. Readers of the Aeneid *will be reminded of Virgil by Apollonius. The difference between Euripides' Medea and Apollonius' heroine and also Virgil's Dido is in its degree a measure of what Greek tragedy was.*

The first hero in Europe who undertook a great journey was the leader of the Quest of the Golden Fleece. He was supposed to have lived a generation earlier than the most famous Greek traveler, the hero of the *Odyssey*. It was of course a journey by water. Rivers, lakes, and seas, were the only highways; there were no roads. All the same, a voyager had to face perils not only on the deep, but on the land as well. Ships did not sail by night, and any place where sailors put in might harbor a monster or a magician who could work more deadly harm than storm and shipwreck. High courage was necessary to travel, especially outside of Greece.

No story proved this fact better than the account of what the heroes suffered who sailed in the ship *Argo* to find the Golden Fleece. It may be doubted, indeed, if there ever was a voyage on which sailors had to face so many and such varied dangers. However, they were all heroes of renown, some of them the greatest in Greece, and they were quite equal to their adventures.

The tale of the Golden Fleece begins with a Greek king named Athamas, who got tired of his wife, put her away, and married another, the Princess Ino. Nephele, the first wife, was afraid for her two children, especially the boy, Phrixus. She thought the second wife would try to kill him so that her own son could inherit the kingdom, and she was right. This second wife came from a great family. Her father was Cadmus, the excellent King of Thebes; her mother and her three sisters were women of blameless lives. But she herself, Ino, determined to bring about the little boy's death, and she made an elaborate plan how this was to be done. Somehow she got possession of all the seed-corn and parched it before the men went out for the sowing, so that, of course, there was no harvest at all. When the King sent a man to ask the oracle what he should do in this fearful distress, she persuaded or, more probably, bribed the messenger to say that the oracle had declared the corn would not grow again unless they offered up the young Prince as a sacrifice.

The people, threatened with starvation, forced the King to yield and permit the boy's death. To the later Greeks the idea of such a sacrifice was as horrible as it is to us, and when it played a part in a story they almost always changed it into something less shocking. As this tale has come down to us, when the boy had been taken to the altar a wondrous ram, with a fleece of pure gold, snatched him and his sister up and bore them away through the air. Hermes had sent him in answer to their mother's prayer.

While they were crossing the strait which separates Europe and Asia, the girl, whose name was Helle, slipped and fell into the water. She was drowned; and the strait was named for her: the Sea of Helle, the Hellespont. The boy came safely to land, to the country of Colchis on the Unfriendly Sea (the Black Sea, which had not yet become friendly). The Colchians were a fierce people. Nevertheless, they were kind to Phrixus; and their King, Æetes, let him marry one of his daughters. It seems odd that Phrixus sacrificed to Zeus the ram that had saved him, in gratitude for having been saved; but he did so, and he gave the precious Golden Fleece to King Æetes.

Phrixus had an uncle who was by rights a king in Greece, but had had his kingdom taken away from him by his nephew, a man named Pelias. The King's young son, Jason, the rightful heir to the kingdom, had been sent secretly away to a place of safety, and when he was grown he came boldly back to claim the kingdom from his wicked cousin.

The usurper Pelias had been told by an oracle that he would die at the hands of kinsmen, and that he should beware of anyone whom he saw shod with only a single sandal. In due time such a man came to the town. One foot was bare, although in all other ways he was well-clad—a garment fitting close to his splendid limbs, and around his shoulders a leopard's skin to turn the showers. He had not shorn the bright locks of his hair; they ran rippling down his back. He went straight into the town and entered the marketplace fearlessly, at the time when the multitude filled it.

None knew him, but one and another wondered at him and said, "Can he be Apollo? Or Aphrodite's lord? Not one of Poseidon's bold sons, for they are dead." So they questioned each other. But Pelias came in hot haste at the tidings and when he saw the single sandal he was afraid. He hid his terror in his heart, however, and addressed the stranger: "What country is your fatherland? No hateful and defiling lies, I beg you. Tell me the truth." With gentle words the other answered: "I have come to my home to recover the ancient honor of my house, this land no longer ruled aright, which Zeus gave to my father. I am your cousin, and they call me by the name of Jason. You and I must rule ourselves by the law of right—not appeal to brazen swords or spears. Keep all the wealth you have taken, the flocks and the tawny herds of cattle and the fields, but the sovereign scepter and the throne release to me, so that no evil quarrel will arise from them."

Pelias gave him a soft answer. "So shall it be. But one thing must first be done. The dead Phrixus bids us bring back the Golden Fleece and thus bring back his spirit to his home. The oracle has spoken. But for me, already old age is my companion, while the flower of your youth is only now coming into full bloom. Do you go upon this quest, and I swear with Zeus as witness that I will give up the kingdom and the sovereign rule to you." So he spoke, believing in his heart that no one could make the attempt and come back alive.

The idea of the great adventure was delightful to Jason. He agreed, and let it be known everywhere that this would be a voyage indeed. The young men of Greece joyfully met the challenge. They came, all the best and noblest, to join the company. Hercules, the greatest of all heroes, was there; Orpheus, the master musician; Castor with his brother Pollux; Achilles' father, Peleus; and many another. Hera was helping Jason, and it was she who kindled in each one the desire not to be left behind nursing a life without peril by his mother's side, but even at the price of death to drink with his comrades the peerless elixir of valor. They set sail in the ship *Argo.* Jason took in his hands a golden goblet and, pouring a libation of wine into the sea, called upon Zeus whose lance is the lightning to speed them on their way.

Great perils lay before them, and some of them paid with their lives for drinking that peerless elixir. They put in first at Lemnos, a strange island where only women lived. They had risen up against the men and had killed them all, except one, the old king. His daughter, Hypsipyle, a leader among the women, had spared her father and set him afloat on the sea in a hollow chest, which finally carried him to safety. These fierce creatures, however, welcomed the Argonauts, and helped them with good gifts of food and wine and garments before they sailed away.

Soon after they left Lemnos the Argonauts lost Hercules from the company. A lad named Hylas, his armor-bearer, very dear to him, was drawn under the water as he dipped his pitcher in a spring, by a water nymph who saw the rosy flush of his beauty and wished to kiss him. She threw her arms around his neck and drew him down into the depths and he was seen no more. Hercules sought him madly everywhere, shouting his name and plunging deeper and deeper into the forest away from the sea. He had forgotten the Fleece and the *Argo* and his comrades: everything except Hylas. He did not come back, and finally the ship had to sail without him.

Their next adventure was with the Harpies, frightful flying creatures with hooked beaks and claws who always left behind them a loathsome stench, sickening to all living creatures. Where the Argonauts had beached their boat for the night lived a lonely and wretched old man, to whom Apollo, the truth-teller, had given the gift of prophecy. He foretold unerringly what would happen, and this had displeased Zeus, who always liked to wrap in mystery what he would do—and very sensibly, too, in the opinion of all who knew Hera. So he inflicted a terrible punishment upon the old man. Whenever he was about to dine, the Harpies who were called "the hounds of Zeus" swooped down and defiled the food, leaving it so foul that no one could bear to be near it, much less eat it. When the Argonauts saw the poor old creature—his name was Phineus—he was like a lifeless dream, creeping on withered feet, trembling for weakness, and only the skin on his body held his bones together. He welcomed them gladly and begged them to help him. He knew through his gift of prophecy that he could be defended from the Harpies by two men alone, who were among the company on the *Argo*—the sons of Boreas, the great North Wind. All listened to him with pity and the two gave him eagerly their promise to help.

While the others set forth food for him, Boreas' sons took their stand beside him with drawn swords. He had hardly put a morsel to his lips when the hateful monsters darted down from the sky and in a moment had devoured everything and were flying off, leaving the intolerable odor behind them. But the wind-swift sons of the North Wind followed them; they caught up with them and struck at them with their swords. They would assuredly have cut them to pieces if Iris, the rainbow messenger of the gods, gliding down from heaven, had not checked them. They must forbear to kill the hounds of Zeus, she said, but she swore by the waters of the Styx, the oath that none can break, that they would never again trouble Phineus. So the two returned gladly and comforted the old man, who in his joy sat feasting with the heroes all through the night.

He gave them wise advice, too, about the dangers before them, in especial about the Clashing Rocks, the Symplegades, that rolled perpetually against one another while the sea boiled up around them. The way to pass between them, he said, was first to make trial with a dove. If she passed through safely, then the chances were that they too would get through. But if the dove were crushed, they must turn back and give up all hope of the Golden Fleece.

The next morning they started, with a dove, of course, and were soon in sight of the great rolling rocks. It seemed impossible that there could be a way between them, but they freed the dove and watched her. She flew through and came out safe. Only the tips of her tail-feathers were caught between the rocks as they rolled back together; and those were torn away. The heroes went after her as swiftly as they could. The rocks parted, the rowers put forth all their strength, and they too came through safely. Just in time, however, for as the rocks clashed together again the extreme end of the stern ornament was shorn off. By so little they escaped destruction. But ever since they passed them, the rocks have been rooted fast to each other and have never any more brought disaster to sailors.

Not far from there was the country of the warrior women, the Amazons—the daughters, strangely enough, of that most peace-loving nymph, sweet Harmony. But their father was Ares, the terrible god of war, whose ways they followed and not their mother's. The heroes would gladly have halted and closed in battle with them, and it would not have been a battle without bloodshed, for the Amazons were not gentle foes. But the wind was favorable and they hurried on. They caught a glimpse of the Caucasus as they sped past, and of Prometheus on his rock high above them, and they heard the fanning of the eagle's huge wings as it darted down to its bloody feast. They stopped for nothing, and that same day at sunset they reached Colchis, the country of the Golden Fleece.

They spent the night facing they knew not what and feeling that there was no help for them anywhere except in their own valor. Up in Olympus, however, a consultation was being held about them. Hera, troubled at the danger they were in, went to ask Aphrodite's help. The Goddess of Love was surprised at the visit, for Hera was no friend of hers. Still, when the great Queen of Olympus begged for her aid, she was awed and promised to do all she could. Together they planned that Aphrodite's son Cupid should make the daughter of the Colchian King fall in love with Jason. That was an excellent plan—for Jason. The maiden, who was named Medea, knew how to work very powerful magic, and could undoubtedly save the Argonauts if she would use her dark knowledge for them. So Aphrodite went to Cupid and told him she would give him a lovely plaything, a ball of shining gold and deep blue enamel, if he would do what she wanted. He was delighted, seized his bow and quiver, and swept down from Olympus through the vast expanse of air to Colchis.

Meantime the heroes had started for the city to ask the King for the Golden Fleece. They were safe from any trouble on the way, for Hera wrapped them in a thick mist, so that they reached the palace unseen. It dissolved when they approached the entrance, and the warders, quick to notice the band of splendid young strangers, led them courteously within and sent word to the King of their arrival.

He came at once and bade them welcome. His servants hastened to make all ready, build fires and heat water for the baths and prepare food. Into this busy scene stole the Princess Medea, curious to see the visitors. As her eyes fell upon Jason, Cupid swiftly drew his bow and shot a shaft deep into the maiden's heart. It burned there like a flame and her soul melted with sweet pain, and her face went now white, now red. Amazed and abashed she stole back to her chamber.

Only after the heroes had bathed and refreshed themselves with meat and drink could King Æetes ask them who they were and why they had come. It was accounted great discourtesy to put any question to a guest before his wants had been satisfied. Jason answered that they were all men of noblest birth, sons or grandsons of the gods, who had sailed from Greece in the hope that he would give them the Golden Fleece in return for whatever service he would ask of them. They would conquer his enemies for him, or do anything he wished.

A great anger filled King Æetes' heart as he listened. He did not like foreigners, any more than the Greeks did; he wanted them to keep away from his country, and he said to himself, "If these strangers had not eaten at my table I would kill them." In silence he pondered what he should do, and a plan came to him.

He told Jason that he bore no grudge against brave men and that if they proved themselves such he would give the Fleece to them. "And the trial of your courage," he said, "shall be only what I myself have done." This was to yoke two bulls he had, whose feet were of bronze and whose breath was flaming fire, and with them to plow a field. Then the teeth of a dragon must be cast into the furrows, like seed-corn—which would spring up at once into a crop of armed men. These must be cut down as they advanced to the attack—a fearful harvesting. "I have done all this myself," he said; "and I will give the Fleece to no man less brave than I." For a time Jason sat speechless. The contest seemed impossible, beyond the strength of anyone. Finally he answered, "I will make the trial, monstrous though it is, even if it is my doom to die." With that he rose up and led his comrades back to the ship for the night, but Medea's thoughts followed after him. All through the long night when he had left the palace she seemed to see him, his beauty and his grace, and to hear the words he had uttered. Her heart was tormented with fear for him. She guessed what her father was planning.

Returned to the ship, the heroes held a council and one and another urged Jason to let him take the trial upon himself; but in vain, Jason would yield to none of them. As they talked there came to them one of the King's grandsons whose life Jason once had saved, and he told them of Medea's magic power. There was nothing she could not do, he said, check the stars, even, and the moon. If she were persuaded to help, she could make Jason able to conquer the bulls and the dragon-teeth men. It seemed the only plan that offered any hope and they urged the prince to go back and try to win Medea over, not knowing that the God of Love had already done that.

She sat alone in her room, weeping and telling herself she was shamed forever because she cared so much for a stranger that she wanted to yield to a mad passion and go against her father. "Far better die," she said. She took in her hand a casket which held herbs for killing, but as she sat there with it, she thought of life and the delightful things that are in the world; and the sun seemed sweeter than ever before. She put the casket away; and no longer wavering she determined to use her power for the man she loved. She had a magic ointment which would make him who rubbed it on his body safe for that day; he could not be harmed by anything. The plant it was made from sprang up first when Prometheus' blood dripped down upon the earth. She put it in her bosom and went to find her nephew, the prince whom Jason had helped. She met him as he was looking for her to beg her to do just what she had already decided on. She agreed at once to all he said and sent him to the ship to tell Jason to meet her without delay in a certain place. As soon as he heard the message Jason started, and as he went Hera shed radiant grace upon him, so that all who saw him marveled at him. When he reached Medea it seemed to her as if her heart left her to go to him; a dark mist clouded her eyes and she had no strength to move. The two stood face to face without a word, as lofty pine trees when the wind is still. Then again when the wind stirs they murmur; so these two also, stirred by the breath of love, were fated to tell out all their tale to each other.

He spoke first and implored her to be kind to him. He could not but have hope, he said, because her loveliness must surely mean that she excelled in gentle courtesy. She did not know how to speak to him; she wanted to pour out all she felt at once. Silently she drew the box of ointment from her bosom and gave it to him. She would have given her soul to him if he had asked her. And now both were fixing their eyes on the ground abashed, and again were throwing glances at each other, smiling with love's desire.

At last Medea spoke and told him how to use the charm and that when it was sprinkled on his weapons it would make them as well as himself invincible for a day. If too many of the dragon-teeth men rushed to attack him, he must throw a stone into their midst, which would make them turn against each other and fight until all were killed. "I must go back to the palace now," she said. "But when you are once more safe at home remember Medea, as I will remember you forever." He answered passionately, "Never by night and never by day will I forget you. If you will come to Greece, you shall be worshiped for what you have done for us, and nothing except death will come between us."

They parted, she to the palace to weep over her treachery to her father, he to the ship to send two of his comrades for the dragon's teeth. Meantime he made trial of the ointment and at the touch of it a terrible, irresistible power entered into him and the heroes all exulted. Yet, even so, when they reached the field where the King and the Colchians were waiting, and the bulls rushed out from their lair breathing forth flames of fire, terror overcame them. But Jason withstood the fearful creatures as a great rock in the sea withstands the waves. He forced first one and then the other down on its knees and fastened the yoke upon them, while all wondered at his mighty prowess. Over the field he drove them, pressing the plow down firmly and casting the dragon's teeth into the furrows. By the time the plowing was done the crop was springing up, men bristling with arms who came rushing to attack him. Jason remembered Medea's words and flung a huge stone into their midst. With that, the warriors turned upon each other and fell beneath their own spears while the furrows ran with blood. So Jason's contest was ended in victory, bitter to King Æetes.

The King went back to the palace planning treachery against the heroes and vowing they should never have the Golden Fleece. But Hera was working for them. She made Medea, all bewildered with love and misery, determine to fly with Jason. That night she stole out of the house and sped along the dark path to the ship, where they were rejoicing in their good fortune with no thought of evil. She fell on her knees before them and begged them to take her with them. They must get the Fleece at once, she told them, and then make all haste away or they would be killed. A terrible serpent guarded the Fleece, but she would lull it to sleep so that it would do them no harm. She spoke in anguish, but Jason rejoiced and raised her gently and embraced her, and promised her she would be his own wedded wife when once they were back in Greece. Then taking her on board they went where she directed and reached the sacred grove where the Fleece hung. The guardian serpent was very terrible, but Medea approached it fearlessly and singing a sweet magical song she charmed it to sleep. Swiftly Jason lifted the golden wonder from the tree it hung on, and hurrying back they reached the ship as dawn was breaking. The strongest were put at the oars and they rowed with all their might down the river to the sea.

By now what had happened was known to the King, and he sent his son in pursuit—Medea's brother, Apsyrtus. He led an army so great that it seemed impossible for the little band of heroes either to conquer it or to escape, but Medea saved them again, this time by a horrible deed. She killed her brother. Some say she sent him word that she was longing to go back to her home and that she had the Fleece for him if he would meet her that night at a certain spot. He came all unsuspecting and Jason struck him down and his dark blood dyed his sister's silvery robe as she shrank away. With its leader dead, the army scattered in disorder and the way to the sea lay open to the heroes.

Others say that Apsyrtus set sail on the *Argo* with Medea, although why he did so is not explained, and that it was the King who pursued them. As his ship gained on them, Medea herself struck her brother down and cutting him limb from limb cast the pieces into the sea. The King stopped to gather them, and the *Argo* was saved.

By then the adventures of the Argonauts were almost over. One terrible trial they had while passing between the smooth, sheer rock of Scylla and the whirlpool of Charybdis, where the sea forever spouted and roared and the furious waves mounting up touched the very sky.

But Hera had seen to it that sea nymphs should be at hand to guide them and send the ship on to safety.

Next came Crete—where they would have landed but for Medea. She told them that Talus lived there, the last man left of the ancient bronze race, a creature made all of bronze except one ankle where alone he was vulnerable. Even as she spoke, he appeared, terrible to behold, and threatened to crush the ship with rocks if they drew nearer. They rested on their oars, and Medea kneeling prayed to the hounds of Hades to come and destroy him. The dread powers of evil heard her. As the bronze man lifted a pointed crag to hurl it at the *Argo* he grazed his ankle and the blood gushed forth until he sank and died. Then the heroes could land and refresh themselves for the voyage still before them.

Upon reaching Greece they disbanded, each hero going to his home, and Jason with Medea took the Golden Fleece to Pelias. But they found that terrible deeds had been done there. Pelias had forced Jason's father to kill himself and his mother had died of grief. Jason, bent upon punishing this wickedness, turned to Medea for the help which had never failed him. She brought about the death of Pelias by a cunning trick. To his daughters she said that she knew a secret, how to make the old young again; and to prove her words she cut up before them a ram worn out with many years, and put the pieces into a pot of boiling water. Then she uttered a charm and in a moment out from the water sprang a lamb and ran frisking away. The maidens were convinced. Medea gave Pelias a potent sleeping-draught and called upon his daughters to cut him into bits. With all their longing to make him young again they could hardly force themselves to do so, but at last the dreadful task was done, the pieces in the water, and they looked to Medea to speak the magic words that would bring him back to them and to his youth. But she was gone—gone from the palace and from the city, and horrified they realized that they were their father's murderers. Jason was revenged, indeed.

There is a story, too, that Medea restored Jason's father to life and made him young again, and that she gave to Jason the secret of perpetual youth. All that she did of evil and of good was done for him alone, and in the end, all the reward she got was that he turned traitor to her.

They came to Corinth after Pelias' death. Two sons were born to them and all seemed well, even to Medea in her exile, lonely as exile must always be. But her great love for Jason made the loss of her family and her country seem to her a little thing. And then Jason showed the meanness that was in him, brilliant hero though he had seemed to be: he engaged himself to marry the daughter of the King of Corinth. It was a splendid marriage and he thought of ambition only, never of love or of gratitude. In the first amazement at his treachery and in the passion of her anguish, Medea let fall words which made the King of Corinth fear she would do harm to his daughter,—he must have been a singularly unsuspicious man not to have thought of that before,—and he sent her word that she and her sons must leave the country at once. That was a doom almost as bad as death. A woman in exile with little helpless children had no protection for herself or them.

As she sat brooding over what she should do and thinking of her wrongs and her wretchedness,—wishing for death to end the life she could no longer bear; sometimes remembering with tears her father and her home; sometimes shuddering at the stain nothing could wash out of her brother's blood, of Pelias', too; conscious above all of the wild passionate devotion that had brought her to this evil and this misery,—as she sat thus, Jason appeared before her. She looked at him; she did not speak. He was there beside her, yet she was far away from him, alone with her outraged love and her ruined life. His feelings had nothing in them to make him silent. He told her coldly that he had always known how uncontrolled her spirit was. If it had not been for her foolish, mischievous talk about his bride she might have stayed on comfortably in Corinth. However, he had done his best for her. It was entirely through his efforts that she was only to be exiled, not killed. He had had a very hard time indeed to persuade the King, but he had spared no pains. He had come to her now because he was not a man to fail a friend, and he would see that she had plenty of gold and everything necessary for her journey.

This was too much. The torrent of Medea's wrongs burst forth. "You come to me?" she said—

To me, of all the race of men?
Yet it is well you came.
For I shall ease the burden of my heart
If I can make your baseness manifest.
I saved you. Every man in Greece knows that.
The bulls, the dragon-men, the serpent warder of the Fleece,
I conquered them. I made you victor.
I held the light that saved you.
Father and home—I left them
For a strange country.
I overthrew your foes,
Contrived for Pelias the worst of deaths.
Now you forsake me.
Where shall I go? Back to my father's house?
To Pelias' daughters? I have become for you
The enemy of all.
Myself, I had no quarrel with them.
Oh, I have had in you
A loyal husband, to be admired of men.
An exile now, O God, O God.
No one to help. I am alone.

His answer was that he had been saved not by her, but by Aphrodite, who had made her fall in love with him, and that she owed him a great deal for bringing her to Greece, a civilized country. Also that he had done very well for her in letting it be known how she had helped the Argonauts, so that people praised her. If only she could have had some common sense, she would have been glad of his marriage, as such a connection would have been profitable for her and the children, too. Her exile was her own fault only.

Whatever else she lacked Medea had plenty of intelligence. She wasted no more words upon him except to refuse his gold. She would take nothing, no help from him. Jason flung away angrily from her. "Your stubborn pride," he told her—

> It drives away all those who would be kind.
> But you will grieve the more for it.

From that moment Medea set herself to be revenged, as well she knew how.

> By death, oh, by death, shall the conflict of life be decided,
> Life's little day ended.

She determined to kill Jason's bride, and then—then? But she would not think of what else she saw before her. "Her death first," she said.

She took from a chest a most lovely robe. This she anointed with deadly drugs and placing it in a casket she sent her sons with it to the new bride. They must ask her, she told them, to show that she accepted the gift by wearing it at once. The Princess received them graciously, and agreed. But no sooner had she put it on than a fearful, devouring fire enveloped her. She dropped dead; her very flesh had melted away.

When Medea knew the deed was done she turned her mind to one still more dreadful. There was no protection for her children, no help for them anywhere. A slave's life might be theirs, nothing more. "I will not let them live for strangers to ill-use," she thought—

> To die by other hands more merciless than mine.
> No; I who gave them life will give them death.
> Oh, now no cowardice, no thought how young they are,
> How dear they are, how when they first were born—
> Not that—I will forget they are my sons
> One moment, one short moment—then forever sorrow.

When Jason came full of fury for what she had done to his bride and determined to kill her, the two boys were dead, and Medea on the roof of the house was stepping into a chariot drawn by dragons. They carried her away through the air out of his sight as he cursed her, never himself, for what had come to pass.

One-Way Traffic
Why Some Men Are Loutish Brutes

AESOP

ONE-WAY TRAFFIC

An old lion, who was too weak to hunt or fight for his food, decided that he must get it by his wits. He lay down in a cave, pretending to be ill, and whenever any animals came to visit him, he seized them and ate them. When many had perished in this way, a fox who had seen through the trick came and stood at a distance from the cave, and inquired how he was. "Bad," the lion answered, and asked why he did not come in. "I would have come in," said the fox, "but I saw a lot of tracks going in and none coming out."

¶A wise man recognizes danger signals in time to avoid injury.

WHY SOME MEN ARE LOUTISH BRUTES

On the orders of Zeus, Prometheus fashioned men and beasts. Seeing that the beasts were much more numerous, Zeus commanded him to unmake some of them and turn them into men, and he did as he was told. But those who had not originally been fashioned as men, even though they now had a human form, still had the minds of beasts.

Considerations

1. What elements of style are common to the two fables? Why are they appropriate?
2. What are the advantages of using imaginary people or animals instead of realistic characters in fables?
3. Is the fable an appropriate medium for moralizing? Is that its primary purpose?

Sunrise in His Pocket

Davy Crockett

One January morning it was so all-screwen-up cold that the forest trees war so stiff that they couldn't shake, and the very day-break froze fast as it war tryin' to dawn. The tinder-box in my cabin would no more ketch fire than a sunk raft at the bottom o' the sea. Seein' that daylight war so far behind time, I thought creation war in a fair way for freezin' fast.

"So," thinks I, "I must strike a leetle fire from my fingers, light my pipe, travel out a few leagues, and see about it."

Then I brought my knuckles together like two thunder clouds, but the sparks froze up afore I could begin to collect 'em—so out I walked, and endeavored to keep myself unfriz by goin' at a hop, step and jump gait, and whistlin' the tune of "fire in the mountains!" as I went along in three double quick time. Well, arter I had walked about twenty-five miles up the peak o' Daybreak Hill, I soon discovered what war the matter. The airth had actually friz fast in her axis, and couldn't turn round; the sun had got jammed between two cakes o' ice under the wheels, an' thar he had bin shinin' and workin' to get loose, till he friz fast in his cold sweat.

"C-r-e-a-t-i-o-n!" thought I, "this are the toughest sort o' suspension, and it mustn't be endured—somethin' must be done, or human creation is done for."

It war then so antedeluvian and premature cold that my upper and lower teeth an' tongue war all collapsed together as tight as a friz oyster. I took a fresh twenty pound bear off o' my back that I'd picked up on the road, an' beat the animal agin the ice till the hot ile began to walk out on him at all sides. I then took an' held him over the airth's axes, an' squeezed him till I thaw'd 'em loose, poured about a ton on it over the sun's face, give the airth's cog-wheel one kick backward, till I got the sun loose—whistled "Push along, keep movin'!" an' in about fifteen seconds the airth gin a grunt, and begun movin'—the sun walked up beautiful, salutin' me with sich a wind o' gratitude that it made me sneeze. I lit my pipe by the blaze o' his top-knot, shouldered my bear, an' walked home, introducin' the people to fresh daylight with a piece of sunrise in my pocket, with which I cooked my bear steaks, an' enjoyed one o' the best breakfasts I had tasted for some time. If I didn't, jist wake some mornin' and go with me to the office o' sunrise!

They Have Yarns

FROM *The People Yes*

CARL SANDBURG

They have yarns
Of a skyscraper so tall they had to put hinges
On the two top stories so to let the moon go by,
Of one corn crop in Missouri when the roots
Went so deep and drew off so much water
The Mississippi riverbed that year was dry,
Of pancakes so thin they only had one side,
Of "a fog so thick we shingled the barn and six feet out on the fog,"
Of Pecos Pete straddling a cyclone in Texas and riding it to the west coast where "it rained out under him,"
Of the man who drove a swarm of bees across the Rocky Mountains and the Desert "and didn't lose a bee,"
Of a mountain railroad curve where the engineer in his cab can touch the caboose and spit in the conductor's eye,
Of the boy who climbed a cornstalk growing so fast he would have starved to death if they hadn't shot biscuits up to him,
Of the old man's whiskers: "When the wind was with him his whiskers arrived a day before he did,"
Of the hen laying a square egg and cackling "Ouch!" and of hens laying eggs with the dates printed on them,
Of the ship captain's shadow: it froze to the deck one cold winter night,
Of mutineers on that same ship put to chipping rust with rubber hammers,
Of the sheep counter who was fast and accurate: "I just count their

---

2 **skyscraper so tall.** The structure so tall that hinges are needed to protect the sun and the moon turns up frequently in American folklore. Captain Stormalong, hero of New England tall tales, built a mast with such an arrangement, according to Charles Edward Brown's *Old Stormalong Yarns.* Paul Bunyan built an oil rig with a similar arrangement, according to John Lee Brooks' "Paul Bunyan, Oil Man" in *Follow de Drinkin' Gourd* 9 **Pecos Pete**, or Pecos Bill (the name usually given him in Texas windies), thus busted a cyclone. See Edward O'Reilly, "The Saga of Pecos Bill," *Century,* October 1923 10 **swarm of bees.** The boast about herding the swarm of bees occurs in the play *Lightnin'* (1918) by Winchell Smith and Frank Bacon 12 **the boy . . . cornstalk.** This story is told of Paul Bunyan's handyman, Swede Charlie, in Ida Turney's "The Scissorbills" in *Paul Bunyan Marches on* 15 **ship captain's shadow.** In Mark Twain's *Following the Equator,* Ch. XXVI, the ship's mate had this difficulty on an arctic voyage

feet and divide by four,"
Of the man so tall he must climb a ladder to shave himself,
Of the runt so teeny-weeny it takes two men and a boy to see him,
Of mosquitoes: one can kill a dog, two of them a man,
Of a cyclone that sucked cookstoves out of the kitchen, up the chimney flue, and on to the next town,
Of the same cyclone picking up wagon-tracks in Nebraska and dropping them over in the Dakotas,
Of the hook-and-eye snake unlocking itself into forty pieces, each piece two inches long, then in nine seconds flat snapping itself together again,
Of the watch swallowed by the cow—when they butchered her a year later the watch was running and had the correct time,
Of horned snakes, hoop snakes that roll themselves where they want to go, and rattlesnakes carrying bells instead of rattles on their tails,
Of the herd of cattle in California getting lost in a giant redwood tree that had hollowed out,
Of the man who killed a snake by putting its tail in its mouth so it swallowed itself,
Of railroad trains whizzing along so fast they reach the station before the whistle,
Of pigs so thin the farmer had to tie knots in their tails to keep them from crawling through the cracks in their pens,
Of Paul Bunyan's big blue ox, Babe, measuring between the eyes forty-two axhandles and a plug of Star tobacco exactly,
Of John Henry's hammer and the curve of its swing and his singing of it as "a rainbow round my shoulder."

"Do tell!"
"I want to know!"
"You don't say so!"
"For the land's sake!"
"Gosh all fish-hooks!"
"Tell me some more.
I don't believe a word you say
but I love to listen
to your sweet harmonica
to your chin-music.
Your fish stories hang together
when they're just a pack of lies:

---

20 **mosquitoes.** Snadburg may be recalling the mosquitoes described by a steamboat mate, Mr. H., in Ch. XXXIV of Mark Twain's *Life on the Mississippi.* If so he errs in his statistics. Says Twain of Mr. H.: "He said that two of them could whip a dog, and that four of them could hold a man down. . . 'butcher' him." Mr. Sandburg appears to be exaggerating somewhat 25 **horned snakes.** Sandburg may have confused these with "horn-snakes," which are described in H. E. Taliaferro's *Fisher River Scenes and Characters.* This snake, as described by Uncle Davy, an eyewitness, was ten feet long, had a head as big as a saucer, and had a stinger in his tail which was "six inches long and sharp as a needle." "This snake," said Uncle Davy, "he cotched the eend uv his tail in his mouth, he did, and come rollin' down the mounting . . . jist like a hoop." The snake landed, by chance, so that his stinger caught in a tree, and soon the tree was "dead as a herrin'; all the leaves was wilted like a fire had gone through its branches." This happened in North Carolina 30 **blue ox,** Babe, a wonderful animal, very helpful in logging operations. Babe could pull great sleds of logs, could pile lumber with his tail, and make himself useful in many other ways 31 **John Henry,** folk hero of the Negroes, was a great steel-driver who died in a contest with a steel-driving machine. See "John Henry of the Cape Fear" in *Bundles of Troubles and Other Tarheel Tales*

you ought to have a leather medal:
you ought to have a statue carved of butter: you deserve a large bouquet of turnips."

"Yessir," the traveler drawled,
"Away out there in the petrified forest
everything goes on the same as usual.
The petrified birds sit in their petrified nests
and hatch their petrified young from petrified eggs."

A high pressure salesman jumped off the Brooklyn Bridge and was saved by a policeman. But it didn't take him long to sell the idea to the policeman. So together they jumped off the bridge.

One of the oil men in heaven started a rumor of a gusher down in hell. All the other oil men left in a hurry for hell. As he gets to thinking about the rumor he had started he says to himself there might be something in it after all. So he leaves for hell in a hurry.

"The number 42 will win this raffle, that's my number" And when he won they asked him whether he guessed the number or had a system. He said he had a system, "I took up the old family album and there on page 7 was my grandfather and grandmother both on page 7. I said to myself this is easy for 7 times 7 is the number that will win and 7 times 7 is 42."

Once a shipwrecked sailor caught hold of a stateroom door and floated for hours till friendly hands from out of the darkness threw him a rope. And he called across the night, "What country is this?" and hearing voices answer, "New Jersey," he took a fresh hold of the floating stateroom door and called back half-wearily, "I guess I'll float a little farther."

An Ohio man bundled up the tin roof of a summer kitchen and sent it to a motorcar maker with a complaint of his car not giving service. In three weeks a new car arrived for him and a letter: "We regret delay in shipment but your car was received in a very bad order."

A Dakota cousin of this Ohio man sent six years of tin can accumulations to the same works, asking them to overhaul his car. Two weeks later came a rebuilt car, five old tin cans, and a letter: "We are also forwarding you five parts not necessary in our new model."

Thus fantasies heard at filling stations in the midwest. Another relates to a Missouri mule who took aim with his heels at an automobile rattling by. The car turned a somersault, lit next a fence, ran right along through a cornfield till it came to a gate, moved onto the road and went on its way as though nothing had happened. The mule heehawed with desolation, "What's the use?"

---

49 **the petrified forest,** a forest in Yellowstone Park apparently discovered by the guide Jim Bridger. See biographies by J. C. Alter (1925; rev. ed., 1962) and Stanley Vestal (1946). One of the most remarkable facts about this forest was that there the law of gravity was petrified

Another tells of a farmer and his family stalled on a railroad crossing, how they jumped out in time to see a limited express knock it into flinders, the farmer calling, "Well, I always did say that car was no shucks in a real pinch."

When the Masonic Temple in Chicago was the tallest building in the United States west of New York, two men who would cheat the eyes out of you if you gave 'em a chance, took an Iowa farmer to the top of the building and asked him, "How is this for high?" They told him that for $25 they would go down in the basement and turn the building around on its turntable for him while he stood on the roof and saw how this seventh wonder of the world worked. He handed them $25. They went. He waited. They never came back.

This is told in Chicago as a folk tale, the same as the legend of Mrs. O'Leary's cow kicking over the barn lamp that started the Chicago fire, when the Georgia visitor, Robert Toombs, telegraphed an Atlanta crony, "Chicago is on fire, the whole city burning down, God be praised!"

Nor is the prize sleeper Rip Van Winkle and his scolding wife forgotten, nor the headless horseman scooting through Sleepy Hollow
Nor the sunken treasure-ships in coves and harbors, the hideouts of gold and silver sought by Coronado, nor the Flying Dutchman rounding the Cape doomed to nevermore pound his ear nor ever again take a snooze for himself
Nor the sailor's caretaker Mother Carey seeing to it that every seafaring man in the afterworld has a seabird to bring him news of ships and women, an albatross for the admiral, a gull for the deckhand
Nor the sailor with a sweetheart in every port of the world, nor the ships that set out with flying colors and all the promises you could ask, the ships never heard of again,
Nor Jim Liverpool, the riverman who could jump across any river and back without touching land he was that quick on his feet,
Nor Mike Fink along the Ohio and the Mississippi, half wild horse and half cock-eyed alligator, the rest of him snags and snapping turtle. "I can out-run, out-jump, out-shoot, out-brag, out-drink, and out-fight, rough and tumble, no holts barred, any man on both sides of the river from Pittsburgh to New Orleans and back again to St. Louis. My trigger finger itches and I want to go redhot. War, famine and bloodshed puts flesh on my bones, and hardship's my daily bread."
Nor the man so lean he threw no shadow: six rattlesnakes struck at him at one time and every one missed him.

A Fable

Samuel Clemens

Once upon a time an artist who had painted a small and very beautiful picture placed it so that he could see it in the mirror. He said, "This doubles the distance and softens it, and it is twice as lovely as it was before."

The animals out in the woods heard of this through the housecat, who was greatly admired by them because he was so learned, and so refined and civilized, and so polite and high-bred, and could tell them so much which they didn't know before, and were not certain about afterward. They were much excited about this new piece of gossip, and they asked questions, so as to get at a full understanding of it. They asked what a picture was, and the cat explained.

"It is a flat thing," he said; "wonderfully flat, marvelously flat, enchantingly flat and elegant. And, oh, so beautiful!"

That excited them almost to a frenzy, and they said they would give the world to see it. Then the bear asked:

"What is it that makes it so beautiful?"

"It is the looks of it," said the cat.

This filled them with admiration and uncertainty, and they were more excited than ever. Then the cow asked:

"What is a mirror?"

"It is a hole in the wall," said the cat. "You look in it, and there you see the picture, and it is so dainty and charming and ethereal and inspiring in its unimaginable beauty that your head turns round and round, and you almost swoon with ecstasy."

The ass had not said anything as yet; he now began to throw doubts. He said there had never been anything as beautiful as this before, and probably wasn't now. He said that when it took a whole basketful of sesquipedalian adjectives to whoop up a thing of beauty, it was time for suspicion.

It was easy to see that these doubts were having an effect upon the animals, so the cat went off offended. The subject was dropped for a couple of days, but in the meantime curiosity was taking a fresh start, and there was a revival of interest perceptible. Then the animals assailed the ass for spoiling what could possibly have been a pleasure to them, on a mere suspicion that the picture was not beautiful, without any evidence that such was the case. The ass was not troubled; he was calm, and said there was one way to find out who was in the right, himself or the cat: he would go and look in that hole, and come back and tell what he found there. The animals felt relieved and grateful, and asked him to go at once—which he did.

But he did not know where he ought to stand; and, so, through error, he stood between the picture and the mirror. The result was that the picture had no chance, and didn't show up. He returned home and said:

"The cat lied. There was nothing in that hole but an ass. There wasn't a sign of a flat thing visible. It was a handsome ass, and friendly, but just an ass, and nothing more."

The elephant asked:

"Did you see it good and clear? Were you close to it?"

"I saw it good and clear, O Hathi, King of Beasts. I was so close that I touched noses with it."

"This is very strange," said the elephant; "the cat was always truthful before—as far as we could make out. Let another witness try. Go, Baloo, look in the hole, and come and report."

So the bear went. When he came back, he said:

"Both the cat and the ass have lied; there was nothing in the hole but a bear."

Great was the surprise and puzzlement of the animals. Each was now anxious to make the test himself and get at the straight truth. The elephant sent them one at a time.

First, the cow. She found nothing in the hole but a cow.

The tiger found nothing in it but a tiger.

The lion found nothing in it but a lion.

The leopard found nothing in it but a leopard.

The camel found a camel, and nothing more.

The Hathi was wroth, and said he would have the truth, if he had to go and fetch it himself. When he returned, he abused his whole subjectry for liars, and was in an unappeasable fury with the moral and mental blindness of the cat. He said anybody but a near-sighted fool could see that there was nothing in the hole but an elephant.

Moral, by the Cat

You can find in a text whatever you bring, if you will stand between it and the mirror of your imagination. You may not see your ears, but they will be there.

1909

The Cowboy

DUNCAN EMRICH

It is very difficult to capsule the legendary figure of the cowboy. A full book on him *as legend alone* at least is wanted. Into the making of it would go Owen Wister, B. M. Bowers, Zane Grey, Luke Short, *The Illustrated Police News, Harper's Illustrated Weekly,* Theodore Roosevelt, Frederick Remington, Willard Thorpe, Con Price, Will Rogers, Charlie Russel, Tom Mix, Buck Jones, Hoot Gibson, John Wayne, millions of American youngsters playing cowboys and Indians, millions of American men (some of whom should know better) wearing cowboy boots and ten-gallon hats, and millions of American men, women, and children watching him at the movies or on TV (half a dozen shows per week, or more?), and innumerable other matters—his speech, his food, his clothes (and as the folk say, and I am glad to be able to put this in somewhere) *and etcetera.*

Why all this, and why the legend? Because the cowboy is a symbol of what we as a people and nation have wished as our way of life. He is a projection of our hopes and desires, a projection of our best code of ethics, of our wished-for *mores.*

Santa Claus is a projection of certain of our characteristics—generosity, gift giving, kindness, thoughtfulness—but he is a one-shot annual occurrence. We go all out with him at Christmastime, but the cowboy is with us the year 'round. And the cowboy symbolizes much more of us and for us than Santa.

Let me summarize some of the cowboy's greatness.

[But before doing so, a sideswipe at his denigrators. The little "researchers" are coming along (there have been nitpickers in every generation) saying that the cowboy was in literal fact lousy, often a drunkard, uneducated and illiterate (like Jim Bridger), had himself no concept of anything beyond his forty-dollars-and-beans a month, raised payday hell out of sheer boredom, and so on and on. Let us readily admit every bit of this as it applied to some, and even a goodly number, of cowboys: and sailors, and farmers, and railroaders, and newspapermen, and workers of every sort, and United States senators (percentagewise), and mothers of our children. But let us also quickly reverse tracks and say that on balance the symbol of goodness and greatness in the cowboy knocks all that nitpicking into a cocked hat.—It would amuse me, if it weren't all so boring, to note that Soviet Russia attacks Santa Claus as "a tool of American capitalist interests." And that Soviet Russia praises (follow this) Paul Bunyan because he is a symbol for the American worker of the power of the American worker in the face of bourgeois, ideological, capitalistic oppression. When will they ever learn that Paul Bunyan is a "capitalistic" chamber of commerce creation and is no symbol of anything whatsoever to the worker other than a grand-scale picnic, rib-roast, logrolling, outdoor jamboree competition or holiday? (I wonder who feeds Moscow its pap?)—And the cowboy. I have not myself seen an attack upon the cowboy. And yet if the Russians had any sense they would attempt to undermine him in every possible way, because the cowboy is us. I have the feeling that they may have considered doing so. Considered attacking him and reducing him with their monstrous machine to something *bourgeois, etc., etc. . . . ,* to a nothingness. (How would you feel about that, Tex? Up on the Cimarron? Would you go with it in the Judith Basin? What about around Winnemucca? Along the Ruidoso? Down Durango way?) I think that the Soviets and their representatives here may have considered it, but that even they, in the face of their audience, may have backed away from such idiocy. Every child from the age of seven or eight on up in the United States would have laughed themselves silly, which would have been only a beginning of the snickering assault upon such obscenity. I think we'll keep the cowboy. And I do not feel that Russia will ever attempt to touch him. To attempt to take him for themselves (along with the electric light bulb and radio) would at once deny their "collectivism." To attack him would make everyone forever aware of their humorless, insensitive bureaucracy. Ah, to hell with them.]

Anyhow, these it seems to me are the attributes and attractions going to make up the cowboy, in fact and legend. Many overlap, but that is reinforcement, not repetition. Add your own beliefs and affections in the event I have missed some. The cowboy as legend (and legend based on fact):

Individualism: *"I am my own man. I speak for myself. . . ."*

Independence: *"Nobody owns me. I can pick up my saddle and go. . . ."*

Freedom: *"Don't fence me in!"* (How about *that* phrase over East Berlin way?)

Close to the land, but not bound by it, as a farmer is: *One sees the cowboy against the great spaces of the West, the mountains, the plains, the distances. There is freedom on the land that he sees and rides.*

Not given to bragging: *Very great understatement in his speech and description of anything unusual he may have done: "They just would not go across that swollen river, and it took us four days, and finally we got the fifteen hundred head over by not letting them drink, and then they made a rush for water, and we just kept driving them. . . ."*

Courage: *"Men who followed this life wouldn't tolerate a coward . . . one coward endangered the whole group. He had to have bones in his spinal column and know how to die standin' up."*

Cheerfulness: *"The bigness of the country . . . wouldn't let him listen to the whimpers of a mere human. . . . No one knowed a man was tired; sickness or injury was his own secret unless it couldn't be hid any longer. You'd never know but what he was as happy as a lost soul with hell in a flood, and he was usually grinnin' like a jackass eatin' cactus."*

Pride: *There is no prouder soul on earth than a cowboy. "The man on hossback has always held himself above the man on foot."*

Loyalty: *"He was one class of worker who didn't have to be watched to see that he did his work well. The nature of his work demanded that he be trusted. He took a pride in being faithful to his 'brand' and in performing his job well. He needed no overseer, or advice. He worked long hours and packed no timepiece. He belonged to no union, and no whistle was blowed orderin' him to knock off work. He worked from before dawn to after dark, and even later if need be. His loyalty to the boss came first, and he'd ride night herd on the cattle as faithfully on a rainy night, or in a stingin' sleet, as he would on starry, moonlight nights. . . . He'd lay down his life, if necessary, for the privilege of defendin' his outfit. Once a cowhand had throwed his bedroll into the wagon and turned his private hoss into the remuda of an outfit he'd pledged his allegiance and loyalty."*

True to his word: *His word was as good as law. It had to be. One did not survive on that harsh land on false promises. One did not question a man's word. One never forced him into defensively saying, "If I say so, I'll do it." It was said, and believed implicitly, and done. No questions. Complete faith, complete honesty.*

Generosity: *"The true old-time cowhand had a heart in his brisket as big as a saddle blanket." He shared with friends and strangers, and even enemies when the occasion demanded. "Hearing of some puncher being sick or broke or needing medicine, the whole range would empty its pockets." And this next I have seen: "Far out on the range, a long way from where he could buy more, his supply of 'makin's' might run low, but he never refused another a smoke unless he wanted to offer a direct and intentional insult." It was so natural that I have forgotten now whether I was the giver or the recipient.*

Women: *"One of the strictest codes of the West was to respect women. No other class of men looked upon women with greater reverence. . . . No matter who she was, or her station in life, the cowman held her with respect. . . . A woman might live alone, miles from anyone but she had no fear of any true cowman. She was as safe as in a church, and she knowed it. If any man, at any time, under any circumstances, mistreated a woman, he was culled from society. Men refused to speak to him, doors were shut against him, and he was an outcast. In spite of the movies, if one insulted a woman he was probably killed sooner or later, even if somebody had to get drunk to do it."*

Kindness: *Of course. A basic American trait. You don't think it was invented by GI's giving chewing gum and chocolate to children, do you? They simply carried the tradition.*

The equal of any man: *Fighting fair and square, could anyone beat the cowboy? Impossible.*

Nicknames: *They are good. Tex, Nevada, Luke, Shorty, Red, Mex, Whitey, Bronc. . . .*

The names of their ranches and brands: *These are enough to make the men stand separate from the rest of us: Rocking X, Lazy L, Flying W, R Bar Z, Running M. We envy them for the names. . . .*

Their clothes and gear: *These set the men apart: chaps, sombreros, leather jackets, bandanas, boots, spurs, jeans (Levi's), gloves, saddle, lariat, six-shooter, Remington, blanket, slicker. . . .*

Their way of life: *bunkhouse, corral, range, roundup, trail-herding, fenceiding, cutting out, branding, nightherding, chuckwagon, their special speech and their Western words . . . .*

All of these attributes and individual characteristics go into the making of the cowboy legend and become an inextricable part of it. At random ask any person to describe a cowboy (what makes him different?) and see what you come up with. On balance, it will be good and with elements of legend.

These things are the legend, the base of the legend, but there is more, certainly. The legend grows and is carried in all of the cowboy songs: each one of them is the stuff of legend: "The Streets of Laredo," "The Dying Cowboy," "The Trail to Mexico," "The Chisholm Trail," "Little Joe, the Wrangler." Legend lies back of every cattle brand. Legend rides every one of the great trails. Legend rides every range. Legend is in every cowtown. Legend is at every bar and in every saloon still standing. Legend is in every saddle.

To pick out one or half a dozen tales or legends is not the purpose here. (Read J. Frank Dobie, Con Price, Ramon F. Adams, Will James, and all the others for that.) The purpose here is to give the cowboy—as legendary figure—the greatness which is his due. Legendary and very human.

I am glad that he rides our land.

This is the Way I Was Raised Up

Mrs. Marvin Watts

The following article was given to us by its author, Mrs. Watts, during a recent visit to her home. It was painstakingly written out in pencil on notebook paper that had been folded and refolded many times. It is presented here exactly as it was given to us.—Editor

my dadie raised the stuff we lived one he groed the corn to make our bread he groed they cane to make our syrup allso groed they Beans and Peas to make the soup beans out of and dried leather Britches beans and dried fruit enough to last all winter he Killed enough meat to last all winter

he Killed a beaf and a Sheep and two or three hogs for the winter he diden have mutch money for anything we just had our biskets for sunday morning and when mother ran out of coffie she parched chustnuts and ground them one her coffie mill to make coffie out of and when it rained and the mills coulden grind our bread we ate potatoes for bread my dad usto make our shoes I can remember waring them my mother usto weaved woal cloth to make blankets and cloths out of I have worn woal dresses and my dad has worn home made Britches out of woven woal to my mother also knit our Stockings and socks to I have hope my dad Shear Sheep a lot of times to get that wool my mother would wash it and Spen it make it into thread and then weave it one her loom to make her blankets and cloth out of we usto have corn Shukings to get our corn all shucked

we had our crib full that lasted till the next fall every body in the neighborhood come and my mother cooked a big dinner for the crowd seames as every body was happie to I rember when my mother had to cook one the fire place she cooked her dried fruit and every thing one the fire place it sure was good back in them dayes to I usto help my brothers Saw wood to make fires out of to keep warm we lived in a log house it was pretty hard to keep warm by an open fire place but we never was Sick back then we played out the bigest Snow ever com we had a Spring to cary our watter from and my dad had to take his Shovel and ditch out a way through the Snow for us to get to the Spring the snow was waist deep we usto make our play houses out in the woods make our rag dolls to play with my brothers Sawed pine wagon wheels and made there wagons to play with I have sent to the mountains and hope my dad and brothers Snake out tan bark to get a little money to buy things with One Xmas Santa Clause gave us three or four sticks of candie and a ornge he put it in our Stocking and we was as pleased as if he had give us a box full of candy we lived one a hill out of site of the road and we was toaled the was a car coming through that day it was a teamotel ford tom mitchel was driving it and we sit one the hill all day to get to see it we haden never saw a car that was our firston

De Witch'-ooman an' de Spinnin'-Wheel

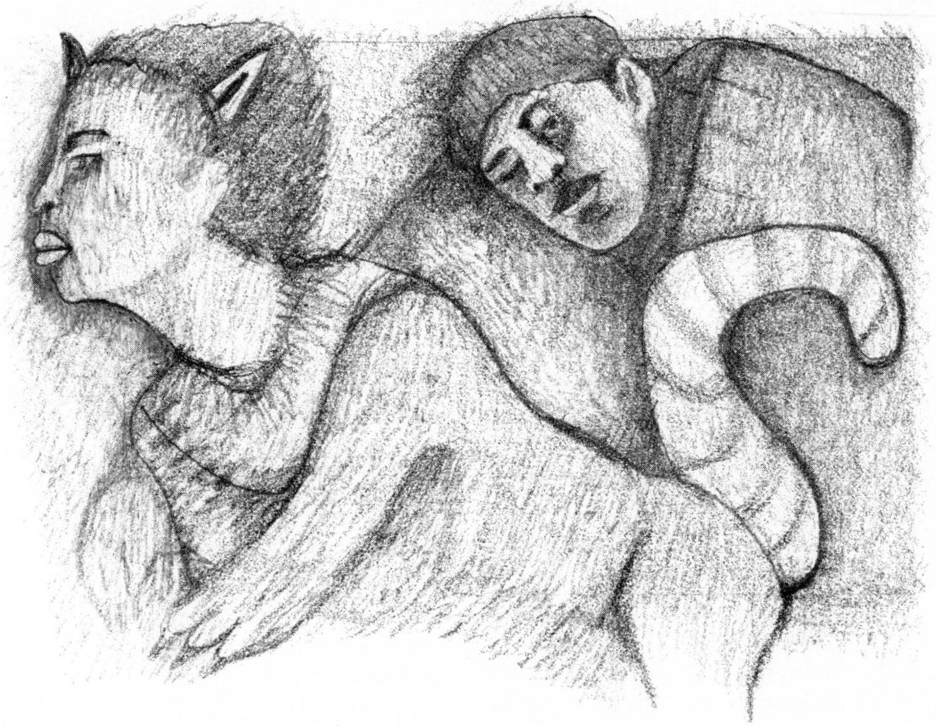

The Witch Prevented From Reentering Her Skin: A Tale from Louisiana.

One time dey wuz a man whar rid up at night ter a cabin in de eedge o' de swamp. He wuz dat hongry an' ti'd dat he say ter hissef: "Ef I kin git a hunk o' co'n-pone and a slice o' bakin', I doan kur what I pays!" On dat here come a yaller-'ooman spankin' out'n de cabin. She wuz spry on her foot ez a catbird, an' her eyes wuz sof' an' shiny. She ax de man fer ter light an' come in de cabin, an' git some supper. An' Lawd! how he mouf do water when he cotch a glimpst er de skillet on de coals! He

Reprinted from JOURNAL OF AMERICAN FOLKLORE XVIII. By permission of Houghton Mifflin Company.

luk it so well dat he stay; an' he sot eroun' in dat cabin ontwel he git so fat dat de grease fa'r run out'n he jaws when he look up at de sun. De yaller-'ooman she spen' her time cookin' fer him, an' waitin' on him wi' so much oberly, dat at las' de man, he up an' marry dat yaller-'ooman.

At fus' dey git erlong tollable well, but a'ter erwhile he gin ter notice dat sump'n curus 'bout dat yaller-'ooman. She ain' never in de cabin when he wake up in de night time! So, he mek up his min' fer ter spy on her. He lay down one night on de fo' pos' bed in de cornder, 'ten luk he sleep. De yaller-'ooman watch him out'n de een o' her eye, an' when she hear him gin a sno' (caze *cose* he 'ten luk he sno') she jump up an' pat a juba in de middle o' de flo'. Den she reach down a big gridi'on fum de wall, an' take out some coals, an' haul de big spinnin'-wheel close ter de ha'th. Den, she sot herself down on dat gridi'on, an' soon ez it wuz red-hot she 'gin ter spin her skin off'n her body on de spinnin'-wheel. "Tu'n an' spin, come off skin, tu'n an' spin, come off skin." An' fo' de Lawd, de skin come off'n dat witch-'ooman's body, berginning at de top o' her head, ez slick es de shush come off de ear o' corn. An' when it wuz fa'r off, dan she wuz a gret big yaller cat. Den, she tuk her skin an' chuck it onder de bed. "Lay dar, skin," she say, "wi' dat fool nigger sno'in' in de bed, ontwel I come back. I gwine ter ha' some fum, I is."

Wi' dat she jump out'n de winder an' lope off. Soon ez she wuz gone de man, he jump out'n de bed an' tuk out skin an' fill it plum full o' salt an' pepper, un' th'ow it back onder de bed. Den he crope out an' watch thro' de key-hole ontwel de witch-'ooman come home. She laugh whilse she wuz rakin' out de skin fum onder de bed, an' shakin' herse'f inter it. But when she feel de salt an' pepper, she laugh on de yether side her mouf. She moan an' groan so you kin hear her a mile! But she ain' able ter git out'n dat skin, an' de man watch her thoo de key-hole twel she fall down an' die on de flo'.

FICTION

Classic
Modern
Contemporary

Introduction to Fiction

Here is a story from a newspaper:

> Miss Jennifer Thompson, 63, of 1712 Brundage Road, was listed in fair condition at St. Francis Hospital here today as a result of last night's fire that caused an estimated $7,500 damage in her small apartment. According to firemen, a cigarette that had been smoldering in a wastebasket apparently burst into flames when Miss Thompson opened the door to her living room.
>
> Miss Thompson managed to call the fire department but was then overcome by smoke inhalation.

Here is another way in which you might read about the same event:

> Jenny slowly brushed her hair back with one hand while she tried sleepily to find the doorknob with the other. She thought, "How odd that I dozed off so early. And where did all this smoke come from? Where's that wretched knob?"
>
> The door was always hard to open. How often she had reached the living room too late to answer the phone just because she had had to fight a stupid door.
>
> Finally it gave, and suddenly the smoke filled gray of the room was shot through with the red of flames. Jenny stumbled to the phone. As she grabbed up the receiver, she watched her lovely chintz-covered couch and the white fur rug become part of the blaze.

The purpose of the first piece is to inform. Theoretically, most of the information could be checked for accuracy. Its tone is objective and impersonal. The second version, on the other hand, is a personal recreation of an experience. The second piece is fiction.

Although the story or narrative is basically an old form, fiction as we know it today is considered to be a relatively new genre compared to poetry and drama. The tradition of fiction started with myth and legend and allegory. But the fictional characters in these imaginary worlds were mostly one-dimensional abstractions, personified as Love, Greed, War, or even Sir Valiant in Faith. The evolution from allegory to novel (and short story), from the sermon about an abstraction in human guise to the story of the individual whose personal experience might have universal application, took a long time. Perhaps the first step toward a new mode was taken in 1382 when Geoffrey Chaucer translated Boccacio's phrase *E con gli occulti ferri i Tradimenti* (literally meaning "And Treachery with hidden weapons") as "The smyler with the knyf under the cloke." Suddenly, this character is a person rather than an abstraction.

For a long time, writing fiction was considered undignified; Sir Walter Scott and Jane Austen published their first works under pseudonyms. Reading fiction was considered even more vulgar, and the romances that filled the lending libraries of Regency England were thought to be suitable only for chambermaids. Perhaps part of the problem lay in the use of the word *fiction,* which implies falseness. This usage was avoided for a while by calling stories *histories,* thus giving an air of respectability to them.

Just what is fiction? The task of definition is difficult because a wide variety of prose writing has borne this label. Most of the fiction—as most of the literature—of Western civilization tends toward invention rather than transcription, toward creation rather than observation. However, the fiction writer may base his story on a situation from real life. He then must add other details in order to make the scene seem real—information he couldn't possibly know about how the people in the situation felt and what they thought. Then he is likely to have the characters act in a way that will reveal something about human nature, details of their backgrounds, and the relation of each to the other characters or to the setting. (In the process, incidentally, the author is likely consciously or unconsciously to reveal something about his own attitudes.)

For example, let us consider a scene in a railroad car that is passing slowly through a town. Two people, a man and a woman, are seated in the car, looking out the same window. It is late at night, and the streets of the town are lit up; the coach is in darkness. The man and woman are spectators of a drama that is taking place outside their window. Under a street light stand another man and woman. The woman's back is to the tracks, but in the few moments it takes the train to pass, the spectators can see her shake her head at the man. He appears to hit her; she bends over and supports herself against the side of the building. The train passes on.

Such are the basic ingredients. The natural question the witnesses ask themselves is "Why did he do that?" They begin to speculate. The woman will tend to interpret the scene by projecting her own feelings and assumptions, and the man will do the same. Now what happened on the street can be interpreted in any number of ways. The interpretation each witness makes reveals something of his or her own personality.

Even in this short sketch you can see the possibilities for expansion into a short story through the development of some of the basic elements of fiction. There is opportunity for *description* of *characters* and *setting,* the development of *atmosphere,* and the use of the *key moment* (seeing the scene). There could be a *plot* involving conflict—either between the characters or within the minds of each of them. The way the events unfold could easily be linked to the outcome or *resolution* of the story. *Dialogue* would probably be included, although not to the same extent as in drama, to reveal something about the characters or to advance the action. (Occasionally dialogue is used to express the author's ideas more personally and directly through one character who acts as his spokesman. For example, Hemingway's male characters are often Hemingway in thin disguise. When this is done the author is said to be using a *persona.*) The *chronology*—the order in which the events are related—can be straightforward, or there can be *flashbacks* to previous experiences in the lives of the major characters that would explain why they are responding in a particular way to the present situation. *Foreshadowing* could be used, in which case the story might open earlier in the evening with the major characters having some sort of argument that gives clues to explain, or prepare the reader for, things that will arise when the outside scene takes place. The story could act as a vehicle for whatever *theme* the author chooses. (Most authors tend to repeat the same basic theme or themes throughout their works, even though the works themselves may vary widely in other respects.)

The theme of a story may be any subject the author feels strongly about. (It should not be confused with a moral.) Usually it is suggested rather than stated. Ideally it will have universality, which makes it meaningful in a larger context. In other words, a story may, on the surface, be nothing more than the description of what happened to a particular group of people in a particular set of circumstances. If that is all there is to the story, readers will probably feel at most a passing interest in it. The stories that are read again and again by generations of readers are those that contain something more, something deeper, than surface description. They contain something—some message, some idea, or an attitude—that is applicable to all readers in all times. Tolstoy's *The Death of Ivan Iych* is an excellent example. Although it was written in the nineteenth century about a member of the Russian middle-class, the underlying feelings expressed in it are very similar to those many people have today. Tolstoy's ideas are still relevant for modern readers.

Just as the theme is very personal to each author, so are the style, the tone, and the use of rhetorical devices such as symbolism and figurative language. The *tone* of a work reflects both the author's attitude toward his subject and his attitude toward the reader. An author's *style* is his particular, characteristic way of writing, and it involves all of the elements of writing, such as sentence structure, diction, tone, and use of figurative language. He may write very long involved sentences or very short clipped sentences; he may use a lot of description or none at all; his statements may be vague and general or very precise. (In the stories in this collection, those by Hemingway, Thurber, and Faulkner are good examples of their authors' very noticeable styles.) One characteristic of an author's style is the extent to which he uses or doesn't use figurative language and symbolism. In the writings of authors such as Hawthorne, many objects and events are laden with symbolic significance. A light is not merely a light—it is hope, a new beginning, or even life itself.

A critical issue in any story is its *point of view*. The importance of point of view may easily be overlooked, but the choice of the narrator influences the total structure of the story. The reader knows only as much as the person acting as narrator, because everything is seen through his eyes. If one character acts as the narrator, the point of view is said to be limited to that character. A character who tells his own story will, of course, know only what goes on inside his own head. The observer who is a participant in the story is less directly and emotionally involved. The omniscient point of view (in which the author acts as an all-knowing narrator, free to comment on the action) would seem most appropriate for retelling the vignette outlined earlier, because all the thoughts and experiences of people inside and outside the railroad car could become part of the story. The author may, however, choose to use a self-effacing, or objective, point of view, in which case actions and conversations are presented objectively, in detail, without authorial comment.

Point of view also dictates distance. Anything written in the first person will seem immediate and personal; the reader will almost feel himself part of the action. To illustrate this, let us consider a familiar story written in the third person:

Again he said: "There was once a man who had two sons; and the younger said to his father, 'Father, give me my share of the property.' So he divided his estate between them. A few days later the younger son turned the whole of his share into cash and left home for a distant country, where he squandered it in reckless living. He had spent it all, when a severe famine fell upon that country and he began to feel the pinch. So he went and attached himself to one of the local landowners, who sent him on to his farm to mind the pigs. He would have been glad to fill his belly with the pods that the pigs were eating; and no one gave him anything. Then he came to his senses and said, 'How many of my father's paid servants have more food than they can eat, and here am I, starving to death! I will set off and go to my father, and say to him, "Father, I have sinned, against God and against you; I am no longer fit to be called your son; treat me as one of your paid servants."' So he set out for his father's house. But while he was still a long way off his father saw him, and his heart went out to him. He ran to meet him, flung his arms round him, and kissed him. The son said, 'Father, I have sinned, against God and against you; I am no longer fit to be called your son.' But the father said to his servants, 'Quick! fetch a robe, my best one, and put it on him; put a ring on his finger and shoes on his feet. Bring the fatted calf and kill it, and let us have a feast to celebrate the day. For this son of mine was dead and has come back to life; he was lost and is found.' And the festivities began.

"Now the elder son was out on the farm; and on his way back, as he approached the house, he heard music and dancing. He called one of the servants and asked what it meant. The servant told him, 'Your brother has come home, and your father has killed the fatted calf because he has him back safe and sound.' But he was angry and refused to go in. His father came out and pleaded with him; but he retorted, 'You know how I have slaved for you all these years; I never once disobeyed your orders; and you never gave me so much as a kid, for a feast with my friends. But now that this son of your turns up, after running through your money with his women, you kill the fatted calf for him.' 'My boy,' said the father, 'you are always with me, and everything I have is yours. How could we help celebrating this happy day? Your brother here was dead and has come back to life, was lost and is found.' "

Now imagine how the victim would begin the tale if he were telling it in the first person:

> When the famine struck the countryside, I was penniless and was forced to work for a landowner tending his pigs. At that point, I was not beyond eating some of their food if I could have gotten it, but the owner watched the whole operation too closely. I felt that if someone did not offer me something to eat soon, I would not know what to do.
>
> I found myself in this horrible situation due to my having spent my share of Father's estate. . .

An equally valid but different point of view would be that of a worker on the father's estate who was an observer yet almost a participant in the drama.

An author must decide what point of view best suits his material and his purpose. In some stories several points of view may be used. When this is done, it is usually for a particular purpose, and paying attention to these shifts will usually tell you something about how the author wants you to feel toward his characters or the theme.

The narrator is not necessarily the character upon whom the story is focused. A story told in the first person by a bystander may focus on a character who particularly intrigues or annoys the storyteller. Only if the teller's character and actions are the major elements in the story's development is he the focus of the story. Often it is clear whose story a particular piece is. There is no question that "My Kinsman, Major Molineux" is Robin's story. But is "Hills Like White Elephants" the man's story, the woman's story, or both? Here the author has used the objective point of view and has not focused on one character more than the other.

The selections that follow are for the most part short stories. Short stories differ from the novel or novella chiefly in matters of complexity, development, number of episodes, and number of loose ends (material that is introduced without being an essential part of the story's development or denouement). The process of selectivity is so keen in a short story, and the scope is so brief (usually 3,000–5,000 words), that there isn't space for the leisurely establishment of mood and setting that there is in a novel. In a well-written short story, each word helps establish the overall impression.

Within these limits, short stories touch on almost as wide a variety of themes as novels. Many of the first short stories written are stories in which adventure is more important than characterization. These stories are highly plotted; there is a quick introduction to the characters, a complication (or complications) of some kind, conflict, a climax, and then a resolution.

Many modern short stories lack an obvious plot or theme. Many of the so-called New Yorker type baffle readers who try to come up with a single definitive statement about what the author was trying to say. A judgment as to when a description of "a slice of life" is merely that and when it becomes a short story involves criteria outside the province of this text. You will find that the stories that have been included here are not of that variety.

An attempt has been made in this collection to balance themes and settings and yet to include representative pieces by the most important writers of our times. You will find a preponderant number of stories about relatively well-to-do urban men and women who are alienated, unhappy, aimless, and unmotivated, aspiring to little and doing less, and yet the sampling is representative. For a number of years during the middle of the twentieth century it seems as though the majority of good writers dealt with this subject at least tangentially.

The struggle against malevolent authority may have preoccupied many novelists and several dramatists, but short story writers seem to have remained more concerned with the human condition as reflected in personal relationships.

My Kinsman, Major Molineux

Nathaniel Hawthorne

After the kings of Great Britain had assumed the right of appointing the colonial governors, the measures of the latter seldom met with the ready and general approbation which had been paid to those of their predecessors, under the original charters. The people looked with most jealous scrutiny to the exercise of power which did not emanate from themselves, and they usually rewarded their rulers with slender gratitude for the compliances by which, in softening their instructions from beyond the sea, they had incurred the reprehension of those who gave them. The annals of Massachusetts Bay will inform us, that of six governors in the space of about forty years from the surrender of the old charter, under James II, two were imprisoned by a popular insurrection; a third, as Hutchinson[1] inclines to believe, was driven from the province by the whizzing of a musket-ball; a fourth, in the opinion of the same historian, was hastened to his grave by continual bickerings with the House of Representatives; and the remaining two, as well as their successors, till the Revolution, were favored with few and brief intervals of peaceful sway. The inferior members of the court party, in times of high political excitement, led scarcely a more desirable life. These remarks may serve as a preface to the following adventures, which chanced upon a summer night, not far from a hundred years ago. The reader, in order to avoid a long and dry detail of colonial affairs, is requested to dispense with an account of the train of circumstances that had caused much temporary inflammation of the popular mind.

It was near nine o'clock of a moonlight evening, when a boat crossed the ferry with a single passenger, who had obtained his conveyance at that unusual hour by the promise of an extra fare. While he stood on the landing-place, searching in either pocket for the means of fulfilling his agreement, the ferryman lifted a lantern, by the aid of which, and the newly risen moon, he took a very accurate survey of the stranger's figure. He was a youth of barely eighteen years, evidently country-bred, and now, as it should seem, upon his first visit to town. He was clad in a coarse gray coat, well worn, but in

1. Thomas Hutchinson (1711–1780), the last royal governor of Massachusetts Bay Colony, and author of *The History of the Colony of Massachusetts Bay, from Its First Settlement in 1628 to the Year 1750,* 2 vols., 1764, 1767.

excellent repair; his under garments[2] were durably constructed of leather, and fitted tight to a pair of serviceable and well-shaped limbs; his stockings of blue yarn were the incontrovertible work of a mother or a sister; and on his head was a three-cornered hat, which in its better days had perhaps sheltered the graver brow of the lad's father. Under his left arm was a heavy cudgel formed of an oak sapling, and retaining a part of the hardened root; and his equipment was completed by a wallet, not so abundantly stocked as to incommode the vigorous shoulders on which it hung. Brown, curly hair, well-shaped features, and bright, cheerful eyes were nature's gifts, and worth all that art could have done for his adornment.

The youth, one of whose names was Robin, finally drew from his pocket the half of a little province bill of five shillings, which, in the depreciation in that sort of currency, did but satisfy the ferryman's demand, with the surplus of a sexangular piece of parchment, valued at three-pence. He then walked forward into the town, with as light a step as if his day's journey had not already exceeded thirty miles, and with as eager an eye as if he were entering London city, instead of the little metropolis of a New England colony. Before Robin had proceeded far, however, it occurred to him that he knew not whither to direct his steps; so he paused, and looked up and down the narrow street, scrutinizing the small and mean wooden buildings that were scattered on either side.

"This low hovel cannot be my kinsman's dwelling," thought he, "nor yonder old house, where the moonlight enters at the broken casement; and truly I see none hereabouts that might be worthy of him. It would have been wise to inquire my way of the ferryman, and doubtless he would have gone with me, and earned a shilling from the Major for his pains. But the next man I meet will do as well."

He resumed his walk, and was glad to perceive that the street now became wider, and the houses more respectable in their appearance. He soon discerned a figure moving on moderately in advance, and hastened his steps to overtake it. As Robin drew nigh, he saw that the passenger was a man in years, with a full periwig of gray hair, a wide-skirted coat of dark cloth, and silk stockings rolled above his knees. He carried a long and polished cane, which he struck down perpendicularly before him at every step; and at regular intervals he uttered two successive hems, of a peculiarly solemn and sepulchral intonation. Having made these observations, Robin laid hold of the skirt of the old man's coat, just when the light from the open door and windows of a barber's shop fell upon both their figures.

"Good-evening to you, honored sir," said he, making a low bow, and still retaining his hold of the skirt. "I pray you tell me whereabouts is the dwelling of my kinsman, Major Molineux."

The youth's question was uttered

2. Knee breeches.

very loudly; and one of the barbers, whose razor was descending on a well-soaped chin, and another who was dressing a Ramillies wig, left their occupations, and came to the door. The citizen, in the mean time, turned a long-favored countenance upon Robin, and answered him in a tone of excessive anger and annoyance. His two sepulchral hems, however, broke into the very centre of his rebuke, with most singular effect, like a thought of the cold grave obtruding among wrathful passions.

"Let go my garment, fellow! I tell you, I know not the man you speak of. What! I have authority, I have—hem, hem—authority; and if this be the respect you show for your betters, your feet shall be brought acquainted with the stocks by daylight, tomorrow morning!"

Robin released the old man's skirt, and hastened away, pursued by an ill-mannered roar of laughter from the barber's shop. He was at first considerably surprised by the result of his question, but, being a shrewd youth, soon thought himself able to account for the mystery.

"This is some country representative," was his conclusion, "who has never seen the inside of my kinsman's door, and lacks the breeding to answer a stranger civilly. The man is old, or verily—I might be tempted to turn back and smite him on the nose. Ah, Robin, Robin! even the barber's boys laugh at you for choosing such a guide! You will be wiser in time, friend Robin."

He now became entangled in a succession of crooked and narrow streets, which crossed each other, and meandered at no great distance from the water-side. The smell of tar was obvious to his nostrils, the masts of vessels pierced the moonlight above the tops of the buildings, and the numerous signs, which Robin paused to read, informed him that he was near the centre of business. But the streets were empty, the shops were closed, and lights were visible only in the second stories of a few dwelling-houses. At length, on the corner of a narrow lane, through which he was passing, he beheld the broad countenance[3] of a British hero swinging before the door of an inn, whence proceeded the voices of many guests. The casement of one of the lower windows was thrown back, and a very thin curtain permitted Robin to distinguish a party at supper, round a well-furnished table. The fragrance of the good cheer steamed forth into the outer air, and the youth could not fail to recollect that the last remnant of his travelling stock of provisions had yielded to his morning appetite, and that noon had found and left him dinnerless.

"O, that a parchment three-penny might give me a right to sit down at yonder table!" said Robin with a sigh. "But the Major will make me welcome to the best of his victuals; so I will even step boldly in, and inquire my way to his dwelling."

He entered the tavern, and was guided by the murmur of voices and the fumes of tobacco to the public-room. It was a long and low apart-

3. Usually a picture of a notable person.

ment, with oaken walls, grown dark in the continual smoke, and a floor which was thickly sanded, but of no immaculate purity. A number of persons—the larger part of whom appeared to be mariners, or in some way connected with the sea—occupied the wooden benches, or leather-bottomed chairs, conversing on various matters, and occasionally lending their attention to some topic of general interest. Three or four little groups were draining as many bowls of punch, which the West India trade had long since made a familiar drink in the colony. Others, who had the appearance of men who lived by regular and laborious handicraft, preferred the insulated bliss of an unshared potation, and became more taciturn under its influence. Nearly all, in short, evinced a predilection for the Good Creature[4] in some of its various shapes, for this is a vice to which, as Fast Day sermons of a hundred years ago will testify, we have a long hereditary claim. The only guests to whom Robin's sympathies inclined him were two or three sheepish countrymen, who were using the inn somewhat after the fashion of a Turkish caravansary;[5] they had gotten themselves into the darkest corner of the room, and, heedless of the Nicotian[6] atmosphere, were supping on the bread of their own ovens, and the bacon cured in their own chimney smoke. But though Robin felt a sort of brotherhood with these strangers, his eyes were attracted from them to a person who stood near the door, holding whispered conversation with a group of ill-dressed associates. His features were separately striking almost to grotesqueness, and the whole face left a deep impression on the memory. The forehead bulged out into a double prominence, with a vale between; the nose came boldly forth in an irregular curve, and its bridge was of more than a finger's breadth; the eyebrows were deep and shaggy, and the eyes glowed beneath them like fire in a cave.

While Robin deliberated of whom to inquire respecting his kinsman's dwelling, he was accosted by the innkeeper, a little man in a stained white apron, who had come to pay his professional welcome to the stranger. Being in the second generation from a French Protestant, he seemed to have inherited the courtesy of his parent nation; but no variety of circumstances was ever known to change his voice from the one shrill note in which he now addressed Robin.

"From the country, I presume, sir?" said he, with a profound bow. "Beg leave to congratulate you on your arrival, and trust you intend a long stay with us. Fine town here, sir, beautiful buildings, and much that may interest a stranger. May I hope for the honor of your commands in respect to supper?"

4. The Good Creature: intoxicating beverages; it has its "long hereditary claim" in *I Timothy,* 4:4: "the Good Creature in some of its various shapes . . . [has] a long hereditary claim."
5. A public place provided for travelers to bring their own food to eat.
6. A smoky atmosphere named after Jacques Nicot who is said to have introduced tobacco into France in 1560.

"The man sees a family likeness! the rogue has guessed that I am related to the Major!" thought Robin, who had hitherto experienced little superfluous civility.

All eyes were now turned on the country lad, standing at the door, in his worn three-cornered hat, gray coat, leather breeches, and blue yarn stockings, leaning on an oaken cudgel, and bearing a wallet on his back.

Robin replied to the courteous innkeeper, with such an assumption of confidence as befitted the Major's relative. "My honest friend," he said, "I shall make it a point to patronize your house on some occasion, when"—here he could not help lowering his voice—"when I may have more than a parchment three-pence in my pocket. My present business," continued he, speaking with lofty confidence, "is merely to inquire my way to the dwelling of my kinsman, Major Molineux."

There was a sudden and general movement in the room, which Robin interpreted as expressing the eagerness of each individual to become his guide. But the innkeeper turned his eyes to a written paper on the wall, which he read, or seemed to read, with occasional recurrences to the young man's figure.

"What have we here?" said he, breaking his speech into little dry fragments. " 'Left the house of the subscriber, bounden servant,[7] Hezeiah Mudge,—had on, when he went away, gray coat, leather breeches, master's third-best hat. One pound currency reward to whosoever shall lodge him in any jail of the province.' Better trudge, boy; better trudge!"

Robin had begun to draw his hand towards the lighter end of the oak cudgel, but a strange hostility in every countenance induced him to relinquish his purpose of breaking the courteous innkeeper's head. As he turned to leave the room, he encountered a sneering glance from the bold-featured personage whom he had before noticed; and no sooner was he beyond the door, than he heard a general laugh, in which the innkeeper's voice might be distinguished, like the dropping of small stones into a kettle.

"Now, is it not strange," thought Robin, with his usual shrewdness,—"is it not strange that the confession of an empty pocket should outweigh the name of my kinsman, Major Molineux? O, if I had one of those grinning rascals in the woods, where I and my oak sapling grew up together, I would teach him that my arm is heavy, though my purse be light!"

On turning the corner of the narrow lane, Robin found himself in a spacious street, with an unbroken line of lofty houses on each side, and a steepled building at the upper end, whence the ringing of a bell announced the hour of nine. The light of the moon, and the lamps from the numerous shop-windows, discovered people promenading on the pavement, and amongst them Robin hoped to recognize his hitherto in-

7. One who earns his liberty by working a contracted period of time; the legal term is "indentured servant."

scrutable relative. The result of his former inquiries made him unwilling to hazard another, in a scene of such publicity, and he determined to walk slowly and silently up the street, thrusting his face close to that of every elderly gentleman, in search of the Major's lineaments. In his progress, Robin encountered many gay and gallant figures. Embroidered garments of showy colors, enormous periwigs, gold-laced hats, and silver-hilted swords glided past him and dazzled his optics. Travelled youths, imitators of the European fine gentlemen of the period, trod jauntily along, half dancing to the fashionable tunes which they hummed, and making poor Robin ashamed of his quiet and natural gait. At length, after many pauses to examine the gorgeous display of goods in the shop-windows, and after suffering some rebukes for the impertinence of his scrutiny into people's faces, the Major's kinsman found himself near the steepled building, still unsuccessful in his search. As yet, however, he had seen only one side of the thronged street; so Robin crossed, and continued the same sort of inquisition down the opposite pavement, with stronger hopes than the philosopher seeking an honest man, but with no better fortune. He had arrived about midway towards the lower end, from which his course began, when he overheard the approach of some one who struck down a cane on the flag-stones at every step, uttering, at regular intervals, two sepulchral hems.

"Mercy on us!" quoth Robin, recognizing the sound.

Turning a corner, which chanced to be close at his right hand, he hastened to pursue his researches in some other part of the town. His patience now was wearing low, and he seemed to feel more fatigue from his rambles since he crossed the ferry, than from his journey of several days on the other side. Hunger also pleaded loudly within him, and Robin began to balance the propriety of demanding, violently, and with lifted cudgel, the necessary guidance from the first solitary passenger whom he should meet. While a resolution to this effect was gaining strength, he entered a street of mean appearance, on either side of which a row of ill-built houses was straggling towards the harbor. The moonlight fell upon no passenger along the whole extent, but in the third domicile which Robin passed there was a half-opened door, and his keen glance detected a woman's garment within.

"My luck may be better here," said he to himself.

Accordingly, he approached the door, and beheld it shut closer as he did so; yet an open space remained, sufficing for the fair occupant to observe the stranger, without a corresponding display on her part. All that Robin could discern was a strip of scarlet petticoat, and the occasional sparkle of an eye, as if the moonbeams were trembling on some bright thing.

"Pretty mistress," for I may call her so with a good conscience, thought the shrewd youth, since I know nothing to the contrary,—"my sweet pretty mistress, will you be kind enough to tell me whereabouts I must seek the dwelling of my kinsman, Major Molineux?"

Robin's voice was plaintive and winning, and the female, seeing nothing to be shunned in the handsome country youth, thrust open the door, and came forth into the moonlight. She was a dainty little figure, with a white neck, round arms, and a slender waist, at the extremity of which her scarlet petticoat jutted out over a hoop, as if she were standing in a balloon. Moreover, her face was oval and pretty, her hair dark beneath the little cap, and her bright eyes possessed a sly freedom, which triumphed over those of Robin.

"Major Molineux dwells here," said this fair woman.

Now, her voice was the sweetest Robin had heard that night, the airy counterpart of a stream of melted silver; yet he could not help doubting whether that sweet voice spoke Gospel truth. He looked up and down the mean street, and then surveyed the house before which they stood. It was a small, dark edifice of two stories, the second of which projected over the lower floor, and the front apartment had the aspect of a shop for petty commodities.

"Now, truly, I am in luck," replied Robin cunningly, "and so indeed is my kinsman, the Major, in having so pretty a housekeeper. But I prithee trouble him to step to the door; I will deliver him a message from his friends in the country, and then go back to my lodgings at the inn."

"Nay, the Major has been abed this hour or more," said the lady of the scarlet petticoat; "and it would be to little purpose to disturb him tonight, seeing his evening draught was of the strongest. But he is a kind-hearted man, and it would be as much as my life's worth to let a kinsman of his turn away from the door. You are the good old gentleman's very picture, and I could swear that was his rainy-weather hat. Also he has garments very much resembling those leather small-clothes. But come in, I pray, for I bid you hearty welcome in his name."

So saying, the fair and hospitable dame took our hero by the hand; and the touch was light, and the force was gentleness, and though Robin read in her eyes what he did not hear in her words, yet the slender-waisted woman in the scarlet petticoat proved stronger than the athletic country youth. She had drawn his half-willing footsteps nearly to the threshold, when the opening of a door in the neighborhood startled the Major's housekeeper, and, leaving the Major's kinsman, she vanished speedily into her own domicile. A heavy yawn preceded the appearance of a man, who, like the Moonshine of Pyramus and Thisbe,[8] carried a lantern, needlessly aiding his sister luminary in the heavens. As he walked sleepily up the street, he turned his broad, dull face on Robin, and displayed a long staff, spiked at the end.

"Home, vagabond, home!" said the watchman, in accents that seemed to fall asleep as soon as they

8. A reference to the tragic love story of Pyramus and Thisbe as ludicrously enacted by a character in Shakespeare's *A Midsummer Night's Dream,* V, i.

were uttered. "Home, or we'll set you in the stocks by peep of day!"

"This is the second hint of the kind," thought Robin. "I wish they would end my difficulties, by setting me there to-night."

Nevertheless, the youth felt an instinctive antipathy towards the guardian of midnight order, which at first prevented him from asking his usual question. But just when the man was about to vanish behind the corner, Robin resolved not to lose the opportunity, and shouted lustily after him,—

"I say, friend! will you guide me to the house of my kinsman, Major Molineux?"

The watchman made no reply, but turned the corner and was gone; yet Robin seemed to hear the sound of drowsy laughter stealing along the solitary street. At that moment, also, a pleasant titter saluted him from the open window above his head; he looked up, and caught the sparkle of a saucy eye; a round arm beckoned to him, and next he heard light footsteps descending the staircase within. But Robin, being of the household of a New England clergyman, was a good youth, as well as a shrewd one; so he resisted temptation, and fled away.

He now roamed desperately, and at random, through the town, almost ready to believe that a spell was on him, like that by which a wizard of his country had once kept three pursuers wandering, a whole winter night, within twenty paces of the cottage which they sought. The streets lay before him, strange and desolate, and the lights were extinguished in almost every house. Twice, however, little parties of men, among whom Robin distinguished individuals in outlandish attire, came hurrying along; but, though on both occasions they paused to address him, such intercourse did not at all enlighten his perplexity. They did but utter a few words in some language of which Robin knew nothing, and perceiving his inability to answer, bestowed a curse upon him in plain English and hastened away. Finally, the lad determined to knock at the door of every mansion that might appear worthy to be occupied by his kinsman, trusting that perseverance would overcome the fatality that had hitherto thwarted him. Firm in this resolve, he was passing beneath the walls of a church, which formed the corner of two streets when, as he turned into the shade of its steeple, he encountered a bulky stranger, muffled in a cloak. The man was proceeding with the speed of earnest business, but Robin planted himself full before him, holding the oak cudgel with both hands across his body as a bar to further passage.

"Halt, honest man, and answer me a question," said he very resolutely. "Tell me, this instant, whereabouts is the dwelling of my kinsman, Major Molineux!"

"Keep your tongue between your teeth, fool, and let me pass!" said a deep, gruff voice, which Robin partly remembered. "Let me pass, I say, or I'll strike you to the earth!"

"No, no, neighbor!" cried Robin, flourishing his cudgel, and then thrusting its larger end close to the man's muffled face. "No, no, I'm not the fool you take me for, nor do you pass till I have an answer to my question. Whereabouts is the dwelling of my kinsman, Major Molineux?"

The stranger, instead of attempting to force his passage, stepped back into the moonlight, unmuffled his face, and stared full into that of Robin.

"Watch here an hour, and Major Molineux will pass by," said he.

Robin gazed with dismay and astonishment on the unprecedented physiognomy of the speaker. The forehead with its double prominence, the broad hooked nose, the shaggy eyebrows, and fiery eyes were those which he had noticed at the inn, but the man's complexion had undergone a singular, or, more properly, a twofold change. One side of the face blazed an intense red, while the other was black as midnight, the division line being in the broad bridge of the nose; and a mouth which seemed to extend from ear to ear was black or red, in contrast to the color of the cheek. The effect was as if two individual devils, a fiend of fire and a fiend of darkness, had united themselves to form this infernal visage. The stranger grinned in Robin's face, muffled his party-colored[9] features, and was out of sight in a moment.

"Strange things we travellers see!" ejaculated Robin.

He seated himself, however, upon the steps of the church door, resolving to wait the appointed time for his kinsman. A few moments were consumed in philosophical speculations upon the species of man who had just left him; but having settled this point shrewdly, rationally, and satisfactorily, he was compelled to look elsewhere for his amusement. And first he threw his eyes along the street. It was of more respectable appearance than most of those into which he had wandered; and the moon, creating, like the imaginative power, a beautiful strangeness in familiar objects, gave something of romance to a scene that might not have possessed it in the light of day. The irregular and often quaint architecture of the houses, some of whose roofs were broken into numerous little peaks, while others ascended, steep and narrow, into a single point, and others again were square; the pure snow-white of some of their complexions, the aged darkness of others, and the thousand sparklings, reflected from bright substances in the walls of many; these matters engaged Robin's attention for a while, and then began to grow wearisome. Next he endeavored to define the forms of distant objects, starting away, with almost ghostly indistinctness, just as his eye appeared to grasp them; and finally he took a minute survey of an edifice which stood on the opposite side of the street, directly in front of the church door, where he was stationed. It was a large, square mansion, distinguished from its neighbors by a balcony, which rested on tall pillars, and by an elaborate Gothic window, communicating therewith.

"Perhaps this is the very house I have been seeking," thought Robin.

9. An obsolete spelling for *parti-colored;* many colored.

Then he strove to speed away the time, by listening to a murmur which swept continually along the street, yet was scarcely audible, except to an unaccustomed ear like his; it was a low, dull, dreamy sound, compounded of many noises, each of which was at too great a distance to be separately heard. Robin marvelled at this snore of a sleeping town, and marvelled more whenever its continuity was broken by now and then a distant shout, apparently loud where it originated. But altogether it was a sleep-inspiring sound, and, to shake off its drowsy influence, Robin arose, and climbed a window frame, that he might view the interior of the church. There the moonbeams came trembling in, and fell down upon the deserted pews, and extended along the quiet aisles. A fainter yet more awful radiance was hovering around the pulpit, and one solitary ray had dared to rest upon the open page of the great Bible. Had nature, in that deep hour, become a worshipper in the house which man had builded? Or was that heavenly light the visible sanctity of the place,—visible because no earthly and impure feet were within the walls? The scene made Robin's heart shiver with a sensation of loneliness stronger than he had ever felt in the remotest depths of his native woods; so he turned away and sat down again before the door. There were graves around the church, and now an uneasy thought obtruded into Robin's breast. What if the object of his search, which had been so often and so strangely thwarted, were all the time mouldering in his shroud? What if his kinsman should glide through yonder gate, and nod and smile to him in dimly passing by?

"O that any breathing thing were here with me!" said Robin.

Recalling his thoughts from this uncomfortable track, he sent them over forest, hill, and stream, and attempted to imagine how that evening of ambiguity and weariness had been spent by his father's household. He pictured them assembled at the door, beneath the tree, the great old tree, which had been spared for its huge twisted trunk and venerable shade, when a thousand leafy brethren fell. There, at the going down of the summer sun, it was his father's custom to perform domestic worship, that the neighbors might come and join with him like brothers of the family, and that the wayfaring man might pause to drink at that fountain, and keep his heart pure by freshening the memory of home. Robin distinguished the seat of every individual of the little audience; he saw the good man in the midst, holding the Scriptures in the golden light that fell from the western clouds; he beheld him close the book and all rise up to pray. He heard the old thanksgivings for daily mercies, the old supplications for their continuance, to which he had so often listened in weariness, but which were now among his dear remembrances. He perceived the slight inequality of his father's voice when he came to speak of the absent one; he noted how his mother turned her face to the broad and knotted trunk; how his elder brother scorned, because the beard was rough upon his upper lip, to permit his features to be moved; how the younger sister drew down a low hanging branch before her eyes; and how the little one of all, whose sports had hitherto broken the decorum of the scene, understood the prayer for her playmate, and burst into clamorous grief. Then he saw them go in at the door; and when Robin would have entered also, the latch tinkled into its place, and he was excluded from his home.

"Am I here, or there?" cried Robin, starting; for all at once, when his thoughts had become visible and audible in a dream, the long, wide, solitary street shone out before him.

He aroused himself, and endeavored to fix his attention steadily upon the large edifice which he had surveyed before. But still his mind kept vibrating between fancy and reality; by turns, the pillars of the balcony lengthened into the tall, bare stems of pines, dwindled down to human figures, settled again into their true shape and size, and then commenced a new succession of changes. For a single moment, when he deemed himself awake, he could have sworn that a visage—one which he seemed to remember, yet could not absolutely name as his kinsman's—was looking towards him from the Gothic window. A deeper sleep wrestled with and nearly overcame him, but fled at the sound of footsteps along the opposite pavement. Robin rubbed his eyes, discerned a man passing at the foot of the balcony, and addressed him in a loud, peevish, and lamentable cry.

"Hallo, friend! must I wait here all night for my kinsman, Major Molineux?"

The sleeping echoes awoke, and answered the voice; and the passenger, barely able to discern a figure sitting in the oblique shade of the steeple, traversed the street to obtain a nearer view. He was himself a gentleman in his prime, of open, intelligent, cheerful, and altogether prepossessing countenance. Perceiving a country youth, apparently homeless and without friends, he accosted him in a tone of real kindness, which had become strange to Robin's ears.

"Well, my good lad, why are you sitting here?" inquired he. "Can I be of service to you in any way?"

"I am afraid not, sir," replied Robin despondingly; "yet I shall take it kindly, if you'll answer me a single question. I've been searching, half the night, for one Major Molineux; now, sir, is there really such a person in these parts, or am I dreaming?"

"Major Molineux! The name is not altogether strange to me," said the gentleman, smiling. "Have you any objection to telling me the nature of your business with him?"

Then Robin briefly related that his father was a clergyman, settled on a small salary, at a long distance back in the country, and that he and Major Molineux were brothers' children. The Major, having inherited riches, and acquired civil and military rank, had visited his cousin, in great pomp, a year or two before; had manifested much interest in Robin and an elder brother, and, being childless himself, had thrown out hints respecting the future establishment of one of them in life. The elder brother was destined to succeed to the farm which his father cultivated in the interval of sacred duties; it was therefore determined that Robin should profit by his kinsman's generous intentions, especially as he seemed to be rather the favorite, and was thought to possess other necessary endowments.

"For I have the name of being a shrewd youth," observed Robin, in this part of his story.

"I doubt not you deserve it," replied his new friend good-naturedly; "but pray proceed."

"Well, sir, being nearly eighteen years old, and well grown, as you see," continued Robin, drawing himself up to his full height, "I thought it high time to begin the world. So my mother and sister put me in handsome trim, and my father gave me half the remnant of his last year's salary, and five days ago I started for this place, to pay the Major a visit. But, would you believe it, sir! I crossed the ferry a little after dark, and have yet found nobody that would show me the way to his dwelling; only, an hour or two since, I was told to wait here, and Major Molineux would pass by."

"Can you describe the man who told you this?" inquired the gentleman.

"O, he was a very ill-favored fellow, sir," replied Robin, "with two great bumps on his forehead, a hook nose, fiery eyes; and, what struck me as the strangest, his face was of two different colors. Do you happen to know such a man, sir?"

"Not intimately," answered the stranger, "but I chanced to meet him a little time previous to your stopping me. I believe you may trust his word, and that the Major will very shortly pass through this street. In the mean time, as I have a singular curiosity to witness your meeting, I will sit down here upon the steps and bear you company."

He seated himself accordingly, and soon engaged his companion in animated discourse. It was but of brief continuance, however, for a noise of shouting, which had long been remotely audible, drew so much nearer that Robin inquired its cause.

"What may be the meaning of this uproar?" asked he. "Truly, if your town be always as noisy, I shall find little sleep while I am an inhabitant."

"Why, indeed, friend Robin, there do appear to be three or four riotous fellows abroad tonight," replied the gentleman. "You must not expect all the stillness of your native woods here in our streets. But the watch will shortly be at the heels of these lads and"—

"Ay, and set them in the stocks by peep of day," interrupted Robin, recollecting his own encounter with the drowsy lantern-bearer. "But, dear sir, if I may trust my ears, an army of watchmen would never make head against such a multitude of rioters. There were at least a thousand voices went up to make that one shout."

"May not a man have several voices, Robin, as well as two complexions?" said his friend.

"Perhaps a man may; but Heaven forbid that a woman should!" responded the shrewd youth, thinking of the seductive tones of the Major's housekeeper.

The sounds of a trumpet in some neighboring street now became so evident and continual, that Robin's curiosity was strongly excited. In addition to the shouts, he heard frequent bursts from many instruments of discord, and a wild and confused laughter filled up the intervals. Robin rose from the steps, and looked wistfully towards a point whither people seemed to be hastening.

"Surely some prodigious merry-making is going on," exclaimed he. "I have laughed very little since I left home, sir, and should be sorry to lose an opportunity. Shall we step round the corner by that darkish house, and take our share of the fun?"

"Sit down again, sit down, good Robin," replied the gentleman, laying his hand on the skirt of the gray coat. "You forget that we must wait here for your kinsman; and there is reason to believe that he will pass by, in the course of a very few moments."

The near approach of the uproar had now disturbed the neighborhood; windows flew open on all sides; and many heads, in the attire of the pillow, and confused by sleep suddenly broken, were protruded to the gaze of whoever had leisure to observe them. Eager voices hailed each other from house to house, all demanding the explanation, which not a soul could give. Half-dressed men hurried towards the unknown commotion, stumbling as they went over the stone steps that thrust themselves into the narrow footwalk. The shouts, the laughter, and the tuneless bray, the antipodes of music, came onwards with increasing din, till scattered individuals, and then denser bodies, began to appear round a corner at the distance of a hundred yards.

"Will you recognize your kinsman, if he passes in this crowd?" inquired the gentleman.

"Indeed, I can't warrant it, sir; but I'll take my stand here, and keep a bright lookout," answered Robin, descending to the outer edge of the pavement.

A mighty stream of people now emptied into the street, and came rolling slowly towards the church. A single horseman wheeled the corner in the midst of them, and close behind him came a band of fearful wind-instruments, sending forth a fresher discord now that no intervening buildings kept it from the ear. Then a redder light disturbed the moonbeams, and a dense multitude of torches shone along the street, concealing, by their glare, whatever object they illuminated. The single horseman, clad in a military dress, and bearing a drawn sword, rode onward as the leader, and, by his fierce and variegated countenance, appeared like war personified; the red of one cheek was an emblem of fire and sword; the blackness of the other betokened the mourning that attends them. In his train were wild figures in the Indian dress, and many fantastic shapes without a model, giving the whole march a visionary air, as if a dream had broken forth from some feverish brain, and were sweeping visibly through the midnight streets. A mass of people, inactive, except as applauding spectators, hemmed the procession in; and several women ran along the sidewalk, piercing the confusion of heavier sounds with their shrill voices of mirth or terror.

"The double-faced fellow has his

eye upon me," muttered Robin, with an indefinite but an uncomfortable idea that he was himself to bear a part in the pageantry.

The leader turned himself in the saddle, and fixed his glance full upon the country youth, as the steed went slowly by. When Robin had freed his eyes from those fiery ones, the musicians were passing before him, and the torches were close at hand; but the unsteady brightness of the latter formed a veil which he could not penetrate. The rattling of wheels over the stones sometimes found its way to his ear, and confused traces of a human form appeared at intervals, and then melted into the vivid light. A moment more, and the leader thundered a command to halt: the trumpets vomited a horrid breath, and then held their peace; the shouts and laughter of the people died away, and there remained only a universal hum, allied to silence. Right before Robin's eyes was an uncovered cart. There the torches blazed the brightest, there the moon shone out like day, and there, in tar-and-feathery dignity, sat his kinsman, Major Molineux!

He was an elderly man, of large and majestic person, and strong, square features, betokening a steady soul; but steady as it was, his enemies had found means to shake it. His face was pale as death, and far more ghastly; the broad forehead was contracted in his agony, so that his eyebrows formed one grizzled line; his eyes were red and wild, and the foam hung white upon his quivering lip. His whole frame was agitated by a quick and continual tremor, which his pride strove to quell, even in those circumstances of overwhelming humiliation. But perhaps the bitterest pang of all was when his eyes met those of Robin; for he evidently knew him on the instant, as the youth stood witnessing the foul disgrace of a head grown gray in honor. They stared at each other in silence, and Robin's knees shook, and his hair bristled, with a mixture of pity and terror. Soon, however, a bewildering excitement began to seize upon his mind; the preceding adventures of the night, the unexpected appearance of the crowd, the torches, the confused din and the hush that followed, the spectre of his kinsman reviled by that great multitude,—all this, and, more than all, a perception of tremendous ridicule in the whole scene, affected him with a sort of mental inebriety. At that moment a voice of sluggish merriment saluted Robin's ears; he turned instinctively, and just behind the corner of the church stood the lantern-bearer, rubbing his eyes, and drowsily enjoying the lad's amazement. Then he heard a peal of laughter like the ringing of silvery bells; a woman twitched his arm, a saucy eye met his, and he saw the lady of the scarlet petticoat. A sharp, dry cachinnation appealed to his memory, and, standing on tiptoe in the crowd, with his white apron over his head, he beheld the courteous little innkeeper. And lastly, there sailed over the heads of the multitude a great, broad laugh, broken in the midst by two sepulchral hems; thus, "Haw, haw, haw,—hem, hem,—haw, haw, haw, haw!"

The sound proceeded from the balcony of the opposite edifice, and thither Robin turned his eyes. In front of the Gothic window stood the old citizen, wrapped in a wide gown, his gray periwig exchanged for a nightcap, which was thrust back from his forehead, and his silk stockings hanging about his legs. He supported himself on his polished cane in a fit of convulsive merriment, which manifested itself on his solemn old features like a funny inscription on a tombstone. Then Robin seemed to hear the voices of the barbers, of the guests of the inn, and of all who had made sport of him that night. The contagion was spreading among the multitude, when all at once it seized upon Robin, and he sent forth a shout of laughter that echoed through the street,—every man shook his sides, every man emptied his lungs, but Robin's shout was the loudest there. The cloud-spirits peeped from their silvery islands, as the congregated mirth went roaring up the sky! The Man in the Moon heard the far bellow. "Oho," quoth he, "the old earth is frolicsome to-night!"

When there was a momentary calm in that tempestuous sea of sound, the leader gave the sign, the procession resumed its march. On they went, like fiends that throng in mockery around some dead potentate, mighty no more, but majestic still in his agony. On they went, in counterfeited pomp, in senseless uproar, in frenzied merriment, trampling all on an old man's heart. On swept the tumult, and left a silent street behind.

"Well, Robin, are you dreaming?" inquired the gentleman, laying his hand on the youth's shoulder.

Robin started, and withdrew his arm from the stone post to which he had instinctively clung, as the living stream rolled by him. His cheek was somewhat pale, and his eye not quite as lively as in the earlier part of the evening.

"Will you be kind enough to show me the way to the ferry?" said he, after a moment's pause.

"You have, then, adopted a new subject of inquiry?" observed his companion with a smile.

"Why, yes, sir," replied Robin rather dryly. "Thanks to you, and to my other friends, I have at last met my kinsman, and he will scarce desire to see my face again. I begin to grow weary of a town life, sir. Will you show me the way to the ferry?"

"No, my good friend Robin,—not to-night, at least," said the gentleman. "Some few days hence, if you wish it, I will speed you on your journey. Or, if you prefer to remain with us, perhaps, as you are a shrewd youth, you may rise in the world without the help of your kinsman, Major Molineux."

Considerations

It would be unreasonable to expect anyone to come up with a definitive explanation of this story. Thus far the numerous critics and scholars who have analyzed it find only elementary points upon which to agree. If it is an allegory, Hawthorne failed to supply a clear key to the meanings of the symbols. The vast areas of ambiguity allow each reader to form his own personalized interpretation, congruent with his view of life itself. Perhaps it is this quality that makes the story a classic. It has been said that classic art is that which can be continually reinterpreted to fit the changing times and tastes.

Critics have seen in the story a rite of passage between innocent childhood and knowledgeable maturity. (What events support this interpretation?) They have attributed to it strong Freudian implications: The respected and honored, but only dimly known, father image of Major Molineux is overthrown as Robin becomes accepted by the community's adults. The story could also be a variation of the archetypal quest of the young man seeking his fortune in spite of great physical or psychic risk. There are obvious similarities to the traditional romance of the rural youth encountering the city. The story has also been read as the embodiment of the conflict between the Puritanical habit of seeing things in terms of their labels and the as yet unbiased view of a young boy.

The above-mentioned ways of viewing the story do not exhaust the possible interpretations. However, the possibility of multiple interpretations does not lessen the impact of the story. Rather it underscores the universal appeal that impels us to try to make the material more comprehensible and therefore more manageable. Or perhaps part of the fascination of the story comes from the challenge of trying to make sense out of things apprehended by means other than reason. Hawthorne believed that only a mental state akin to that borderline state of half-waking half-sleeping can give access to truth. At that time we are not committed to either the fantasy world or to reality, and we can see that both merge, that each is part of the other. When we wake, we feel obligated to make sense out of it all.

The story is excellent structurally. Time is compressed in such a way that a journey which must in actuality have taken quite some time takes place in only a few pages. The events are linked by a variety of transitional devices. Characters are introduced one by one as Robin encounters them and are then shown later in a group. The sequence of events is parallel to Robin's physical journey through the town. There is repetition of key phrases such as "shrewd youth" and "my kinsman." The colors of red and black run through almost every scene: the night, the woman in scarlet, the fire, and of course the man whose face was half red and half black.

What aspects of this story are just as relevant today as they were when it was written? In what sense can many young people of our time sympathize with Robin's feelings of alienation and disillusionment? Do you agree that this story is a classic? Why or why not?

The Death of Ivan Ilych

Leo Tolstoy

I

During an interval in the Melvinski trial in the large building of the Law Courts, the members and public prosecutor met in Ivan Egorovich Shebek's private room, where the conversation turned on the celebrated Krasovski case. Fëdor Vasilievich warmly maintained that it was not subject to their jurisdiction, Ivan Egorovich maintained the contrary, while Peter Ivanovich, not having entered into the discussion at the start, took no part in it but looked through the *Gazette* which had just been handed in.

"Gentlemen," he said, "Ivan Ilych has died!"

"You don't say so!"

"Here, read it yourself," replied Peter Ivanovich, handing Fëdor Vasilievich the paper still damp from the press. Surrounded by a black border were the words: "Praskovya Fëdorovna Golovina, with profound sorrow, informs relatives and friends of the demise of her beloved husband Ivan Ilych Golovin, Member of the Court of Justice, which occurred on February the 4th of this year 1882. The funeral will take place on Friday at one o'clock in the afternoon."

Ivan Ilych had been a colleague of the gentlemen present and was liked by them all. He had been ill for some weeks with an illness said to be incurable. His post had been kept open for him, but there had been conjectures that in case of his death Alexeev might receive his appointment, and that either Vinnikov or Shtabel would succeed Alexeev. So on receiving the news of Ivan Ilych's death the first thought of each of the gentlemen in that private room was of the changes and promotions it might occasion among themselves or their acquaintances.

"I shall be sure to get Shtabel's place or Vinnikov's," thought Fëdor Vasilievich. "I was promised that long ago, and the promotion means an extra eight hundred rubles a year for me beside the allowance."

"Now I must apply for my brother-in-law's transfer from Kaluga," thought Peter Ivanovich. "My wife will be very glad, and then she won't be able to say that I never do anything for her relations."

"I thought he would never leave his bed again," said Peter Ivanovich aloud. "It's very sad."

"But what really was the matter with him?"

from IVAN ILYCH, HADJI MURAD AND OTHER STORIES by Leo Tolstoy, translated by Louise and Aylmer Maude and published by Oxford University Press.

"The doctors couldn't say—at least they could, but each of them said something different. When last I saw him I thought he was getting better."

"And I haven't been to see him since the holidays. I always meant to go."

"Had he any property?"

"I think his wife had a little—but something quite trifling."

"We shall have to go to see her, but they live so terribly far away."

"Far away from you, you mean. Everything's far away from your place."

"You see, he never can forgive my living on the other side of the river," said Peter Ivanovich, smiling at Shebek. Then, still talking of the distances between different parts of the city, they returned to the Court.

Besides considerations as to the possible transfers and promotions likely to result from Ivan Ilych's death, the mere fact of the death of a near acquaintance aroused, as usual, in all who heard of it the complacent feeling that, "it is he who is dead and not I."

Each one thought or felt, "Well, he's dead but I'm alive!" But the more intimate of Ivan Ilych's acquaintances, his so-called friends, could not help thinking also that they would now have to fulfil the very tiresome demands of propriety by attending the funeral service and paying a visit of condolence to the widow.

Fëdor Vasilievich and Peter Ivanovich had been his nearest acquaintances. Peter Ivanovich had studied law with Ivan Ilych and had considered himself to be under obligations to him.

Having told his wife at dinner-time of Ivan Ilych's death and of his conjecture that it might be possible to get her brother transferred to their circuit, Peter Ivanovich sacrificed his usual nap, put on his evening clothes, and drove to Ivan Ilych's house.

At the entrance stood a carriage and two cabs. Leaning against the wall in the hall downstairs near the cloak-stand was a coffin-lid covered with cloth of gold, ornamented with gold cord and tassels, that had been polished up with metal powder. Two ladies in black were taking off their fur cloaks. Peter Ivanovich recognized one of them as Ivan Ilych's sister, but the other was a stranger to him. His colleague Schwartz was just coming downstairs, but on seeing Peter Ivanovich enter he stopped and winked at him, as if to say: "Ivan Ilych has made a mess of things—not like you and me."

Schwartz's face with his Piccadilly whiskers and his slim figure in evening dress, had as usual an air of elegant solemnity which contrasted with the playfulness of his character and had a special piquancy here, or so it seemed to Peter Ivanovich.

Peter Ivanovich allowed the ladies to precede him and slowly followed them upstairs. Schwartz did not come down but remained where he was, and Peter Ivanovich understood that he wanted to arrange where they should play bridge that evening. The ladies went upstairs to the widow's room, and Schwartz with seriously compressed lips but a playful look in his eyes, indicated by a twist of his eyebrows the room to the right where the body lay.

Peter Ivanovich, like everyone else on such occasions, entered feeling uncertain what he would have to do. All he knew was that at such times it is always safe to cross oneself. But he was not quite sure whether one should make obeisances while doing so. He therefore adopted a middle course. On entering the room he began crossing himself and made a slight movement resembling a bow. At the same time, as far as the motion of his head and arm allowed, he surveyed the room. Two young men—apparently nephews, one of whom was a high-school pupil—were leaving the room, crossing themselves as they did so. An old woman was standing motionless, and a lady with strangely arched eyebrows was saying something to her in a whisper. A vigorous, resolute Church Reader, in a frock-coat, was reading something in a loud voice with an expression that precluded any contradiction. The butler's assistant, Gerasim, stepping lightly in front of Peter Ivanovich, was strewing something on the floor. Noticing this, Peter Ivanovich was immediately aware of a faint odour of a decomposing body.

The last time he had called on Ivan Ilych, Peter Ivanovich had seen Gerasim in the study. Ivan Ilych had been particularly fond of him and he was performing the duty of a sick nurse.

Peter Ivanovich continued to make the sign of the cross slightly inclining his head in an intermediate direction between the coffin, the Reader, and the icons on the table in a corner of the room. Afterwards, when it seemed to him that this movement of his arm in crossing himself had gone on too long, he stopped and began to look at the corpse.

The dead man lay, as dead men always lie, in a specially heavy way, his rigid limbs sunk in the soft cushions of the coffin, with the head forever bowed on the pillow. His yellow waxen brow with bald patches over his sunken temples was thrust up in the way peculiar to the dead, the protruding nose seeming to press on the upper lip. He was much changed and had grown even thinner since Peter Ivanovich had last seen him, but, as is always the case with the dead, his face was handsomer and above all more dignified than when he was alive. The expression on the face said that what was necessary had been accomplished, and accomplished rightly. Besides this there was in that expression a reproach and a warning to the living. This warning seemed to Peter Ivanovich out of place, or at least not applicable to him. He felt a certain discomfort and so he hurriedly crossed himself once more and turned and went out of the door—too hurriedly and too regardless of propriety, as he himself was aware.

Schwartz was waiting for him in the adjoining room with legs spread wide apart and both hands toying with his top-hat behind his back. The mere sight of that playful, well-groomed, and elegant figure refreshed Peter Ivanovich. He felt that Schwartz was above all these happenings and would not surrender to any depressing influences. His very look said that this incident of a church service for Ivan Ilych could not be a sufficient reason for infringing the order of the session—in other words, that it would certainly not prevent his unwrapping a new pack of cards and shuffling them that evening while a footman placed four fresh candles on the table: in fact, that there was no reason for supposing that this incident would hinder their spending the evening agreeably. Indeed he said this in a whisper as Peter Ivanovich passed him, proposing that they should meet for a game at Fëdor Vasilievich's. But apparently Peter Ivanovich was not destined to play bridge that evening. Praskovya Fëdorovna (a short, fat woman who despite all efforts to the contrary had continued to broaden steadily from her shoulders downwards and who had the same extraordinarily arched eyebrows as the lady who had been standing by the coffin), dressed all in black, her head covered with lace, came out of her own room with some other ladies, conducted them to the room where the dead body lay, and said: "The service will begin immediately. Please go in."

Schwartz, making an indefinite bow, stood still, evidently neither accepting nor declining this invitation. Praskovya Fëdorovna, recognizing Peter Ivanovich, sighed, went close up to him, took his hand, and said: "I know you were a true friend to Ivan Ilych . . ." and looked at him awaiting some suitable response. And Peter Ivanovich knew that, just as it had been the right thing to cross himself in that room, so what he had to do here was to press her hand, sigh, and say, "Believe me. . . ." So he did all this and as he did it felt that the desired result had been achieved: that both he and she were touched.

"Come with me. I want to speak to you before it begins," said the widow. "Give me your arm."

Peter Ivanovich gave her his arm and they went to the inner rooms, passing Schwartz, who winked at Peter Ivanovich compassionately.

"That does for our bridge! Don't object if we find another player. Perhaps you can cut in when you do escape," said his playful look.

Peter Ivanovich sighed still more deeply and despondently, and Praskovya Fëdorovna pressed his arm gratefully. When they reached the drawing-room, upholstered in pink cretonne and lighted by a dim lamp, they sat down at the table—she on a sofa and Peter Ivanovich on a low pouffe, the springs of which yielded spasmodically under his weight. Praskovya Fëdorovna had been on the point of warning him to take another seat, but felt that such a warning was out of keeping with her present condition and so changed her mind. As he sat down on the pouffe Peter Ivanovich recalled how Ivan Ilych had arranged this room and had consulted him regarding this pink cretonne with green leaves. The whole room was full of furniture and knick-knacks, and on her way to the sofa the lace of the widow's black shawl caught on the carved edge of the table. Peter Ivanovich rose to detach it, and the springs of the pouffe, relieved of his weight, rose also and gave him a push. The widow began detaching her shawl herself, and Peter Ivanovich again sat down, suppressing the rebellious springs of the pouffe under him. But the widow had not quite freed herself and Peter Ivanovich got up again, and again the pouffe rebelled and even creaked. When this was all over she took out a clean cambric handkerchief and began to weep. The episode with the shawl and the struggle with the pouffe had cooled Peter Ivanovich's emotions and he sat there with a sullen look on his face. This awkward situation was interrupted by Sokolov, Ivan Ilych's butler, who came to report that the plot in the cemetery that Praskovya Fëdorovna had chosen would cost two hundred rubles. She stopped weeping and, looking at Peter Ivanovich with the air of a victim, remarked in French that it was very hard for her. Peter Ivanovich made a silent gesture signifying his full conviction that it must indeed be so.

"Please smoke," she said in a magnanimous yet crushed voice, and turned to discuss with Sokolov the price of the plot for the grave.

Peter Ivanovich while lighting his cigarette heard her inquiring very circumstantially into the prices of different plots in the cemetery and finally decide which she would take. When that was done she gave instructions about engaging the choir. Sokolov then left the room.

"I look after everything myself," she told Peter Ivanovich, shifting the albums that lay on the table; and noticing that the table was endangered by his cigarette-ash, she immediately passed him an ash-tray, saying as she did so: "I consider it an affectation to say that my grief prevents my attending to practical affairs. On the contrary, if anything can—I won't say console me, but—distract me, it is seeing to everything concerning him." She again took out her handkerchief as if preparing to cry, but suddenly, as if mastering her feeling, she shook herself and began to speak calmly. "But there is something I want to talk to you about."

Peter Ivanovich bowed, keeping control of the springs of the pouffe, which immediately began quivering under him.

"He suffered terribly the last few days."

"Did he?" said Peter Ivanovich.

"Oh, terribly! He screamed unceasingly, not for minutes but for hours. For the last three days he screamed incessantly. It was unendurable. I cannot understand how I bore it; you could hear him three rooms off. Oh, what I have suffered!"

"Is it possible that he was conscious all that time?" asked Peter Ivanovich.

"Yes," she whispered. "To the last moment. He took leave of us a quarter of an hour before he died, and asked us to take Volodya away."

The thought of the sufferings of this man he had known so intimately, first as a merry little boy, then as a school-mate, and later as a grown-up colleague, suddenly struck Peter Ivanovich with horror, despite an unpleasant consciousness of his own and this woman's dissimulation. He again saw that brow, and that nose pressing down on the lip, and felt afraid for himself.

"Three days of frightful suffering and then death! Why, that might suddenly, at any time, happen to me," he thought, and for a moment felt terrified. But—he did not himself know how—the customary reflection at once occurred to him that this had happened to Ivan Ilych and not to him, and that it should not and could not happen to him, and to think that it could would be yielding to depression which he ought not to do, as Schwartz's expression plainly showed. After which reflection Peter Ivanovich felt reassured, and began to ask with interest about the details of Ivan Ilych's death, as though death was an accident natural to Ivan Ilych but certainly not to himself.

After many details of the really dreadful physical sufferings Ivan Ilych had endured (which details he learnt only from the effect those sufferings had produced on Praskovya Fëdorovna's nerves) the widow apparently found it necessary to get to business.

"Oh, Peter Ivanovich, how hard it is! How terribly, terribly hard!" and she again began to weep.

Peter Ivanovich sighed and waited for her to finish blowing her nose. When she had done so he said, "Believe me . . ." and she again began talking and brought out what was evidently her chief concern with him—namely, to question him as to how she could obtain a grant of money from the government on the occasion of her husband's death. She made it appear that she was asking Peter Ivanovich's advice about her pension, but he soon saw that she already knew about that to the minutest detail, more even than he did himself. She knew how much could be got out of the government in consequence of her husband's death, but wanted to find out whether she could not possibly extract something more. Peter Ivanovich tried to think of some means of doing so, but after reflecting for a while and, out of propriety, condemning the government for its niggardliness, he said he thought that nothing more could be got. Then she sighed and evidently began to devise means of getting rid of her visitor. Noticing this, he put out his cigarette, rose, pressed her hand, and went out into the anteroom.

In the dining-room where the clock stood that Ivan Ilych had liked so much and had bought at an antique shop, Peter Ivanovich met a priest and a few acquaintances who had come to attend the service, and he recognized Ivan Ilych's daughter, a handsome young woman. She was in black and her slim figure appeared slimmer than ever. She had a gloomy, determined, almost angry expression, and bowed to Peter Ivanovich as though he were in some way to blame. Behind her, with the same offended look, stood a wealthy young man, an examining magistrate, whom Peter Ivanovich also knew and who was her fiancé, as he had heard. He bowed mournfully to them and was about to pass into the death-chamber, when from under the stairs appeared the figure of Ivan Ilych's schoolboy son, who was extremely like his father. He seemed a little Ivan Ilych, such as Peter Ivanovich remembered when they studied law together. His tear-stained eyes had in them the look that is seen in the eyes of boys of thirteen or fourteen who are not pure-minded. When he saw Peter Ivanovich he scowled morosely and shamefacedly. Peter Ivanovich nodded to him and entered the death-chamber. The service began: candles, groans, incense, tears, and sobs. Peter Ivanovich stood looking gloomily down at his feet. He did not look once at the dead man, did not yield to any depressing influence, and was one of the first to leave the room. There was no one in the anteroom, but Gerasim darted out of the dead man's room, rummaged with his strong hands among the fur coats to find Peter Ivanovich's and helped him on with it.

"Well, friend Gerasim," said Peter Ivanovich, so as to say something. "It's a sad affair, isn't it?"

"It's God's will. We shall all come to it some day," said Gerasim, displaying his teeth—the even, white teeth of a healthy peasant—and, like a man in the thick of urgent work, he briskly opened the front door, called the coachman, helped Peter Ivanovich into the sledge, and sprang back to the porch as if in readiness for what he had to do next.

Peter Ivanovich found the fresh air particularly pleasant after the smell of incense, the dead body, and carbolic acid.

"Where to, sir?" asked the coachman.

"It's not too late even now. . . . I'll call round on Fëdor Vasilievich."

He accordingly drove there and found them just finishing the first rubber, so that it was quite convenient for him to cut it.

II

Ivan Ilych's life had been most simple and most ordinary and therefore most terrible.

He had been a member of the Court of Justice, and died at the age of forty-five. His father had been an official who after serving in various ministries and departments in Petersburg had made the sort of career which brings men to positions from which by reason of their long service they cannot be dismissed, though they are obviously unfit to hold any responsible position, and for whom therefore posts are especially created, which though fictitious carry salaries of from six to ten thousand rubles that are not fictitious, and in receipt of which they live on to a great age.

Such was the Privy Councillor and superfluous member of various superfluous institutions, Ilya Epimovich Golovin.

He had three sons, of whom Ivan Ilych was the second. The eldest son was following in his father's footsteps only in another department, and was already approaching that stage in the service at which a similar sinecure would be reached. The third son was a failure. He had ruined his prospects in a number of positions and was now serving in the railway department. His father and brothers, and still more their wives, not merely disliked meeting him, but avoided remembering his existence unless compelled to do so. His sister had married Baron Greff, a Petersburg official of her father's type. Ivan Ilych was *le phénix de la famille* as people said. He was neither as cold and formal as his elder brother nor as wild as the younger, but was a happy mean between them—an intelligent, polished, lively and agreeable man. He had studied with his younger brother at the School of Law, but the latter had failed to complete the course and was expelled when he was in the fifth class. Ivan Ilych finished the course well. Even when he was at the School of Law he was just what he remained for the rest of his life: a capable, cheerful, good-natured, and sociable man, though strict in the fulfilment of what he considered to be his duty: and he considered his duty to be what was so considered by those in authority. Neither as a boy nor as a man was he a toady, but from early youth was by nature attracted to people of high station as a fly is drawn to the light, assimilating their ways and views of life and establishing friendly relations with them. All the enthusiasms of childhood and youth passed without leaving much trace on him; he succumbed to sensuality, to vanity, and latterly among the highest classes to liberalism, but always within limits which his instinct unfailingly indicated to him as correct.

At school he had done things which had formerly seemed to him very horrid and made him feel disgusted with himself when he did them; but when later on he saw that such actions were done by people of good position and that they did not regard them as wrong, he was able not exactly to regard them as right, but to forget about them entirely or not be at all troubled at remembering them.

Having graduated from the School of Law and qualified for the tenth rank of the civil service, and having received money from his father for his equipment, Ivan Ilych ordered himself clothes at Scharmer's, the fashionable tailor, hung a medallion inscribed *respice finem** on his watch-chain, took leave of his professor and the prince who was patron of the school, had a farewell dinner with his comrades at Donon's first-class restaurant, and with his new and fashionable portmanteau, linen, clothes, shaving and other toilet appliances, and a travelling rug, all purchased at the best shops, he set off for one of the provinces where, through his father's influence, he had been attached to the Governor as an official for special service.

In the province Ivan Ilych soon arranged as easy and agreeable a position for himself as he had had at the School of Law. He performed his official tasks, made his career, and at the same time amused himself pleasantly and decorously. Occasionally he paid official visits to country districts, where he behaved with dignity both to his superiors and inferiors, and performed the duties entrusted to him, which related chiefly to the sectarians, with an exactness and incorruptible honesty of which he could not but feel proud.

In official matters, despite his youth and taste for frivolous gaiety, he was exceedingly reserved, punctilious, and even severe; but in society he was often amusing and witty, and always good-natured, correct in his manner, and *bon enfant,*† as the governor and his wife—with whom he was like one of the family—used to say of him.

In the province he had an affair with a lady who made advances to the elegant young lawyer, and there was also a milliner; and there were carousals with aides-de-camp who visited the district, and after-supper visits to a certain outlying street of doubtful reputation; and there was too some obsequiousness to his chief and even

---

**respice finem:* look to the end. †*bon enfant:* a good child.

to his chief's wife, but all this was done with such a tone of good breeding that no hard names could be applied to it. It all came under the heading of the French saying: *"Il faut que jeunesse se passe."** It was all done with clean hands, in clean linen, with French phrases, and above all among people of the best society and consequently with the approval of people of rank.

So Ivan Ilych served for five years and then came a change in his official life. The new and reformed judicial institutions were introduced, and new men were needed. Ivan Ilych became such a new man. He was offered the post of examining magistrate, and he accepted it though the post was in another province and obliged him to give up the connexions he had formed and to make new ones. His friends met to give him a send-off; they had a group-photograph taken and presented him with a silver cigarette-case, and he set off to his new post.

As examining magistrate Ivan Ilych was just as *comme il faut* and decorous a man, inspiring general respect and capable of separating his official duties from his private life, as he had been when acting as an official on special service. His duties now as examining magistrate were far more interesting and attractive than before. In his former position it had been pleasant to wear an undress uniform made by Scharmer, and to pass through the crowd of petitioners and officials who were timorously awaiting an audience with the governor, and who envied him as with free and easy gait he went straight into his chief's private room to have a cup of tea and a cigarette with him. But not many people had then been directly dependent on him—only police officials and the sectarians when he went on special missions—and he liked to treat them politely, almost as comrades, as if he were letting them feel that he who had the power to crush them was treating them in this simple, friendly way. There were then but few such people. But now, as an examining magistrate, Ivan Ilych felt that everyone without exception, even the most important and self-satisfied, was in his power, and that he need only write a few words on a sheet of paper with a certain heading, and this or that important, self-satisfied person would be brought before him in the role of an accused person or a witness, and if he did not choose to allow him to sit down, would have to stand before him and answer his questions. Ivan Ilych never abused his power; he tried on the contrary to soften its expression, but the consciousness of it and of the possibility of softening its effect, supplied the chief interest and attraction of his office. In his work itself, especially in his examinations, he very soon acquired a method of eliminating all considerations irrelevant to the legal aspect of the case, and reducing even the most complicated case to a form in which it would be presented on paper only in its externals, completely excluding his personal opinion of the matter, while above all observ-

***Il faut . . . passe:* You're only young once.

ing every prescribed formality. The work was new and Ivan Ilych was one of the first men to apply the new Code of 1864.

On taking up the post of examining magistrate in a new town, he made new acquaintances and connexions, placed himself on a new footing, and assumed a somewhat different tone. He took up an attitude of rather dignified aloofness towards the provincial authorities, but picked out the best circle of legal gentlemen and wealthy gentry living in the town and assumed a tone of slight dissatisfaction with the government, of moderate liberalism, and of enlightened citizenship. At the same time, without at all altering the elegance of his toilet, he ceased shaving his chin and allowed his beard to grow as it pleased.

Ivan Ilych settled down very pleasantly in this new town. The society there, which inclined towards opposition to the Governor, was friendly, his salary was larger, and he began to play *vint,* which he found added not a little to the pleasure of life, for he had a capacity for cards, played good-humouredly, and calculated rapidly and astutely, so that he usually won.

After living there for two years he met his future wife, Praskovya Fëdorovna Mikhel, who was the most attractive, clever, and brilliant girl of the set in which he moved, and among other amusements and relaxations from his labours as examining magistrate, Ivan Ilych established light and playful relations with her.

While he had been an official on special service he had been accustomed to dance, but now as an examining magistrate it was exceptional for him to do so. If he danced now, he did it as if to show that though he served under the reformed order of things, and had reached the fifth official rank, yet when it came to dancing he could do it better than most people. So at the end of an evening he sometimes danced with Praskovya Fëdorovna, and it was chiefly during these dances that he captivated her. She fell in love with him. Ivan Ilych had at first no definite intention of marrying, but when the girl fell in love with him he said to himself: "Really, why shouldn't I marry?"

Praskovya Fëdorovna came of a good family, was not bad looking, and had some little property. Ivan Ilych might have aspired to a more brilliant match, but even this was good. He had his salary, and she, he hoped, would have an equal income. She was well connected, and was a sweet, pretty, and thoroughly correct young woman. To say that Ivan Ilych married because he fell in love with Praskovya Fëdorovna and found that she sympathized with his views of life would be as incorrect as to say that he married because his social circle approved of the match. He was swayed by both these considerations: the marriage gave him personal satisfaction, and at the same time it was considered the right thing by the most highly placed of his associates.

So Ivan Ilych got married.

The preparations for marriage and the beginning of married life, with its conjugal caresses, the new furniture, new crockery, and new linen, were very pleasant until his wife became pregnant—so that Ivan Ilych had begun to think that marriage would not impair the easy, agreeable gay and always decorous character of his life, approved of by society and regarded by himself as natural, but would even improve it. But from the first months of his wife's pregnancy, something new, unpleasant, depressing, and unseemly, and from which there was no way of escape, unexpectedly showed itself.

His wife, without any reason—*de gaieté de coeur** as Ivan Ilych expressed it to himself—began to disturb the pleasure and propriety of their life. She began to be jealous without any cause, expected him to devote his whole attention to her, found fault with everything, and made coarse and ill-mannered scenes.

At first Ivan Ilych hoped to escape from the unpleasantness of this state of affairs by the same easy and decorous relation to life that had served him heretofore: he tried to ignore his wife's disagreeable moods, continued to live in his usual easy and pleasant way, invited friends to his house for a game of cards, and also tried going out to his club or spending his evenings with friends. But one day his wife began upbraiding him so vigorously, using such coarse words, and continued to abuse him every time he did not fulfil her demands, so resolutely and with such evident determination not to give way till he submitted—that is, till he stayed at home and was bored just as she was—that he became alarmed. He now realized that matrimony—at any rate with Praskovya Fëdorovna—was not always conducive to the pleasures and amenities of life, but on the contrary often infringed both comfort and propriety, and that he must therefore entrench himself against such infringement. And Ivan Ilych began to seek for means of doing so. His official duties were the one thing that imposed upon Praskovya Fëdorovna, and by means of his official work and the duties attached to it he began struggling with his wife to secure his own independence.

With the birth of their child, the attempts to feed it and the various failures in doing so, and with the real and imaginary illnesses of mother and child, in which Ivan Ilych's sympathy was demanded but about which he understood nothing, the need of securing for himself an existence outside his family life became still more imperative.

As his wife grew more irritable and exacting and Ivan Ilych transferred the centre of gravity of his life more and more to his official work, so did he grow to like his work better and became more ambitious than before.

Very soon, within a year of his wedding, Ivan Ilych had realized that marriage, though it may add some comforts to life, is in fact a very intricate and difficult affair towards which in order to perform one's duty, that is, to lead a decorous life approved of by society, one must adopt a definite attitude just as towards one's official duties.

And Ivan Ilych evolved such an attitude towards married life. He only

---

**de gaieté de coeur:* out of sheer wantonness.

required of it those conveniences—dinner at home, housewife, and bed—which it could give him, and above all that propriety of external forms required by public opinion. For the rest he looked for light-hearted pleasure and propriety, and was very thankful when he found them, but if he met with antagonism and querulousness he at once retired into his separate fenced-off world of official duties, where he found satisfaction.

Ivan Ilych was esteemed a good official, and after three years was made Assistant Public Prosecutor. His new duties, their importance, the possibility of indicting and imprisoning anyone he chose, the publicity his speeches received, and the success he had in all these things, made his work still more attractive.

More children came. His wife became more and more querulous and ill-tempered, but the attitude Ivan Ilych had adopted towards his home life rendered him almost impervious to her grumbling.

After seven year's service in that town he was transferred to another province as Public Prosecutor. They moved, but were short of money and his wife did not like the place they moved to. Though the salary was higher the cost of living was greater, besides which two of their children died and family life became still more unpleasant for him.

Praskovya Fëdorovna blamed her husband for every inconvenience they encountered in their new home. Most of the conversations between husband and wife, especially as to the children's education, led to topics which recalled former disputes, and those disputes were apt to flare up again at any moment. There remained only those rare periods of amorousness which still came to them at times but did not last long. These were islets at which they anchored for a while and then again set out upon that ocean of veiled hostility which showed itself in their aloofness from one another. This aloofness might have grieved Ivan Ilych had he considered that it ought not to exist, but he now regarded the position as normal, and even made it the goal at which he aimed in family life. His aim was to free himself more and more from those unpleasantnesses and to give them a semblance of harmlessness and propriety. He attained this by spending less and less time with his family, and when obliged to be at home he tried to safeguard his position by the presence of outsiders. The chief thing however was that he had his official duties. The whole interest of his life now centred in the official world and that interest absorbed him. The consciousness of his power, being able to ruin anybody he wished to ruin, the importance, even the external dignity of his entry into court, or meetings with his subordinates, his success with superiors and inferiors, and above all his masterly handling of cases, of which he was conscious—all this gave him pleasure and filled his life, together with chats with his colleagues, dinners, and bridge. So that on the whole Ivan Ilych's life continued to flow as he considered it should do—pleasantly and properly.

So things continued for another seven years. His eldest daughter was already sixteen, another child had died, and only one son was left, a schoolboy and a subject of dissension. Ivan Ilych wanted to put him in the School of Law, but to spite him Praskovya Fëdorovna entered him at the High School. The daughter had been educated at home and had turned out well: the boy did not learn badly either.

III

So Ivan Ilych lived for seventeen years after his marriage. He was already a Public Prosecutor of long standing, and had declined several proposed transfers while awaiting a more desirable post, when an unanticipated and unpleasant occurrence quite upset the peaceful course of his life. He was expecting to be offered the post of presiding judge in a University town, but Happe somehow came to the front and obtained the appointment instead. Ivan Ilych became irritable, reproached Happe, and quarrelled both with him and with his immediate superiors—who became colder to him and again passed him over when other appointments were made.

This was in 1880, the hardest year of Ivan Ilych's life. It was then that it became evident on the one hand that his salary was insufficient for them to live on, and on the other that he had been forgotten, and not only this, but that what was for him the greatest and most cruel injustice appeared to others a quite ordinary occurrence. Even his father did not consider it his duty to help him. Ivan Ilych felt himself abandoned by everyone, and that they regarded his position with a salary of 3,500 rubles as quite normal and even fortunate. He alone knew that with the consciousness of the injustices done him, with his wife's incessant nagging, and with the debts he had contracted by living beyond his means, his position was far from normal.

In order to save money that summer he obtained leave of absence and went with his wife to live in the country at her brother's place.

In the country, without his work, he experienced *ennui* for the first time in his life, and not only *ennui* but intolerable depression, and he decided that it was impossible to go on living like that, and that it was necessary to take energetic measures.

Having passed a sleepless night pacing up and down the veranda, he decided to go to Petersburg and bestir himself, in order to punish those who had failed to appreciate him and to get transferred to another ministry.

Next day, despite many protests from his wife and her brother, he started for Petersburg with the sole object of obtaining a post with a salary of five thousand rubles a year. He was no longer bent on any particular department, or tendency, or kind of activity. All he now wanted was an appointment to another post with a salary of five thousand rubles, either in the administration, in the banks, with the railways, in one of the Empress Marya's Institutions, or even in the customs—but it had to carry with it a salary of five thousand rubles and be in a ministry other than that in which they had failed to appreciate him.

And this quest of Ivan Ilych's was crowned with remarkable and unexpected success. At Kursk an acquaintance of his, F. I. Ilyin, got into the first-class carriage, sat down beside Ivan Ilych, and told him of a telegram just received by the Governor of Kursk announcing that a change was about to take place in the ministry: Peter Ivanovich was to be superseded by Ivan Semënovich.

The proposed change, apart from its significance for Russia, had a special significance for Ivan Ilych, because by bringing forward a new man, Peter Petrovich, and consequently his friend Zachar Ivanovich, it was highly favourable for Ivan Ilych, since Zachar Ivanovich was a friend and colleague of his.

In Moscow this news was confirmed, and on reaching Petersburg Ivan Ilych found Zachar Ivanovich and received a definite promise of an appointment in his former department of Justice.

A week later he telegraphed to his wife: "Zachar in Miller's place. I shall receive appointment on presentation of report."

Thanks to this change of personnel, Ivan Ilych had unexpectedly obtained an appointment in his former ministry which placed him two stages above his former colleagues besides giving him five thousand rubles salary and three thousand five hundred rubles for expenses connected with his removal. All his ill humour towards his former enemies and the whole department vanished, and Ivan Ilych was completely happy.

He returned to the country more cheerful and contented than he had been for a long time. Praskovya Fëdorovna also cheered up and a truce was arranged between them. Ivan Ilych told of how he had been fêted by everybody in Petersburg, how all those who had been his enemies were put to shame and now fawned on him, how envious they were of his appointment, and how much everybody in Petersburg had liked him.

Praskovya Fëdorovna listened to all this and appeared to believe it. She did not contradict anything, but only made plans for their life in the town to which they were going. Ivan Ilych saw with delight that these plans were his plans, that he and his wife agreed, and that, after a stumble, his life was regaining its due and natural character of pleasant lightheartedness and decorum.

Ivan Ilych had come back for a short time only, for he had to take up his new duties on the 10th of September. Moreover, he needed time to settle into the new place, to move all his belongings from the province, and to buy and order many additional things: in a word, to make such arrangements as he had resolved on, which were almost exactly what Praskovya Fëdorovna too had decided on.

Now that everything had happened so fortunately, and that he and his wife were at one in their aims and moreover saw so little of one another, they got on together better than they had done since the first years of marriage. Ivan Ilych had thought of taking his family away with him at once, but the insistence of his wife's brother and her sister-in-law, who had suddenly become particularly amiable and friendly to him and his family, induced him to depart alone.

So he departed, and the cheerful state of mind induced by his success and by the harmony between his wife and himself, the one intensifying the other, did not leave him. He found a delightful house, just the thing both he and his wife had dreamt of—spacious, lofty reception rooms in the old style, a convenient and dignified study, rooms for his wife and daughter, a study for his son—it might have been specially built for them. Ivan Ilych himself superintended the arrangements, chose the wallpapers, supplemented the furniture (preferably with antiques which he considered particularly *comme il faut*), and supervised the upholstering. Everything progressed and progressed and approached the ideal he had set himself: even when things were only half completed they exceeded his expectations. He saw what a refined and elegant character, free from vulgarity, it would all have when it was ready. On falling asleep he pictured to himself how the reception-room would look. Looking at the yet unfinished drawing-room he could see the fireplace, the screen, the what-not, the little chairs dotted here and there, the dishes and plates on the walls, and the bronzes, as they would be when everything was in place. He was pleased by the thought of how his wife and daughter, who shared his taste in this matter, would be impressed by it. They were certainly not expecting as much. He had been particularly successful in finding, and buying cheaply, antiques which gave a particularly aristocratic character to the whole place. But in his letters he intentionally understated everything in order to be able to surprise them. All this so absorbed him that his new duties—though he liked his official work—interested him less than he had expected. Sometimes he even had moments of absentmindedness during the Court Sessions, and would consider whether he should have straight or curved cornices for his curtains. He was so interested in it all that he often did things himself, rearranging the furniture, or rehanging the curtains. Once when mounting a step-ladder to show the upholsterer, who did not understand, how he wanted the hangings draped, he made a false step and slipped, but being a strong and agile man he clung on and only knocked his side against the knob of the window frame. The bruised place was painful but the pain soon passed, and he felt particularly bright and well just then. He wrote: "I feel fifteen years younger." He thought he would have everything ready by September, but it dragged on till mid-October. But the result was charming not only in his eyes but to everyone who saw it.

In reality it was just what is usually seen in the houses of people of moderate means who want to appear rich, and therefore succeed only in resembling others like themselves: there were damasks, dark wood, plants, rugs, and dull and polished bronzes—all the things people of a certain class have in order to resemble other people of that class. His house was so like the others that it would never have been noticed, but to him it all seemed to be quite exceptional. He was very happy when he met his family at the station and brought them to the newly furnished house all lit up, where a footman in a white tie opened the door into the hall decorated with plants, and when they went on into the drawing-room and the study uttering exclamations of delight. He conducted them everywhere, drank in their praises eagerly, and beamed with pleasure. At tea that evening, when Praskovya Fëdorovna among other things asked him about his fall, he laughed and showed them how he had gone flying and had frightened the upholsterer.

"It's a good thing I'm a bit of an athlete. Another man might have been killed, but I merely knocked myself, just here; it hurts when it's touched, but it's passing off already—it's only a bruise."

So they began living in their new home—in which, as always happens, when they got thoroughly settled in they found they were just one room short—and with the increased income, which as always was just a little (some five hundred rubles) too little, but it was all very nice.

Things went particularly well at first, before everything was finally arranged and while something had still to be done: this thing bought, that thing ordered, another thing moved, and something else adjusted. Though there were some disputes between husband and wife, they were both so well satisfied and had so much to do that it all passed off without any serious quarrels. When nothing was left to arrange it became rather dull and something seemed to be lacking, but they were then making acquaintances, forming habits, and life was growing fuller.

Ivan Ilych spent his mornings at the law court and came home to dinner, and at first he was generally in a good humour, though he occasionally became irritable just on account of his house. (Every spot on the tablecloth or the upholstery, and every broken window-blind string, irritated him. He had devoted so much trouble to arranging it all that every disturbance of it distressed him.) But on the whole his life ran its course as he believed life should do: easily, pleasantly, and decorously.

He got up at nine, drank his coffee, read the paper, and then put on his undress uniform and went to the law courts. There the harness in which he worked had already been stretched to fit him and he donned it without a hitch: petitioners, inquiries at the chancery, the chancery itself, and the sittings public and administrative. In all this the thing was to exclude everything fresh and vital, which always disturbs the regular course of official business, and to admit only official relations with people, and then only on official grounds. A man would come, for instance, wanting some information. Ivan Ilych, as one in whose sphere the matter did not lie, would have nothing to do with him: but if the man had some business with him in his official capacity, something that could be expressed on officially stamped paper, he would do everything, positively everything he could within the limits of such relations, and in doing so would maintain the semblance of friendly human relations, that is, would observe the courtesies of life. As soon as the official relations ended, so did everything else. Ivan Ilych possessed this capacity to separate his real life from the official side of affairs and not mix the two, in the highest degree, and by long practice and natural aptitude had brought it to such a pitch that sometimes, in the manner of a virtuoso, he would even allow himself to let the human and official relations mingle. He let himself do this just because he felt that he could at any time he chose resume the strictly official attitude again and drop the human relation. And he did it all easily, pleasantly, correctly, and even artistically. In the intervals between the sessions he smoked, drank tea, chatted a little about politics, a little about general topics, a little about cards, but most of all about official appointments. Tired, but with the feelings of a virtuoso—one of the first violins who has played his part in an orchestra with precision—he would return home to find that his wife and daughter had been out paying calls, or had a visitor, and that his son had been to school, had done his homework with his tutor, and was duly learning what is taught at High Schools. Everything was as it should be. After dinner, if they had no visitors, Ivan Ilych sometimes read a book that was being much discussed at the time, and in the evening settled down to work, that is, read official papers, compared the depositions of witnesses, and noted paragraphs of the Code applying to them. This was neither dull nor amusing. It was dull when he might have been playing bridge, but if no bridge was available it was at any rate better than doing nothing or sitting with his wife. Ivan Ilych's chief pleasure was giving little dinners to which he invited men and women of good social position, and just as his drawing-room resembled all other drawing-rooms so did his enjoyable little parties resemble all other such parties.

Once they even gave a dance. Ivan Ilych enjoyed it and everything went off well, except that it led to a violent quarrel with his wife about the cakes and sweets. Praskovya Fëdorovna had made her own plans, but Ivan Ilych insisted on getting everything from an expensive confectioner and ordered too many cakes, and the quarrel occurred because some of those cakes were left over and the confectioner's bill came to forty-five rubles. It was a great and disagreeable quarrel. Praskovya Fëdorovna called him "a fool and an imbecile," and he clutched at his head and made angry allusions to divorce.

But the dance itself had been enjoyable. The best people were there, and Ivan Ilych had danced with Princess Trufonova, a sister of the distinguished founder of the Society "Bear my Burden."

The pleasures connected with his work were pleasures of ambition; his social pleasures were those of vanity; but Ivan Ilych's greatest pleasure was playing bridge. He acknowledged that whatever disagreeable incident happened in his life, the pleasure that beamed like a ray of light above everything else was to sit down to bridge with good players, not noisy partners, and of course to four-handed bridge (with five players it was annoying to have to stand out, though one pretended not to mind), to play a clever and serious game (when the cards allowed it) and then to have supper and drink a glass of wine. After a game of bridge, especially if he had won a little (to win a large sum was unpleasant), Ivan Ilych went to bed in specially good humour.

So they lived. They formed a circle of acquaintances among the best people and were visited by people of importance and by young folk. In their views as to their acquaintances, husband, wife and daughter were entirely agreed, and tacitly and unanimously kept at arm's length and shook off the shabby friends and relations who, with much show of affection, gushed into the drawing-room with its Japanese plates on the walls. Soon these shabby friends ceased to obtrude themselves and only the best people remained in the Golovins' set.

Young men made up to Lisa, and Petrishchev, an examining magistrate and Dmitri Ivanovich Petrishchev's son and sole heir, began to be so attentive to her that Ivan Ilych had already spoken to Praskovya Fëdorovna about it, and considered whether they should not arrange a party for them, or get up some private theatricals.

So they lived, and all went well, without change, and life flowed pleasantly.

IV

They were all in good health. It could not be called ill health if Ivan Ilych sometimes said that he had a queer taste in his mouth and felt some discomfort in his left side.

But this discomfort increased and, though not exactly painful, grew into a sense of pressure in his side accompanied by ill humour. And his irritability became worse and worse and began to mar the agreeable, easy, and correct life that had established itself in the Golovin family. Quarrels between husband and wife became more and more frequent, and soon the ease and amenity disappeared and even the decorum was barely maintained. Scenes again became frequent, and very few of those islets remained on which husband and wife could meet without an explosion. Praskovya Fëdorovna now had good reason to say that her husband's temper was trying. With characteristic exaggeration she said he had always had a dreadful temper, and that it had needed all her good nature to put up with it for twenty years. It was true that now the quarrels were started by him. His bursts of temper always came just before dinner, often just as he began to eat his soup. Sometimes he noticed that a plate or dish was chipped, or the food was not right, or his son put his elbow on the table, or his daughter's hair was not done as he liked it, and for all this he blamed Praskovya Fëdorovna. At first she retorted and said disagreeable things to him, but once or twice he fell into such a rage at the beginning of dinner that she realized it was due to some physical derangement brought on by taking food, and so she restrained herself and did not answer, but only hurried to get the dinner over. She regarded this self-restraint as highly praiseworthy. Having come to the conclusion that her husband had a dreadful temper and made her life miserable, she began to feel sorry for herself, and the more she pitied herself the more she hated her husband. She began to wish he would die; yet she did not want him to die because then his salary would cease. And this irritated her against him still more. She considered herself dreadfully unhappy just because not even his death could save her, and though she concealed her exasperation, that hidden exasperation of hers increased his irritation also.

After one scene in which Ivan Ilych had been particularly unfair and after which he had said in explanation that he certainly was irritable but that it was due to his not being well, she said that if he was ill it should be attended to, and insisted on his going to see a celebrated doctor.

He went. Everything took place as he had expected and as it always does. There was the usual waiting and the important air assumed by the doctor, with which he was so familiar (resembling that which he himself assumed in court), and the sounding and listening, and the questions which called for answers that were foregone conclusions and were evidently unnecessary, and the look of importance which implied that "if only you put yourself in our hands we will arrange everything—we know indubitably how it has to be done, always in the same way for everybody alike." It was all just as it was in the law courts. The doctor put on just the same air towards him as he himself put on towards an accused person.

The doctor said that so-and-so indicated that there was so-and-so inside the patient, but if the investigation of so-and-so did not confirm this, then he must assume that and that. If he assumed that and that, then . . . and so on. To Ivan Ilych only one question was important: was his case serious or not? But the doctor ignored that inappropriate question. From his point of view it was not the one under consideration, the real question was to decide between a floating kidney, chronic catarrh, or appendicitis. It was not a question of Ivan Ilych's life or death, but one between a floating kidney and appendicitis. And that question the doctor solved brilliantly, as it seemed to Ivan Ilych, in favour of the appendix, with the reservation that should an examination of the urine give fresh indications the matter would be reconsidered. All this was just what Ivan Ilych had himself brilliantly accomplished a thousand times in dealing with men on trial. The doctor summed up just as brilliantly, looking over his spectacles triumphantly and even gaily at the accused. From the doctor's summing up Ivan Ilych concluded that things were bad, but that for the doctor, and perhaps for everybody else, it was a matter of indifference, though for him it was bad. And this conclusion struck him painfully, arousing in him a great feeling of pity for himself and of bitterness towards the doctor's indifference to a matter of such importance.

He said nothing of this, but rose, placed the doctor's fee on the table, and remarked with a sigh: "We sick people probably often put inappropriate questions. But tell me, in general, is this complaint dangerous, or not? . . ."

The doctor looked at him sternly over his spectacles with one eye, as if to say: "Prisoner, if you will not keep to the questions put to you, I shall be obliged to have you removed from the court."

"I have already told you what I consider necessary and proper. The analysis may show something more." And the doctor bowed.

Ivan Ilych went out slowly, seated himself disconsolately in his sledge, and drove home. All the way home he was going over what the doctor had said, trying to translate those complicated, obscure, scientific phrases into plain language and find in them an answer to the question: "Is my condition bad? Is it very bad? or is there as yet nothing much wrong?" And it seemed to him that the meaning of what the doctor had said was that it was very bad. Everything in the streets seemed depressing. The cabmen, the houses, the passers-by, and the shops, were dismal. His ache, this dull gnawing ache that never ceased for a moment, seemed to have acquired a new and more serious significance from the doctor's dubious remarks. Ivan Ilych now watched it with a new and oppressive feeling.

He reached home and began to tell his wife about it. She listened, but in the middle of his account his daughter came in with her hat on, ready to go out with her mother. She sat down reluctantly to listen to this tedious story, but could not stand it long, and her mother too did not hear him to the end.

"Well, I am very glad," she said. "Mind now to take your medicine regularly. Give me the prescription and I'll send Gerasim to the chemist's." And she went to get ready to go out.

While she was in the room Ivan Ilych had hardly taken time to breathe, but he sighed deeply when she left it.

"Well," he thought, "perhaps it isn't so bad after all."

He began taking his medicine and following the doctor's directions, which had been altered after the examination of the urine. But then it happened that there was a contradiction between the indications drawn from the examination of the urine and the symptoms that showed themselves. It turned out that what was happening differed from what the doctor had told him, and that he had either forgotten, or blundered, or hidden something from him. He could not, however, be blamed for that, and Ivan Ilych still obeyed his orders implicitly and at first derived some comfort from doing so.

From the time of his visit to the doctor, Ivan Ilych's chief occupation was the exact fulfilment of the doctor's instructions regarding hygiene and the taking of medicine, and the observation of his pain and his excretions. His chief interests came to be people's ailments and people's health. When sickness, deaths, or recoveries were mentioned in his presence, especially when the illness resembled his own, he listened with agitation which he tried to hide, asked questions, and applied what he heard to his own case.

The pain did not grow less, but Ivan Ilych made efforts to force himself to think that he was better. And he could do this so long as nothing agitated him. But as soon as he had any unpleasantness with his wife, or a lack of success in his official work, or held bad cards at bridge, he was at once acutely sensible of his disease. He had formerly borne such mischances, hoping soon to adjust what was wrong, to master it and attain success, or make a grand slam. But now every mischance upset him and plunged him into despair. He would say to himself: "There now, just as I was beginning to get better and the medicine had begun to take effect, comes this accursed misfortune, or unpleasantness . . ." And he was furious with the mishap, or with the people who were causing the unpleasantness and killing him, for he felt that this fury was killing him but could not restrain it. One would have thought that it should have been clear to him that this exasperation with circumstances and people aggravated his illness, and that he ought therefore to ignore unpleasant occurrences. But he drew the very opposite conclusion: he said that he needed peace, and he watched for everything that might disturb it and became irritable at the slightest infringement of it. His condition was rendered worse by the fact that he read medical books and consulted doctors. The progress of his disease was so gradual that he could deceive himself when comparing one day with another—the difference was so slight. But when he consulted the doctors it seemed to him that he was getting worse, and even very rapidly. Yet despite this he was continually consulting them.

That month he went to see another celebrity, who told him almost the same as the first had done but put his questions rather differently, and the interview with this celebrity only increased Ivan Ilych's doubts and fears. A friend of a friend of his, a very good doctor, diagnosed his illness again quite differently from the others, and though he predicted recovery, his questions and suppositions bewildered Ivan Ilych still more and increased his doubts. A homoeopathist diagnosed the disease in yet another way, and prescribed medicine which Ivan Ilych took secretly for a week. But after a week, not feeling any improvement and having lost confidence both in the former doctor's treatment and in this one's, he became still more despondent. One day a lady acquaintance mentioned a cure effected by a wonder-working icon. Ivan Ilych caught himself listening attentively and beginning to believe that it had occurred. This incident alarmed him. "Has my mind really weakened to such an extent?" he asked himself. "Nonsense! It's all rubbish. I mustn't give way to nervous fears but having chosen a doctor must keep strictly to his treatment. That is what I will do. Now it's all settled. I won't think about it, but will follow the treatment seriously till summer, and then we shall see. From now there must be no more of this wavering!" This was easy to say but impossible to carry out. The pain in his side oppressed him and seemed to grow worse and more incessant, while the taste in his mouth grew stranger and stranger. It seemed to him that his breath had a disgusting smell, and he was conscious of a loss of appetite and strength. There was no deceiving himself: something terrible, new, and more important than anything before in his life, was taking place within him of which he alone was aware. Those about him did not understand or would not understand it, but thought everything in the world was going on as usual. That tormented Ivan Ilych more than anything. He saw that his household, especially his wife and daughter who were in a perfect whirl of visiting, did not understand anything of it and were annoyed that he was so depressed and so exacting, as if he were to blame for it. Though they tried to disguise it he saw that he was an obstacle in their path, and that his wife had adopted a definite line in regard to his illness and kept to it regardless of anything he said or did. Her attitude was this: "You know," she would say to her friends, "Ivan Ilych can't do as other people do, and keep to the treatment prescribed for him. One day he'll take his drops and keep strictly to his diet and go to bed in good time, but the next day unless I watch him he'll suddenly forget his medicine, eat sturgeon—which is forbidden—and sit up playing cards till one o'clock in the morning."

"Oh, come, when was that?" Ivan Ilych would ask in vexation. "Only once at Peter Ivanovich's."

"And yesterday with Shebek."

"Well, even if I hadn't stayed up, this pain would have kept me awake."

"Be that as it may you'll never get well like that, but will always make us wretched."

Praskovya Fëdorovna's attitude to Ivan Ilych's illness, as she expressed it both to others and to him, was that it was his own fault and was another of the annoyances he caused her. Ivan Ilych felt that this opinion escaped her involuntarily—but that did not make it easier for him.

At the law courts too, Ivan Ilych noticed, or thought he noticed, a strange attitude towards himself. It sometimes seemed to him that people were watching him inquisitively as a man whose place might soon be vacant. Then again, his friends would suddenly begin to chaff him in a friendly way about his low spirits, as if the awful, horrible, and unheard-of thing that was going on within him, incessantly gnawing at him and irresistibly drawing him away, was a very agreeable subject for jests. Schwartz in particular irritated him by his jocularity, vivacity, and *savoir-faire,* which reminded him of what he himself had been ten years ago.

Friends came to make up a set and they sat down to cards. They dealt, bending the new cards to soften them, and he sorted the diamonds in his hand and found he had seven. His partner said "No trumps" and supported him with two diamonds. What more could be wished for? It ought to be jolly and lively. They would make a grand slam. But suddenly Ivan Ilych was conscious of that gnawing pain, that taste in his mouth, and it seemed ridiculous that in such circumstances he should be pleased to make a grand slam.

He looked at his partner Mikhail Mikhaylovich, who rapped the table with his strong hand and instead of snatching up the tricks pushed the cards courteously and indulgently towards Ivan Ilych that he might have the pleasure of gathering them up without the trouble of stretching out his hand for them. "Does he think I am too weak to stretch out my arm?" thought Ivan Ilych, and forgetting what he was doing he over-trumped his partner, missing the grand slam by three tricks. And what was most awful of all was that he saw how upset Mikhail Mikhaylovich was about it but did not himself care. And it was dreadful to realize why he did not care.

They all saw that he was suffering, and said: "We can stop if you are tired. Take a rest." Lie down? No, he was not at all tired, and he finished the rubber. All were gloomy and silent. Ivan Ilych felt that he had diffused this gloom over them and could not dispel it. They had supper and went away, and Ivan Ilych was left alone with the consciousness that his life was poisoned and was poisoning the lives of others, and that this poison did not weaken but penetrated more and more deeply into his whole being.

With this consciousness, and with physical pain besides that terror, he must go to bed, often to lie awake the greater part of the night. Next morning he had to get up again, dress, go to the law courts, speak, and write; or if he did not go out, spend at home those twenty-four hours a day each of which was a torture. And he had to live thus all alone on the brink of an abyss, with no one who understood or pitied him.

V

So one month passed and then another. Just before the New Year his brother-in-law came to town and stayed at their house. Ivan Ilych was at the law courts and Praskovya Fëdorovna had gone shopping. When Ivan Ilych came home and entered his study he found his brother-in-law there—a healthy, florid man—unpacking his portmanteau himself. He raised his head on hearing Ivan Ilych's footsteps and looked up at him for a moment without a word. That stare told Ivan Ilych everything. His brother-in-law opened his mouth to utter an exclamation of surprise but checked himself, and that action confirmed it all.

"I have changed, eh?"

"Yes, there is a change."

And after that, try as he would to get his brother-in-law to return to the subject of his looks, the latter would say nothing about it. Praskovya Fëdorovna came home and her brother went out to her. Ivan Ilych locked the door and began to examine himself in the glass, first full face, then in profile. He took up a portrait of himself taken with his wife, and compared it with what he saw in the glass. The change in him was immense. Then he bared his arms to the elbow, looked at them, drew the sleeves down again, sat down on an ottoman, and grew blacker than night.

"No, no, this won't do!" he said to himself, and jumped up, went to the table, took up some law papers and began to read them, but could not continue. He unlocked the door and went into the reception-room. The door leading to the drawing-room was shut. He approached it on tiptoe and listened.

"No, you are exaggerating!" Praskovya Fëdorovna was saying.

"Exaggerating! Don't you see it? Why, he's a dead man! Look at his eyes—there's no light in them. But what is it that is wrong with him?"

"No one knows. Nikolaevich [that was another doctor] said something, but I don't know what. And Leshchetitsky [this was the celebrated specialist] said quite the contrary . . ."

Ivan Ilych walked away, went to his own room, lay down, and began musing: "The kidney, a floating kidney." He recalled all the doctors had told him of how it detached itself and swayed about. And by an effort of imagination he tried to catch that kidney and arrest it and support it. So little was needed for this, it seemed to him. "No, I'll go to see Peter Ivanovich again." [That was the friend whose friend was a doctor.] He rang, ordered the carriage, and got ready to go.

"Where are you going, Jean?" asked his wife, with a specially sad and exceptionally kind look.

This exceptionally kind look irritated him. He looked morosely at her.

"I must go to Peter Ivanovich."

He went to see Peter Ivanovich, and together they went to see his friend, the doctor. He was in, and Ivan Ilych had a long talk with him.

Reviewing the anatomical and physiological details of what in the doctor's opinion was going on inside him, he understood it all.

There was something, a small thing, in the vermiform appendix. It might all come right. Only stimulate the energy of one organ and check the activity of another, then absorption would take place and everything would come right. He got home rather late for dinner, ate his dinner, conversed cheerfully, but could not for a long time bring himself to go back to work in his room. At last, however, he went to his study and did what was necessary, but the consciousness that he had put something aside—an important, intimate matter which he would revert to when his work was done—never left him. When he had finished his work he remembered that this intimate matter was the thought of his vermiform appendix. But he did not give himself up to it, and went to the drawing-room for tea. There were callers there, including the examining magistrate who was a desirable match for his daughter, and they were conversing, playing the piano, and singing. Ivan Ilych, as Praskovya Fëdorovna remarked, spent that evening more cheerfully than usual, but he never for a moment forgot that he had postponed the important matter of the appendix. At eleven o'clock he said good-night and went to his bedroom. Since his illness he had slept alone in a small room next to his study. He undressed and took up a novel by Zola, but instead of reading it fell into thought, and in his imagination that desired improvement in the vermiform appendix occurred. There was the absorption and evacuation and the re-establishment of normal activity. "Yes, that's it!" he said to himself. "One need only assist nature, that's all." He remembered his medicine, rose, took it, and lay down on his back watching for the beneficent action of the medicine and for it to lessen the pain. "I need only take it regularly and avoid all injurious influences. I am already feeling better, much better." He began touching his side: it was not painful to the touch. "There, I really don't feel it. It's much better already." He put out the light and turned on his side . . . "The appendix is getting better, absorption is occurring." Suddenly he felt the old, familiar, dull gnawing pain, stubborn and serious. There was the same familiar loathsome taste in his mouth. His heart sank and he felt dazed. "My God! My God!" he muttered. "Again, again! and it will never cease." And suddenly the matter presented itself in a quite different aspect. "Vermiform appendix! Kidney!" he said to himself. "It's not a question of appendix or kidney, but of life and . . . death. Yes, life was there and now it is going, going and I cannot stop it. Yes. Why deceive myself? Isn't it obvious to everyone but me that I'm dying, and that it's only a question of weeks, days . . . it may happen this moment. There was light and now there is darkness. I was here and now I'm going there! Where?" A chill came over him, his breathing ceased, and he felt only the throbbing of his heart.

"When I am not, what will there be? There will be nothing. Then where shall I be when I am no more? Can this be dying? No, I don't want to!" He jumped up and tried to light the candle, felt for it with trembling hands, dropped candle and candlestick on the floor, and fell back on his pillow.

"What's the use? It makes no difference," he said to himself, staring with wide-open eyes into the darkness. "Death. Yes, death. And none of them know or wish to know it, and they have no pity for me. Now they are playing." (He heard through the door the distant sound of a song and its accompaniment.) "It's all the same to them, but they will die too! Fools! I first, and they later, but it will be the same for them. And now they are merry . . . the beasts!"

Anger choked him and he was agonizingly, unbearably, miserable. "It is impossible that all men have been doomed to suffer this awful horror!" He raised himself.

"Something must be wrong. I must calm myself—must think it all over from the beginning." And he again began thinking. "Yes, the beginning of my illness: I knocked my side, but I was quite well that day and the next. It hurt a little, then rather more. I saw the doctor, then followed despondency and anguish, more doctors, and I drew nearer to the abyss. My strength grew less and I kept coming nearer and nearer, and now I have wasted away and there is no light in my eyes. I think of the appendix—but this is death! I think of mending the appendix, and all the while here is death! Can it really be death?" Again terror seized him and he gasped for breath. He leant down and began feeling for the matches, pressing with his elbow on the stand beside the bed. It was in the way and hurt him, he grew furious with it, pressed on it still harder, and upset it. Breathless and in despair he fell on his back, expecting death to come immediately.

Meanwhile the visitors were leaving. Praskovya Fëdorovna was seeing them off. She heard something fall and came in.

"What has happened?"

"Nothing. I knocked it over accidentally."

She went out and returned with a candle. He lay there panting heavily, like a man who has run a thousand yards, and stared upwards at her with a fixed look.

"What is it, Jean?"

"No . . . o . . . thing. I upset it." ("Why speak of it? She won't understand," he thought.)

And in truth she did not understand. She picked up the stand, lit his candle, and hurried away to see another visitor off. When she came back he still lay on his back, looking upwards.

"What is it? Do you feel worse?"

"Yes."

She shook her head and sat down.

"Do you know, Jean, I think we must ask Leshchetitsky to come and see you here."

This meant calling in the famous specialist, regardless of expense. He smiled malignantly and said "No." She remained a little longer and then went up to him and kissed his forehead.

While she was kissing him he hated her from the bottom of his soul and with difficulty refrained from pushing her away.

"Good-night. Please God you'll sleep."

"Yes."

VI

Ivan Ilych saw that he was dying, and he was in continual despair.

In the depth of his heart he knew he was dying, but not only was he not accustomed to the thought, he simply did not and could not grasp it.

The syllogism he had learnt from Kiezewetter's Logic: "Caius is a man, men are mortal, therefore Caius is mortal," had always seemed to him correct as applied to Caius, but certainly not as applied to himself. That Caius—man in the abstract—was mortal, was perfectly correct, but he was not Caius, not an abstract man, but a creature quite, quite separate from all others. He had been little Vanya, with a mamma and a papa, with Mitya and Volodya, with the toys, a coachman and a nurse, afterwards with Katenka and with all the joys, griefs, and delights of childhood, boyhood, and youth. What did Caius know of the smell of that striped leather ball Vanya had been so fond of? Had Caius kissed his mother's hand like that, and did the silk of her dress rustle so for Caius? Had he rioted like that at school when the pastry was bad? Had Caius been in love like that? Could Caius preside at a session as he did? "Caius really was mortal, and it was right for him to die; but for me, little Vanya, Ivan Ilych, with all my thoughts and emotions, it's altogether a different matter. It cannot be that I ought to die. That would be too terrible."

Such was his feeling.

"If I had to die like Caius, I should have known it was so. An inner voice would have told me so, but there was nothing of the sort in me and I and all my friends felt that our case was quite different from that of Caius. And now here it is!" he said to himself. "It can't be. It's impossible! But here it is. How is this? How is one to understand it?"

He could not understand it, and tried to drive this false, incorrect, morbid thought away and to replace it by other proper and healthy thoughts. But that thought, and not the thought only but the reality itself, seemed to come and confront him.

And to replace that thought he called up a succession of others, hoping to find in them some support. He tried to get back into the former current of thoughts that had once screened the thought of death from him. But strange to say, all that had formerly shut off, hidden, and destroyed, his consciousness of death, no longer had that effect. Ivan Ilych now spent most of his time in attempting to re-establish that old current. He would say to himself: "I will take up my duties again—after all I used to live by them." And banishing all doubts he would go to the law courts, enter into conversation with his colleagues, and sit carelessly as was his wont, scanning the crowd with a thoughtful look and leaning both his emaciated arms on the arms of his oak chair; bending over as usual to a colleague and drawing his papers nearer he would interchange whispers with him, and then suddenly raising his eyes and sitting erect would pronounce certain words and open the proceedings. But suddenly in the midst of those proceedings the pain in his side, regardless of the stage the proceedings had reached, would begin its own gnawing work. Ivan Ilych would turn his attention to it and try to drive the thought of it away, but without success. *It* would come and stand before him and look at him, and he would be petrified and the light would die out of his eyes, and he would again begin asking himself whether *It* alone was true. And his colleagues and subordinates would see with surprise and distress that he, the brilliant and subtle judge, was becoming confused and making mistakes. He would shake himself, try to pull himself together, manage somehow to bring the sitting to a close, and return home with the sorrowful consciousness that his judicial labours could not as formerly hide from him what he wanted them to hide, and could not deliver him from *It.* And what was worst of all was that *It* drew his attention to itself not in order to make him take some action but only that he should look at *It,* look it straight in the face: look at it and without doing anything, suffer inexpressibly.

And to save himself from this condition Ivan Ilych looked for consolations—new screens—and new screens were found and for a while seemed to save him, but then immediately fell to pieces or rather became transparent, as if *It* penetrated them and nothing could veil *It.*

In these latter days he would go into the drawing-room he had arranged—that drawing-room where he had fallen and for the sake of which (how bitterly ridiculous it seemed) he had sacrificed his life—for he knew that his illness originated with that knock. He would enter and see that something had scratched the polished table. He would look for the cause of this and find that it was the bronze ornamentation of an album, that had got bent. He would take up the expensive album which he had lovingly arranged, and feel vexed with his daughter and her friends for their untidiness—for the album was torn here and there and some of the photographs turned upside down. He would put it carefully in order and bend the ornamentation back into position. Then it would occur to him to place all those things in another corner of the room, near the plants. He would call the footman, but his daughter or wife would come to help him. They would not agree, and his wife would contradict him, and he would dispute and grow angry. But that was all right, for then he did not think about *It. It* was invisible.

But then, when he was moving something himself, his wife would say: "Let the servants do it. You will hurt yourself again." And suddenly *It* would flash through the screen and he would see it. It was just a flash, and he hoped it would disappear, but he would involuntarily pay attention to his side. "It sits there as before, gnawing just the same!" And he could no longer forget *It,* but could distinctly see it looking at him from behind the flowers. "What is it all for?"

"It really is so! I lost my life over that curtain as I might have done when storming a fort. Is that possible? How terrible and how stupid. It can't be true! It can't, but it is."

He would go to his study, lie down, and again be alone with *It:* face to face with *It.* And nothing could be done with *It* except to look at it and shudder.

VII

How it happened it is impossible to say because it came about step by step, unnoticed, but in the third month of Ivan Ilych's illness, his wife, his daughter, his son, his acquaintances, the doctors, the servants, and above all he himself, were aware that the whole interest he had for other people was whether he would soon vacate his place, and at last release the living from the discomfort caused by his presence and be himself released from his sufferings.

He slept less and less. He was given opium and hypodermic injections of morphine, but this did not relieve him. The dull depression he experienced in a somnolent condition at first gave him a little relief, but only as something new, afterwards it became as distressing as the pain itself or even more so.

Special foods were prepared for him by the doctors' orders, but all those foods became increasingly distasteful and disgusting to him.

For his excretions also special arrangements had to be made, and this was a torment to him every time—a torment from the uncleanliness, the unseemliness, and the smell, and from knowing that another person had to take part in it.

But just through this most unpleasant matter, Ivan Ilych obtained comfort. Gerasim, the butler's young assistant, always came in to carry the things out. Gerasim was a clean, fresh peasant lad, grown stout on town food and always cheerful and bright. At first the sight of him, in his clean Russian peasant costume, engaged in that disgusting task embarrassed Ivan Ilych.

Once when he got up from the commode too weak to draw up his trousers, he dropped into a soft armchair and looked with horror at his bare, enfeebled thighs with the muscles so sharply marked on them.

Gerasim with a firm light tread, his heavy boots emitting a pleasant smell of tar and fresh winter air, came in wearing a clean Hessian apron, the sleeves of his print shirt tucked up over his strong bare young arms; and refraining from looking at his sick master out of consideration for his feelings, and restraining the joy of life that beamed from his face, he went up to the commode.

"Gerasim!" said Ivan Ilych in a weak voice.

Gerasim started, evidently afraid he might have committed some blunder, and with a rapid movement turned his fresh, kind, simple young face which just showed the first downy signs of a beard.

"Yes, sir?"

"That must be very unpleasant for you. You must forgive me. I am helpless."

"Oh, why, sir," and Gerasim's eyes beamed and he showed his glistening white teeth, "what's a little trouble? It's a case of illness with you, sir."

And his deft strong hands did their accustomed task, and he went out of the room stepping lightly. Five minutes later he as lightly returned.

Ivan Ilych was still sitting in the same position in the armchair.

"Gerasim," he said when the latter had replaced the freshly-washed utensil. "Please come here and help me." Gerasim went up to him. "Lift me up. It is hard for me to get up, and I have sent Dmitri away."

Gerasim went up to him, grasped his master with his strong arms deftly but gently, in the same way that he stepped—lifted him, supported him with one hand, and with the other drew up his trousers and would have set him down again, but Ivan Ilych asked to be led to the sofa. Gerasim, without an effort and without apparent pressure, led him, almost lifting him, to the sofa and placed him on it.

"Thank you. How easily and well you do it all!"

Gerasim smiled again and turned to leave the room. But Ivan Ilych felt his presence such a comfort that he did not want to let him go.

"One thing more, please move up that chair. No, the other one—under my feet. It is easier for me when my feet are raised."

Gerasim brought the chair, set it down gently in place, and raised Ivan Ilych's legs on to it. It seemed to Ivan Ilych that he felt better while Gerasim was holding up his legs.

"It's better when my legs are higher," he said. "Place that cushion under them."

Gerasim did so. He again lifted the legs and placed them, and again Ivan Ilych felt better while Gerasim held his legs. When he set them down Ivan Ilych fancied he felt worse.

"Gerasim," he said. "Are you busy now?"

"Not at all, sir," said Gerasim, who had learnt from the townfolk how to speak to gentlefolk.

"What have you still to do?"

"What have I to do? I've done everything except chopping the logs for tomorrow."

"Then hold my legs up a bit higher, can you?"

"Of course I can. Why not?" And Gerasim raised his master's legs higher and Ivan Ilych thought that in that position he did not feel any pain at all.

"And how about the logs?"

"Don't trouble about that, sir. There's plenty of time."

Ivan Ilych told Gerasim to sit down and hold his legs, and began to talk to him. And strange to say it seemed to him that he felt better while Gerasim held his legs up.

After that Ivan Ilych would sometimes call Gerasim and get him to hold his legs on his shoulders, and he liked talking to him. Gerasim did it all easily, willingly, simply, and with a good nature that touched Ivan Ilych. Health, strength, and vitality in other people were offensive to him, but Gerasim's strength and vitality did not mortify but soothed him.

What tormented Ivan Ilych most was the deception, the lie, which for some reason they all accepted, that he was not dying but was simply ill, and that he only need keep quiet and undergo a treatment and then something very good would result. He however knew that do what they would nothing would come of it, only still more agonizing suffering and death. This deception tortured him—their not wishing to admit what they all knew and what he knew, but wanting to lie to him concerning his terrible condition, and wishing and forcing him to participate in that lie. Those lies—lies enacted over him on the eve of his death and destined to degrade this awful, solemn act to the level of their visitings, their curtains, their sturgeon for dinner—were a terrible agony for Ivan Ilych. And strangely enough, many times when they were going through their antics over him he had been within a hairbreadth of calling out to them: "Stop lying! You know and I know that I am dying. Then at least stop lying about it!" But he had never had the spirit to do it. The awful, terrible act of his dying was, he could see, reduced by those about him to the level of a casual, unpleasant, and almost indecorous incident (as if someone entered a drawing-room diffusing an unpleasant odour) and this was done by the very decorum which he had served all his life long. He saw that no one felt for him, because no one even wished to grasp his position. Only Gerasim recognized it and pitied him. And so Ivan Ilych felt at ease only with him. He felt comforted when Gerasim supported his legs (sometimes all night long) and refused to go to bed, saying: "Don't you worry, Ivan Ilych. I'll get sleep enough later on," or when he suddenly became familiar and exclaimed: "If you weren't sick it would be another matter, but as it is, why should I grudge a little trouble?" Gerasim alone did not lie; everything showed that he alone understood the facts of the case and did not consider it necessary to disguise them, but simply felt sorry for his emaciated and enfeebled master. Once when Ivan Ilych was sending him away he even said straight out: "We shall all of us die, so why should I grudge a little trouble?"—expressing the fact that he did not think his work burdensome, because he was doing it for a dying man and hoped someone would do the same for him when his time came.

Apart from this lying, or because of it, what most tormented Ivan Ilych was that no one pitied him as he wished to be pitied. At certain moments after prolonged suffering he wished most of all (though he would have been ashamed to confess it) for someone to pity him as a sick child is pitied. He longed to be petted and comforted. He knew he was an important functionary, that he had a beard turning grey, and that therefore what he longed for was impossible, but still he longed for it. And in Gerasim's attitude towards him there was something akin to what he wished for, and so that attitude comforted him. Ivan Ilych wanted to weep, wanted to be petted and cried over, and then his colleague Shebek would come, and instead of weeping and being petted, Ivan Ilych would assume a serious, severe, and profound air, and by force of habit would express his opinion on a decision of the Court of Cassation and would stubbornly insist on that view. This falsity around him and within him did more than anything else to poison his last days.

VIII

It was morning. He knew it was morning because Gerasim had gone, and Peter the footman had come and put out the candles, drawn back one of the curtains, and begun quietly to tidy up. Whether it was morning or evening, Friday or Sunday, made no difference, it was all just the same: the gnawing, unmitigated, agonizing pain, never ceasing for an instant, the consciousness of life inexorably waning but not yet extinguished, the approach of that ever dreaded and hateful Death which was the only reality, and always the same falsity. What were days, weeks, hours, in such a case?

"Will you have some tea, sir?"

"He wants things to be regular, and wishes the gentlefolk to drink tea in the morning," thought Ivan Ilych, and only said "No."

"Wouldn't you like to move onto the sofa, sir?"

"He wants to tidy up the room, and I'm in the way. I am uncleanliness and disorder," he thought, and said only:

"No, leave me alone."

The man went on bustling about. Ivan Ilych stretched out his hand. Peter came up, ready to help.

"What is it, sir?"

"My watch."

Peter took the watch which was close at hand and gave it to his master.

"Half-past eight. Are they up?"

"No, sir, except Vladimir Ivanich" (the son) "who has gone to school. Preskovya Fëdorovna ordered me to wake her if you asked for her. Shall I do so?"

"No, there's no need to." "Perhaps I'd better have some tea," he thought, and added aloud: "Yes, bring me some tea."

Peter went to the door, but Ivan Ilych dreaded being left alone. "How can I keep him here? Oh yes, my medicine." "Peter, give me my medicine." "Why not? Perhaps it may still do me some good." He took a spoonful and swallowed it. "No, it won't help. It's all tomfoolery, all deception," he decided as soon as he became aware of the familiar, sickly, hopeless taste. "No, I can't believe in it any longer. But the pain, why this pain? If it would only cease just for a moment!" And he moaned. Peter turned towards him. "It's all right. Go and fetch me some tea."

Peter went out. Left alone Ivan Ilych groaned not so much with pain, terrible though that was, as from mental anguish. Always and for ever the same, always these endless days and nights. If only it would come quicker! If only *what* would come quicker? Death, darkness? . . . No, no! Anything rather than death!

When Peter returned with the tea on a tray, Ivan Ilych stared at him for a time in perplexity, not realizing who and what he was. Peter was disconcerted by that look and his embarrassment brought Ivan Ilych to himself.

"Oh, tea! All right, put it down. Only help me to wash and put on a clean shirt."

And Ivan Ilych began to wash. With pauses for rest, he washed his hands and then his face, cleaned his teeth, brushed his hair, and looked in the glass. He was terrified by what he saw, especially by the limp way in which his hair clung to his pallid forehead.

While his shirt was being changed he knew that he would be still more frightened at the sight of his body, so he avoided looking at it. Finally he was ready. He drew on a dressing-gown, wrapped himself in a plaid, and sat down in the armchair to take his tea. For a moment he felt refreshed, but as soon as he began to drink the tea he was again aware of the same taste, and the pain also returned. He finished it with an effort, and then lay down stretching out his legs, and dismissed Peter.

Always the same. Now a spark of hope flashes up, then a sea of despair rages, and always pain; always pain, always despair, and always the same. When alone he had a dreadful and distressing desire to call someone, but he knew beforehand that with others present it would be still worse. "Another dose of morphine—to lose consciousness. I will tell him, the doctor, that he must think of something else. It's impossible, impossible, to go on like this."

An hour and another pass like that. But now there is a ring at the door bell. Perhaps it's the doctor? It is. He comes in fresh, hearty, plump, and cheerful, with that look on his face that seems to say: "There now, you're in a panic about something, but we'll arrange it all for you directly!" The doctor knows this expression is out of place here, but he has put it on once for all and can't take it off—like a man who has put on a frock-coat in the morning to pay a round of calls.

The doctor rubs his hands vigorously and reassuringly.

"Brr! How cold it is! There's such a sharp frost; just let me warm myself!" he says, as if it were only a matter of waiting till he was warm, and then he would put everything right.

"Well now, how are you?"

Ivan Ilych feels that the doctor would like to say: "Well, how are your affairs?" but that even he feels that this would not do, and says instead: "What sort of a night have you had?"

Ivan Ilych looks at him as much as to say: "Are you really never ashamed of lying?" But the doctor does not wish to understand this question, and Ivan Ilych says: "Just as terrible as ever. The pain never leaves me and never subsides. If only something . . ."

"Yes, you sick people are always like that . . . There, now I think I am warm enough. Even Praskovya Fëdorovna, who is so particular, could find no fault with my temperature. Well, now I can say good-morning," and the doctor presses his patient's hand.

Then, dropping his former playfulness, he begins with a most serious face to examine the patient, feeling his pulse and taking his temperature, and then begins the sounding and auscultation.

Ivan Ilych knows quite well and definitely that all this is nonsense and pure deception, but when the doctor, getting down on his knee, leans over him, putting the ear first higher than lower, and performs various gymnastic movements over him with a significant expression on his face, Ivan Ilych submits to it all as he used to submit to the speeches of the lawyers, though he knew very well that they were all lying and why they were lying.

The doctor, kneeling on the sofa, is still sounding him when Praskovya Fëdorovna's silk dress rustles at the door and she is heard scolding Peter for not having let her know of the doctor's arrival.

She comes in, kisses her husband, and at once proceeds to prove that she has been up a long time already, and only owing to a misunderstanding failed to be there when the doctor arrived.

Ivan Ilych looks at her, scans her all over, sets against her the whiteness and plumpness and cleanness of her hands and neck, the gloss of her hair, and the sparkle of her vivacious eyes. He hates her with his whole soul. And the thrill of hatred he feels for her makes him suffer from her touch.

Her attitude towards him and his disease is still the same. Just as the doctor had adopted a certain relation to his patient which he could not abandon, so had she formed one towards him—that he was not doing something he ought to do and was himself to blame, and that she reproached him lovingly for this—and she could not now change that attitude.

"You see he doesn't listen to me and doesn't take his medicine at the proper time. And above all he lies in a position that is no doubt bad for him—with his legs up."

She described how he made Gerasim hold his legs up.

The doctor smiled with a contemptuous affability that said: "What's to be done? These sick people do have foolish fancies of that kind, but we must forgive them."

When the examination was over the doctor looked at his watch, and then Praskovya Fëdorovna announced to Ivan Ilych that it was of course as he pleased, but she had sent today for a celebrated specialist who would examine him and have a consultation with Michael Danilovich (their regular doctor).

"Please don't raise any objections. I am doing this for my own sake," she said ironically, letting it be felt that she was doing it all for his sake and only said this to leave him no right to refuse. He remained silent, knitting his brows. He felt that he was so surrounded and involved in a mesh of falsity that it was hard to unravel anything.

Everything she did for him was entirely for her own sake, and she told him she was doing for herself what she actually was doing for herself, as if that was so incredible that he must understand the opposite.

At half-past eleven the celebrated specialist arrived. Again the sounding began and the significant conversations in his presence and in another room, about the kidneys and the appendix, and the questions and answers, with such an air of importance that again, instead of the real question of life and death which now alone confronted him, the question arose of the kidney and appendix which were not behaving as they ought to and would now be attacked by Michael Danilovich and the specialist and forced to mend their ways.

The celebrated specialist took leave of him with a serious though not hopeless look, and in reply to the timid question Ivan Ilych, with eyes glistening with fear and hope, put to him as to whether there was a chance of recovery, said that he could not vouch for it but there was a possibility. The look of hope with which Ivan

Ilych watched the doctor out was so pathetic that Praskovya Fëdorovna, seeing it, even wept as she left the room to hand the doctor his fee.

The gleam of hope kindled by the doctor's encouragement did not last long. The same room, the same pictures, curtains, wall-paper, medicine bottles, were all there, and the same aching suffering body, and Ivan Ilych began to moan. They gave him a subcutaneous injection and he sank into oblivion.

It was twilight when he came to. They brought him his dinner and he swallowed some beef tea with difficulty, and then everything was the same again and night was coming on.

After dinner, at seven o'clock, Praskovya Fëdorovna came into the room in evening dress, her full bosom pushed up by her corset, and with traces of powder on her face. She had reminded him in the morning that they were going to the theatre. Sarah Bernhardt was visiting the town and they had a box, which he had insisted on their taking. Now he had forgotten about it and her toilet offended him, but he concealed his vexation when he remembered that he had himself insisted on their securing a box and going because it would be an instructive and aesthetic pleasure for the children.

Praskovya Fëdorovna came in, self-satisfied but yet with a rather guilty air. She sat down and asked how he was, but, as he saw, only for the sake of asking and not in order to learn about it, knowing that there was nothing to learn—and then went on to what she really wanted to say: that she would not on any account have gone but that the box had been taken and Helen and their daughter were going, as well as Petrishchev (the examining magistrate, their daughter's financé) and that it was out of the question to let them go alone; but that she would have much preferred to sit with him for a while; and he must be sure to follow the doctor's orders while she was away.

"Oh, and Fëdor Petrovich" (the fiancé) "would like to come in. May he? And Lisa?"

"All right."

Their daughter came in in full evening dress, her fresh young flesh exposed (making a show of that very flesh which in his own case caused so much suffering), strong, healthy, evidently in love, and impatient with illness, suffering, and death, because they interfered with her happiness.

Fëdor Petrovich came in too, in evening dress, his hair curled *à la Capoul,* a tight stiff collar round his long sinewy neck, an enormous white shirt-front and narrow black trousers tightly stretched over his strong thighs. He had one white glove tightly drawn on, and was holding his opera hat in his hand.

Following him the schoolboy crept in unnoticed, in a new uniform, poor little fellow, and wearing gloves. Terribly dark shadows showed under his eyes, the meaning of which Ivan Ilych knew well.

His son had always seemed pathetic to him, and now it was dreadful to see the boy's frightened look of pity. It seemed to Ivan Ilych that Vasya was the only one besides Gerasim who understood and pitied him.

They all sat down and again asked how he was. A silence followed. Lisa asked her mother about the opera-glasses, and there was an altercation between mother and daughter as to who had taken them and where they had been put. This occasioned some unpleasantness.

Fëdor Petrovich inquired of Ivan Ilych whether he had ever seen Sarah Bernhardt. Ivan Ilych did not at first catch the question, but then replied: "No, have you seen her before?"

"Yes, in *Adrienne Lecouvreur.*"

Praskovya Fëdorovna mentioned some rôles in which Sarah Bernhardt was particularly good. Her daughter disagreed. Conversation sprang up as to the elegance and realism of her acting—the sort of conversation that is always repeated and is always the same.

In the midst of the conversation Fëdor Petrovich glanced at Ivan Ilych and became silent. Ivan Ilych was staring with glittering eyes straight before him, evidently indignant with them. This had to be rectified, but it was impossible to do so. The silence had to be broken, but for a time no one dared to break it and they all became afraid that the conventional deception would suddenly become obvious and the truth become plain to all. Lisa was the first to pluck up courage and break that silence, but by trying to hide what everybody was feeling, she betrayed it.

"Well, if we are going it's time to start," she said, looking at her watch, a present from her father, and with a faint and significant smile at Fëdor Petrovich relating to something known only to them. She got up with a rustle of her dress.

They all rose, said good-night, and went away.

When they had gone it seemed to Ivan Ilych that he felt better; the falsity had gone with them. But the pain remained—that same pain and that same fear that made everything monotonously alike, nothing harder and nothing easier. Everything was worse.

Again minute followed minute and hour followed hour. Everything remained the same and there was no cessation. And the inevitable end of it all became more and more terrible.

"Yes, send Gerasim here," he replied to a question Peter asked.

IX

His wife returned late at night. She came in on tiptoe, but he heard her, opened his eyes, and made haste to close them again. She wished to send Gerasim away and to sit with him herself, but he opened his eyes and said: "No, go away."

"Are you in great pain?"

"Always the same."

"Take some opium."

He agreed and took some. She went away.

Till about three in the morning he was in a state of stupefied misery. It seemed to him that he and his pain were being thrust into a narrow, deep black sack, but though they were pushed further and further in they could not be pushed to the bottom. And this, terrible enough in itself, was accompanied by suffering. He struggled but yet cooperated. And suddenly he broke through, fell, and regained consciousness. Gerasim was sitting at the foot of the bed dozing quietly, while he himself lay with his emaciated stockinged legs resting on Gerasim's shoulders; the same shaded candle was there and the same unceasing pain.

"Go away, Gerasim," he whispered.

"It's all right, sir. I'll stay a while."

"No. Go away."

He removed his legs from Gerasim's shoulders, turned sideways onto his arm, and felt sorry for himself. He only waited till Gerasim had gone into the next room and then restrained himself no longer but wept like a child. He wept on account of his helplessness, his terrible loneliness, the cruelty of man, the cruelty of God, and the absence of God.

"Why has Thou done all this? Why hast Thou brought me here? Why, why dost Thou torment me so terribly?"

He did not expect an answer and yet wept because there was no answer and could be none. The pain again grew more acute, but he did not stir and did not call. He said to himself: "Go on! Strike me! But what is it for? What have I done to Thee? What is it for?"

Then he grew quiet and not only ceased weeping but even held his breath and became all attention. It was as though he were listening not to an audible voice but to the voice of his soul, to the current of thoughts arising within him.

"What is it you want?" was the first clear conception capable of expression in words, that he heard.

"What do you want? What do you want?" he repeated to himself.

"What do I want? To live and not to suffer," he answered.

And again he listened with such concentrated attention that even his pain did not distract him.

"To live? How?" asked his inner voice.

"Why, to live as I used to—well and pleasantly."

"As you lived before, well and pleasantly?" the voice repeated.

And in imagination he began to recall the best moments of his pleasant life. But strange to say none of those best moments of his pleasant life now seemed at all what they had then seemed—none of them except the first recollections of childhood. There, in childhood, there had been something really pleasant with which it would be possible to live if it could return. But the child who had experienced that happiness existed no longer, it was like a reminiscence of somebody else.

As soon as the period began which had produced the present Ivan Ilych, all that had then seemed joys now melted before his sight and turned into something trivial and often nasty.

And the further he departed from childhood and the nearer he came to the present the more worthless and doubtful were the joys. This began with the School of Law. A little that was really good was still found there—there was light-heartedness, friendship, and hope. But in the upper classes there had already been fewer of such good moments. Then during the first years of his official career, when he was in the service of the Governor, some pleasant moments again occurred: they were the memories of love for a woman. Then all became confused and there was still less of what was good; later on again there was still less that was good, and the further he went the less there was. His marriage, a mere accident, then the disenchantment that followed it, his wife's bad breath and the sensuality and hypocrisy: then that deadly official life and those preoccupations about money, a year of it, and two, and ten, and twenty, and always the same thing. And the longer it lasted the more deadly it became. "It is as if I had been going downhill while I imagined I was going up. And that is really what it was. I was going up in public opinion, but to the same extent life was ebbing away from me. And now it is all done and there is only death."

"Then what does it mean? Why? It can't be that life is so senseless and horrible. But if it really has been so horrible and senseless, why must I die and die in agony? There is something wrong!"

"Maybe I did not live as I ought to have done," it suddenly occurred to him. "But how could that be, when I did everything properly?" he replied, and immediately dismissed from his mind this, the sole solution of all the riddles of life and death, as something quite impossible.

"Then what do you want now? To live? Live how? Live as you lived in the law courts when the usher proclaimed 'The judge is coming!' The judge is coming, the judge!" he repeated to himself. "Here he is, the judge. But I am not guilty!" he exclaimed angrily. "What is it for?" And he ceased crying, but turning his face to the wall continued to ponder on the same question: Why, and for what purpose, is there all this horror? But however much he pondered he found no answer. And whenever the thought occurred to him, as it often did, that it all resulted from his not having lived as he ought to have done, he at once recalled the correctness of his whole life and dismissed so strange an idea.

Another fortnight passed. Ivan Ilych now no longer left his sofa. He would not lie in bed but lay on the sofa, facing the wall nearly all the time. He suffered ever the same unceasing agonies and in his loneliness pondered always on the same insoluble question: "What is this? Can it be that it is Death?" And the inner voice answered: "Yes, it is Death."

"Why these sufferings?" And the voice answered, "For no reason—they just are so." Beyond and besides this there was nothing.

From the very beginning of his illness, ever since he had first been to see the doctor, Ivan Ilych's life had been divided between two contrary and alternating moods: now it was despair and the expectation of this uncomprehended and terrible death, and now hope and an intently interested observation of the functioning of his organs. Now before his eyes there was only a kidney or an intestine that temporarily evaded its duty, and now only that incomprehensible and dreadful death from which it was impossible to escape.

These two states of mind had alternated from the very beginning of his illness, but the further it progressed the more doubtful and fantastic became the conception of the kidney, and the more real the sense of impending death.

He had but to call to mind what he had been three months before and what he was now, to call to mind with what regularity he had been going downhill, for every possibility of hope to be shattered.

Latterly during that loneliness in which he found himself as he lay facing the back of the sofa, a loneliness in the midst of a populous town and surrounded by numerous acquaintances and relations but that yet could not have been more complete anywhere—either at the bottom of the sea or under the earth—during that terrible loneliness Ivan Ilych had lived only in memories of the past. Pictures of his past rose before him one after another. They always began with what was nearest in time and then went back to what was the most remote—to his childhood—and rested there. If he thought of the stewed prunes that had been offered him that day, his mind went back to the raw shrivelled French plums of his childhood, their peculiar flavour and the flow of saliva when he sucked their stones, and along with the memory of that taste came a whole series of memories of those days: his nurse, his brother, and their toys. "No, I mustn't think of that . . . It is too painful," Ivan Ilych said to himself, and brought himself back to the present—to the button on the back of the sofa and the creases in its morocco. "Morocco is expensive, but it does not wear well: there had been a quarrel about it. It was a different kind of quarrel and a different kind of morocco that time when we tore father's portfolio and were punished, and Mamma brought us some tarts . . ." And again his thoughts dwelt on his childhood, and again it was painful and he tried to banish them and fix his mind on something else.

Then again together with that chain of memories another series passed through his mind—of how his illness had progressed and grown worse. There also the further back he looked the more life there had been. There had been more of what was good in life and more of life itself. The two merged together. "Just as the pain went on getting worse and worse, so my life grew worse and worse," he thought. "There is one bright spot there at the back, at the beginning of life, and afterwards all becomes blacker and blacker and proceeds more and more rapidly—in inverse ratio to the square of the distance from death," thought Ivan

Ilych. And the example of a stone falling downwards with increasing velocity entered his mind. Life, a series of increasing sufferings, flies further and further towards its end—the most terrible suffering. "I am flying . . ." He shuddered, shifted himself, and tried to resist, but was already aware that resistance was impossible, and again with eyes weary of gazing but unable to cease seeing what was before them, he stared at the back of the sofa and waited—awaiting that dreadful fall and shock and destruction.

"Resistance is impossible!" he said to himself. "If I could only understand what it is all for! But that too is impossible. An explanation would be possible if it could be said that I have not lived as I ought to. But it is impossible to say that," and he remembered all the legality, correctitude, and propriety of his life. "That at any rate can certainly not be admitted," he thought, and his lips smiled ironically as if someone could see that smile and be taken in by it. "There is no explanation! Agony, death . . . What for?"

XI

Another two weeks went by in this way and during that fortnight an event occurred that Ivan Ilych and his wife had desired. Petrishchev formally proposed. It happened in the evening. The next day Praskovya Fëdorovna came into her husband's room considering how best to inform him of it, but that very night there had been a fresh change for the worse in his condition. She found him still lying on the sofa but in a different position. He lay on his back, groaning and staring fixedly in front of him.

She began to remind him of his medicines, but he turned his eyes towards her with such a look that she did not finish what she was saying; so great an animosity, to her in particular, did that look express.

"For Christ's sake let me die in peace!" he said.

She would have gone away, but just then their daughter came in and went up to say good morning. He looked at her as he had done at his wife, and in reply to her inquiry about his health said dryly that he would soon free them all of himself. They were both silent and after sitting with him for a while went away.

"Is it our fault?" Lisa said to her mother. "It's as if we were to blame! I am sorry for papa, but why should we be tortured?"

The doctor came at his usual time. Ivan Ilych answered "Yes" and "No," never taking his angry eyes from him, and at last said: "You know you can do nothing for me, so leave me alone."

"We can ease your sufferings."

"You can't even do that. Let me be."

The doctor went into the drawing-room and told Praskovya Fëdorovna that the case was very serious and that the only resource left was opium to allay her husband's sufferings, which must be terrible.

It was true, as the doctor said, that Ivan Ilych's physical sufferings were terrible, but worse than the physical sufferings were his mental sufferings, which were his chief torture.

His mental sufferings were due to the fact that that night, as he looked at Gerasim's sleepy, good-natured face with its prominent cheek-bones, the question suddenly occurred to him: "What if my whole life has really been wrong?"

It occurred to him that what had appeared perfectly impossible before, namely that he had not spent his life as he should have done, might after all be true. It occurred to him that his scarcely perceptible attempts to struggle against what was considered good by the most highly placed people, those scarcely noticeable impulses which he had immediately suppressed, might have been the real thing, and all the rest false. And his professional duties and the whole arrangement of his life and of his family, and all his social and official interests, might all have been false. He tried to defend all those things to himself and suddenly felt the weakness of what he was defending. There was nothing to defend.

"But if that is so," he said to himself, "and I am leaving this life with the consciousness that I have lost all that was given me and it is impossible to rectify it—what then?"

He lay on his back and began to pass his life in review in quite a new way. In the morning when he saw first his footman, then his wife, then his daughter, and then the doctor, their every word and movement confirmed to him the awful truth that had been revealed to him during the night. In them he saw himself—all that for which he had lived—and saw clearly that it was not real at all, but a terrible and huge deception which had hidden both life and death. This consciousness intensified his physical suffering tenfold. He groaned and tossed about, and pulled at his clothing which choked and stifled him. And he hated them on that account.

He was given a large dose of opium and became unconscious, but at noon his sufferings began again. He drove everybody away and tossed from side to side.

His wife came to him and said:

"Jean, my dear, do this for me. It can't do any harm and often helps. Healthy people often do it."

He opened his eyes wide.

"What? Take communion? Why? It's unnecessary! However . . ."

She began to cry.

"Yes, do, my dear. I'll send for our priest. He is such a nice man."

"All right. Very well," he muttered.

When the priest came and heard his confession, Ivan Ilych was softened and seemed to feel a relief from his doubts and consequently from his sufferings, and for a moment there came a ray of hope. He again began to think of the vermiform appendix and the possibility of correcting it. He received the sacrament with tears in his eyes.

When they laid him down again afterwards he felt a moment's ease, and the hope that he might live awoke in him again. He began to think of the operation that had been suggested to him. "To live! I want to live!" he said to himself.

His wife came to congratulate him after his communion, and when uttering the usual conventional words she added:

"You feel better, don't you?"

Without looking at her he said "Yes."

Her dress, her figure, the expression of her face, the tone of her voice, all revealed the same thing. "This is wrong, it is not as it should be. All you have lived for and still live for is falsehood and deception, hiding life and death from you." And as soon as he admitted that thought, his hatred and his agonizing physical suffering again sprang up, and with that suffering a consciousness of the unavoidable, approaching end. And to this was added a new sensation of grinding shooting pain and a feeling of suffocation.

The expression of his face when he uttered that "yes" was dreadful. Having uttered it, he looked her straight in the eyes, turned on his face with a rapidity extraordinary in his weak state and shouted:

"Go away! Go away and leave me alone!"

XII

From that moment the screaming began that continued for three days, and was so terrible that one could not hear it through two closed doors without horror. At the moment he answered his wife he realized that he was lost, that there was no return, that the end had come, the very end, and his doubts were still unsolved and remained doubts.

"Oh! Oh! Oh!" he cried in various intonations. He had begun by screaming "I won't!" and continued screaming on the letter *O*.

For three whole days, during which time did not exist for him, he struggled in that black sack into which he was being thrust by an invisible, resistless force.Struggled as a man condemned to death struggles in the hands of the executioner, knowing that he cannot save himself. And every moment he felt that despite all his efforts he was drawing nearer and nearer to what terrified him. He felt that his agony was due to his being thrust into that black hole and still more to his not begin able to get right into it. He was hindered from getting into it by his conviction that his life had been a good one. That very justification of his life held him fast and prevented his moving forward, and it caused him most torment of all.

Suddenly some force struck him in the chest and side, making it still harder to breathe, and he fell through the hole and there at the bottom was a light. What had happened to him was like the sensation one sometimes experiences in a railway carriage when one thinks one is going backwards while one is really going forwards and suddenly becomes aware of the real direction.

"Yes, it was all not the right thing," he said to himself, "but that's no matter. It can be done. But what *is* the right thing?" he asked himself, and suddenly grew quiet.

This occurred at the end of the third day, two hours before his death. Just then his schoolboy son had crept softly in and gone up to the bedside. The dying man was still screaming and waving his arms. His hand fell on the boy's head, and the boy caught it, pressed it to his lips, and began to cry.

At that very moment Ivan Ilych fell through and caught sight of the light, and it was revealed to him that though his life had not been what it should have been, this could still be rectified. He asked himself, "What *is* the right thing?" and grew still, listening. Then he felt that someone was kissing his hand. He opened his eyes, looked at his son, and felt sorry for him. His wife came up to him and he glanced at her. She was gazing at him openmouthed, with undried tears on her nose and cheek and a despairing look on her face. He felt sorry for her too.

"Yes, I am making them wretched," he thought. "They are sorry, but it will be better for them when I die." He wished to say this but had not the strength to utter it. "Besides, why speak? I must act," he thought. With a look at his wife he indicated his son and said: "Take him away . . . sorry for him . . . sorry for you too . . ." He tried to add, "forgive me," but said "forgo" and waved his hand, knowing that He whose understanding mattered would understand.

And suddenly it grew clear to him that what had been oppressing him and would not leave him was dropping away at once from two sides, from ten sides, and from all sides. He was sorry for them, he must act so as not to hurt them and free himself from these sufferings. "How good and how simple!" he thought. "And the pain?" he asked himself. "What has become of it? Where are you, pain?"

He turned his attention it.

"Yes, here it is. Well, what of it? Let the pain be."

"And death . . . where is it?"

He sought his former accustomed fear of death and did not find it. "Where is it? What death?" There was no fear because there was no death.

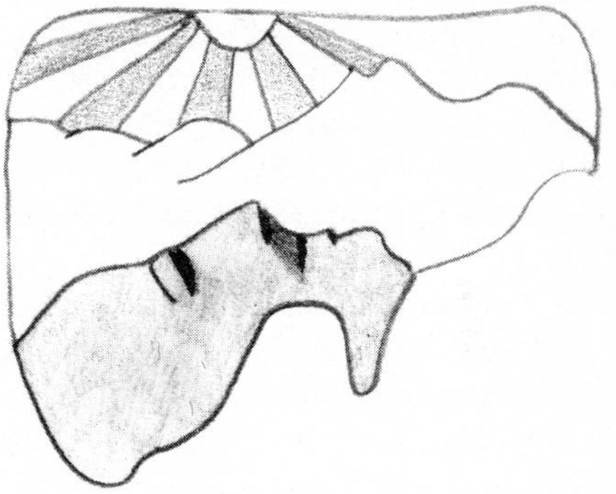

In place of death there was light.

"So that's what it is!" he suddenly exclaimed aloud. "What joy!"

To him all this happened in a single instant, and the meaning of that instant did not change. For those present his agony continued for another two hours. Something rattled in his throat, his emaciated body twitched, then the gasping and rattle became less and less frequent.

"It is finished!" said someone near him.

He heard these words and repeated them in his soul.

"Death is finished," he said to himself. "It is no more!"

He drew in a breath, stopped in the midst of a sigh, stretched out, and died.

Considerations

By beginning the story at the end—with Ivan's death—Tolstoy makes sure that wondering what is going to happen to Ivan does not distract our attention from the story. The point of view we are given is occasionally that of the impartial observer, but most often it is that of Ivan. We share his coping with life, his perception of his friends, relatives, and colleagues, his sickness, his obsessions, and his coming to terms with death.

In the span of one short novel Tolstoy catalogs the life of a man: he grows up, he marries for many of the same reasons that many men marry, his marriage becomes difficult, he enjoys somewhat superficial pleasures, and finally he comes face to face with his own mortality. This confrontation with the self is achieved in the most dramatic and ironic way possible—through a commonplace incident. Why is the use of such an incident so effective? Is it because it recalls to us the countless similar ironies that we have encountered in real life—the simple operation that went wrong, the childhood disease that permanently crippled and disfigured? Is it because it reflects the possible vast consequences something normally considered insignificant? Is it because it shows the absurdity of life itself? Is it because in his almost ludicrous difficulties, Ivan is all too easily us?

While we can understand Ivan and pity him, we find ourselves also disliking him. As long as things are going well, when he has money and health, Ivan is pleasant and generous. He is no better but certainly no worse than the rest of us. Suddenly, however, something occurs to set him apart, and everything turns sour. He is sure that others—including his wife—are more interested in themselves than in him. (How do you suppose he would have acted had he been in his wife's place?) He becomes petulant and fretful. His physical suffering is nothing to the suffering of his mind—on one level because "no one pitied him as he wished to be pitied," and on another because he is unable to comfort himself with the certainty that his life has been worthwhile: "Maybe I did not live as I ought to have done. . . . But how could that be, when I did everything properly?" What comment could Tolstoy be making about the concept of living "properly"?

In a moment of light (which could symbolize afterlife, the infinite, or merely a sudden clear insight) he recognizes that what is done is done, that only a few duties remain to those he is leaving, and that then he will be finished with it all. How such a feeling should come to a man shown earlier as so insensitive and unimaginative is unexplained. Does the ending turn the story of Ivan's essentially tawdry life into something of beauty and hope? Are any of Ivan's (or our) questions about the meaning of life or death answered in this story?

The Revolt of Mother

Mary E. Wilkins Freeman

"Father!"

"What is it?"

"What are them men diggin' over there in the field for?"

There was a sudden dropping and enlarging of the lower part of the old man's face, as if some heavy weight had settled therein; he shut his mouth tight, and went on harnessing the great bay mare. He hustled the collar on to her neck with a jerk.

"Father!"

The old man slapped the saddle upon the mare's back.

"Look here, father, I want to know what them men are diggin' over in the field for, an' I'm goin' to know."

"I wish you'd go into the house, mother, an' 'tend to your own affairs," the old man said then. He ran his words together, and his speech was almost as inarticulate as a growl.

But the woman understood; it was her most native tongue. "I ain't goin' into the house till you tell me what them men are doin' over there in the field," said she.

Then she stood waiting. She was a small woman, short and straight-waisted like a child in her brown cotton gown. Her forehead was mild and benevolent between the smooth curves of gray hair; there were meek downward lines about her nose and mouth; but her eyes, fixed upon the old man, looked as if the meekness had been the result of her own will, never of the will of another.

They were in the barn, standing before the wide open doors. The spring air, full of the smell of growing grass and unseen blossoms, came in their faces. The deep yard in front was littered with farm wagons and piles of wood; on the edges, close to the fence and the house, the grass was a vivid green, and there were some dandelions.

The old man glanced doggedly at his wife as he tightened the last buckles on the harness. She looked as immovable to him as one of the rocks in his pastureland, bound to the earth with generations of blackberry vines. He slapped the reins over the horse, and started forth from the barn.

"Father!" said she.

The old man pulled up. "What is it?"

"I want to know what them men are diggin' over there in that field for."

"They're diggin' a cellar, I s'pose, if you've got to know."

"A cellar for what?"

"A barn."

"A barn? You ain't goin' to build a barn over there where we was goin' to have a house, father?"

The old man said not another

word. He hurried the horse into the farm wagon, and clattered out of the yard, jouncing as sturdily on his seat as a boy.

The woman stood a moment looking after him, then she went out of the barn across a corner of the yard to the house. The house, standing at right angles with the great barn and a long reach of sheds and outbuildings, was infinitesimal compared with them. It was scarcely as commodious for people as the little boxes under the barn eaves were for doves.

A pretty girl's face, pink and delicate as a flower, was looking out of one of the house windows. She was watching three men who were digging over in the field which bounded the yard near the road line. She turned quietly when the woman entered.

"What are they digging for, mother?" said she. "Did he tell you?"

"They're diggin' for—a cellar for a new barn."

"Oh, mother, he ain't going to build another barn?"

"That's what he says."

A boy stood before the kitchen glass combing his hair. He combed slowly and painstakingly, arranging his brown hair in a smooth hillock over his forehead. He did not seem to pay any attention to the conversation.

"Sammy, did you know father was going to build a new barn?" asked the girl.

The boy combed assiduously.

"Sammy!"

He turned, and showed a face like his father's under his smooth crest of hair. "Yes, I s'pose I did," he said, reluctantly.

"How long have you known it?" asked his mother.

"'Bout three months, I guess."

"Why didn't you tell of it?"

"Didn't think 'twould do no good."

"I don't see what father wants another barn for," said the girl, in her sweet, slow voice. She turned again to the window, and stared out at the digging men in the field. Her tender, sweet face was full of a gentle distress. Her forehead was as bald and innocent as a baby's with the light hair strained back from it in a row of curl papers. She was quite large, but her soft curves did not look as if they covered muscles.

Her mother looked sternly at the boy. "Is he goin' to buy more cows?"

The boy did not reply; he was tying his shoes.

"Sammy, I want you to tell me if he's goin' to buy more cows."

"I s'pose he is."

"How many?"

"Four, I guess."

His mother said nothing more. She went into the pantry, and there was a clatter of dishes. The boy got his cap from a nail behind the door, took an old arithmetic from the shelf, and started for school. He was lightly built, but clumsy. He went out of the yard with a curious spring in the hips, that made his loose homemade jacket tilt up in the rear.

The girl went to the sink, and began to wash the dishes that were piled up there. Her mother came promptly out of the pantry, and shoved her aside. "You wipe 'em," said she, "I'll wash. There's a good many this mornin'."

The mother plunged her hands vigorously into the water, the girl wiped the plates slowly and dreamily. "Mother," said she, "don't you think it's too bad father's going to build that new barn, much as we need a decent house to live in?"

Her mother scrubbed a dish fiercely. "You ain't found out yet we're women-folks, Nanny Penn," said she. "You ain't seen enough of men-folks yet to. One of these days you'll find it out, an' then you'll know that we know only what men-folks think we do, so far as any use of it goes, an' how we'd ought to reckon men-folks in with Providence, an' not complain of what they do any more than we do of the weather."

"I don't care; I don't believe George is anything like that, anyhow," said Nanny. Her delicate face flushed pink, her lips pouted softly, as if she were going to cry.

"You wait an' see. I guess George Eastman ain't no better than other men. You hadn't ought to judge father, though. He can't help it, 'cause he don't look at things jest the way we do. An' we've been pretty comfortable here, after all. The roof don't leak—ain't never but once—that's one thing. Father's kept it shingled right up."

"I do wish we had a parlor."

"I guess it won't hurt George Eastman any to come to see you in a nice clean kitchen. I guess a good many girls don't have as good a place as this. Nobody's ever heard me complain."

"I ain't complained either, mother."

"Well, I don't think you'd better, a good father an' a good home as you've got. S'pose your father made you go out an' work for your livin'? Lots of girls have to that ain't no stronger an' better able to than you be."

Sarah Penn washed the frying-pan with a conclusive air. She scrubbed the outside of it as faithfully as the inside. She was a masterly keeper of her box of a house. Her one livingroom never seemed to have in it any of the dust which the friction of life with inanimate matter produces. She swept, and there seemed to be no dirt to go before the broom; she cleaned, and one could see no difference. She was like an artist so perfect that he has apparently no art. To-day she got out a mixing bowl and a board, and rolled some pies, and there was no more flour upon her than upon her daughter who was doing finer work. Nanny was to be married in the fall, and she was sewing on some white cambric and embroidery. She sewed industriously while her mother cooked; her soft milkwhite hands and wrists showed whiter than her delicate work.

"We must have the stove moved out in the shed before long," said Mrs. Penn. "Talk about not havin' things, it's been a real blessin' to be able to put a stove up in that shed in hot weather. Father did one good thing when he fixed that stove-pipe out there."

Sarah Penn's face as she rolled her pies had that expression of meek vigor which might have characterized one of the New Testament saints. She was making mince-pies. Her husband, Adoniram Penn, liked them better than any other kind. She baked twice a week. Adoniram often liked a piece of pie between meals. She hurried this morning. It had been later than usual when she began, and she wanted to have a pie baked for dinner. However deep a resentment she might be forced to hold against her husband, she would never fail in sedulous attention to his wants.

Nobility of character manifests itself at loopholes when it is not provided with large doors. Sarah Penn's showed itself to-day in flaky dishes of pastry. So she made the pies faithfully, while across the table she could see, when she glanced up from her work, the sight that rankled in her patient and steadfast soul—the digging of the cellar of the new barn in the place where Adoniram forty years ago had promised her their new house should stand.

The pies were done for dinner. Adoniram and Sammy were home a few minutes after twelve o'clock. The dinner was eaten with serious haste. There was never much conversation at the table in the Penn family. Adoniram asked a blessing, and they ate promptly, then rose up and went about their work.

Sammy went back to school, taking soft sly lopes out of the yard like a rabbit. He wanted a game of marbles before school, and feared his father would give him some chores to do. Adoniram hastened to the door and called after him, but he was out of sight.

"I don't see what you let him go for, mother," said he. "I wanted him to help me unload that wood."

Adoniram went to work out in the yard unloading wood from the wagon. Sarah put away the dinner dishes, while Nanny took down her curl papers and changed her dress. She was going down to the store to buy some more embroidery and thread.

When Nanny was gone, Mrs. Penn went to the door. "Father!" she called.

"Well, what is it!"

"I want to see you jest a minute, father."

"I can't leave this wood nohow. I've got to git it unloaded an' go for a load of gravel afore two o'clock. Sammy had ought to helped me. You hadn't ought to let him go to school so early."

"I want to see you jest a minute."

"I tell ye I can't, nohow, mother."

"Father, you come here." Sarah Penn stood in the door like a queen; she held her head as if it bore a crown; there was that patience which makes authority royal in her voice. Adoniram went.

Mrs. Penn led the way into the kitchen, and pointed to a chair. "Sit down, father," said she; "I've got somethin' I want to say to you."

He sat down heavily; his face was quite stolid, but he looked at her with restive eyes. "Well, what is it, mother?"

"I want to know what you're buildin' that new barn for, father?"

"I ain't got nothin' to say about it."

"It can't be you think you need another barn?"

"I tell ye I ain't got nothin' to say

about it, mother; an' I ain't goin' to say nothin'."

"Be you goin' to buy more cows?"

Adoniram did not reply; he shut his mouth tight.

"I know you be, as well as I want to. Now, father, look here"—Sarah Penn had not sat down; she stood before her husband in the humble fashion of a Scripture woman—"I'm goin' to talk real plain to you; I never have sence I married you, but I'm goin' to now. I ain't never complained, an' I ain't goin' to complain now, but I'm goin' to talk plain. You see this room here, father; you look at it well. You see there ain't no carpet on the floor, an' you see the paper is all dirty, an' droppin' off the wall. We ain't had no new paper on it for ten year, an' then I put it on myself, an' it didn't cost but ninepence a roll. You see this room, father; it's all the one I've had to work in an' eat in an' sit in sence we was married. There ain't another woman in the whole town whose husband ain't got half the means you have but what's got better. It's all the room Nanny's got to have her company in; an' there ain't one of her mates but what's got better, an' their fathers not so able as hers is. It's all the room she'll have to be married in. What would you have thought, father, if we had had our weddin' in a room no better than this? I was married in my mother's parlor, with a carpet on the floor, an' stuffed furniture, an' a mahogany card-table. An' this is all the room my daughter will have to be married in. Look here, father!"

Sarah Penn went across the room as though it were a tragic stage. She flung open a door and disclosed a tiny bedroom, only large enough for a bed and bureau, with a path between. "There father," said she—"there's all the room I've had to sleep in forty year. All my children were born there—the two that died, an' the two that's livin'. I was sick with a fever there."

She stepped to another door and opened it. It led into the small, ill-lighted pantry. "Here," said she, "is all the buttery I've got—every place I've got for my dishes, to set away my victuals in, an' to keep my milkpans in. Father, I've been takin' care of the milk of six cows in this place, an' now you're goin' to build a new barn, an' keep more cows, an' give me more to do in it."

She threw open another door. A narrow crooked flight of stairs wound upward from it. "There, father," said she, "I want you to look at the stairs that go up to them two unfinished chambers that are all the places our son an' daughter have had to sleep in all their lives. There ain't a prettier girl in town nor a more ladylike one than Nanny, an' that's the place she has to sleep in. It ain't so good as your horse's stall; it ain't so warm an' tight."

Sarah Penn went back and stood before her husband. "Now, father," said she, "I want to know if you think you're doin' right an' accordin' to what you profess. Here, when we was married, forty year ago, you promised me faithful that we should have a new house built in that lot over in the field before the year was out. You said you had money enough, an' you wouldn't ask me to live in no such place as this. It is forty year now, an' you've been makin' more money, an' I've been savin' of it for you ever since, an' you ain't built no house yet. You've built sheds an' cow-houses an' one new barn, an' now you're goin' to build another. Father, I want to know if you think it's right. You're lodgin' your dumb beasts better than you are your own flesh an' blood. I want to know if you think it's right."

"I ain't got nothin' to say."

"You can't say nothin' without ownin' it ain't right, father. An' there's another thing—I ain't complained; I've got along forty year, an' I s'pose I should forty more, if it wasn't for that—if we don't have another house, Nanny she can't live with us after she's married. She'll have to go somewhere else to live away from us, an' it don't seem as if I could have it so, noways, father. She wasn't ever strong. She's got considerable color, but there wasn't never any backbone to her. I've always took the heft of everything off her, an' she ain't fit to keep house an' do everything herself. She'll be all worn out inside of a year. Think of her doin' all the washin' an' ironin' an' bakin' with them soft white hands an' arms, an' sweepin'! I can't have it so, noways, father."

Mrs. Penn's face was burning; her mild eyes gleamed. She had pleaded her little cause like a Webster; she had ranged from severity to pathos; but her opponent employed that obstinate silence which makes eloquence futile with mocking echoes. Adoniram arose clumsily.

"Father, ain't you got nothin' to say?" said Mrs. Penn.

"I've got to go off after that load of gravel. I can't stan' here talkin' all day."

"Father, won't you think it over, an' have a house built there instead of a barn?"

"I ain't got nothin' to say."

Adoniram shuffled out. Mrs. Penn went into her bedroom. When she came out, her eyes were red. She had a roll of unbleached cotton cloth. She spread it out on the kitchen table, and began cutting out some shirts for her husband. The men over in the field had a team to help them this afternoon; she could hear their halloos. She had a scanty pattern for the shirts; she had to plan and piece the sleeves.

Nanny came home with her embroidery, and sat down with her needlework. She had taken down her curl papers, and there was a soft roll of fair hair like an aureole over her forehead; her face was as delicately fine and clear as porcelain. Suddenly she looked up, and the tender red flamed all over her face and neck. "Mother," said she.

"What say?"

"I've been thinking—I don't see how we're goin' to have any—wedding in this room. I'd be ashamed to have his folks come if we didn't have anybody else."

"Mebee we can have some new paper before then; I can put it on. I guess you won't have no call to be ashamed of your belongin's."

"We might have the wedding in the new barn," said Nanny, with gentle pettishness. "Why, mother, what makes you look so?"

Mrs. Penn had started, and was staring at her with a curious expression. She turned again to her work, and spread out a pattern carefully on the cloth. "Nothin'," said she.

Presently Adoniram clattered out of the yard in his two-wheeled dump cart, standing as proudly upright as a Roman charioteer. Mrs. Penn opened the door and stood there a minute looking out; the halloos of the men sounded louder.

It seemed to her all through the spring months that she heard nothing but the halloos and the noises of saws and hammers. The new barn grew fast. It was a fine edifice for this little village. Men came on pleasant Sundays, in their meeting suits and clean shirt bosoms, and stood around it admiringly. Mrs. Penn did not speak of it, and Adoniram did not mention it to her, although sometimes, upon a return from inspecting it, he bore himself with injured dignity.

"It's a strange thing how your mother feels about the new barn," he said, confidentially, to Sammy one day.

Sammy only grunted after an odd fashion for a boy; he had learned it from his father.

The barn was all completed ready for use by the third week in July. Adoniram had planned to move his stock in on Wednesday; on Tuesday he received a letter which changed his plans. He came in with it early in the morning, "Sammy's been to the post-office," said he, "an' I've got a letter from Hiram." Hiram was Mrs. Penn's brother, who lived in Vermont.

"Well," said Mrs. Penn, "what does he say about the folks?"

"I guess they're all right. He says he thinks if I come up country right off there's a chance to buy jest the kind of a horse I want." He stared reflectively out of the window at the new barn.

Mrs. Penn was making pies. She went on clapping the rolling-pin into the crust, although she was very pale, and her heart beat loudly.

"I dun' know but what I'd better go," said Adoniram. "I hate to go off jest now, right in the midst of hayin', but the ten-acre lot's cut, an' I guess Rufus an' the others can git along without me three or four days. I can't get a horse round here to suit me, nohow, an' I've got to have another for all that wood-haulin' in the fall. I told Hiram to watch out, an' if he got wind of a good horse to let me know. I guess I'd better go."

"I'll get out your clean shirt an' collar," said Mrs. Penn calmly.

She laid out Adoniram's Sunday suit and his clean clothes on the bed in the little bedroom. She got his shaving-water and razor ready. At last she buttoned on his collar and fastened his black cravat.

Adoniram never wore his collar and cravat except on extra occasions. He held his head high, with a rasped dignity. When he was all ready, with his coat and hat brushed, and a lunch of pie and cheese in a paper bag, he hesitated on the threshold of the door. He looked at his wife, and his manner was definitely apologetic. "*If* them cows come to-day, Sammy can drive 'em into the new barn," said he; "an' when they bring the hay up, they can pitch it in there."

"Well," replied Mrs. Penn.

Adoniram set his shaven face ahead and started. When he had

cleared the door-step, he turned and looked back with a kind of nervous solemnity. "I shall be back by Saturday if nothin' happens," said he.

"Do be careful, father," returned his wife.

She stood in the door with Nanny at her elbow and watched him out of sight. Her eyes had a strange, doubtful expression in them; her peaceful forehead was contracted. She went in, and about her baking again. Nanny sat sewing. Her wedding-day was drawing nearer, and she was getting pale and thin with her steady sewing. Her mother kept glancing at her.

"Have you got that pain in your side this mornin'?" she asked.

"A little."

Mrs. Penn's face, as she worked, changed, her perplexed forehead smoothed, her eyes were steady, her lips firmly set. She formed a maxim for herself, although incoherently with her unlettered thoughts. "Unsolicited opportunities are the guide-posts of the Lord to the new roads of life," she repeated in effect, and she made up her mind to her course of action.

"S'posin' I *had* wrote to Hiram," she muttered once, when she was in the pantry—"s'posin' I had wrote, an' asked him if he knew of any horse? But I didn't, an' father's goin' wa'n't none of my doin'. It looks like a providence." Her voice rang out quite loud at the last.

"What you talkin' about, mother?" called Nanny.

"Nothin'."

Mrs. Penn hurried her baking; at eleven o'clock it was all done. The load of hay from the west field came slowly down the cart track, and drew up at the new barn. Mrs. Penn ran out. "Stop!" she screamed, "stop!"

The men stopped and looked; Sammy upreared from the top of the load, and stared at his mother.

"Stop!" she cried out again. "Don't you put the hay in that barn; put it in the old one."

"Why, he said to put it in here," returned one of the haymakers, wonderingly. He was a young man, a neighbor's son, whom Adoniram hired by the year to help on the farm.

"Don't you put the hay in the new barn; there's room enough in the old one, ain't there?" said Mrs. Penn.

"Room enough," returned the hired man, in his thick, rustic tones. "Didn't need the new barn, nohow, far as room's concerned. Well, I s'pose he changed his mind." He took hold of the horses' bridles.

Mrs. Penn went back to the house. Soon the kitchen windows were darkened, and a fragrance like warm honey came into the room.

Nanny laid down her work. "I thought father wanted them to put the hay into the new barn?" she said, wonderingly.

"It's all right," replied her mother.

Sammy slid down from the load of hay, and came in to see if dinner was ready.

"I ain't goin' to get a regular dinner to-day, as long as father's gone," said his mother. "I've let the fire go out. You can have some bread an' milk an' pie. I thought we could get along." She set out some bowls of milk, some bread, and a pie on the kitchen table. "You'd better eat your dinner now," said she. "You might jest as well get through with it. I want you to help me afterwards."

Nanny and Sammy stared at each other. There was something strange in their mother's manner. Mrs. Penn did not eat anything herself. She went into the pantry, and they heard her moving dishes while they ate. Presently she came out with a pile of plates. She got the clothes-basket out of the shed, and packed them in it. Nanny and Sammy watched. She brought out cups and saucers, and put them in with the plates.

"What you goin' to do, mother?" inquired Nanny, in a timid voice. A sense of something unusual made her tremble, as if it were a ghost. Sammy rolled his eyes over his pie.

"You'll see what I'm goin' to do," replied Mrs. Penn. "If you're through, Nanny, I want you to go up-stairs an' pack up your things; an' I want you, Sammy, to help me take down the bed in the bedroom."

"Oh, mother, what for?" gasped Nanny.

"You'll see."

During the next few hours a feat was performed by this simple, pious New England mother which was equal in its way to Wolfe's storming of the Heights of Abraham. It took no more genius and audacity of bravery for Wolfe to cheer his wondering soldiers up those steep precipices, under the sleeping eyes of the enemy, than for Sarah Penn, at the head of her children, to move all their little household goods into the new barn while her husband was away.

Nanny and Sammy followed their mother's instructions without a murmur; indeed, they were overawed. There is a certain uncanny and superhuman quality about all such purely original undertakings as their mother's was to them. Nanny went back and forth with her light load, and Sammy tugged with sober energy.

At five o'clock in the afternoon the little house in which the Penns had lived for forty years had emptied itself into the new barn.

Every builder builds somewhat for unknown purposes, and is in a measure a prophet. The architect of Adoniram Penn's barn, while he designed it for the comfort of four-footed animals, had planned better than he knew for the comfort of humans. Sarah Penn saw at a glance its possibilities. Those great box-stalls, with quilts hung before them, would make better bedrooms than the one she had occupied for forty years, and there was a tight carriage-room. The harness-room, with its chimney and shelves, would make a kitchen of her dreams. The great middle space would make a parlor, by-and-by, fit for a palace. Up-stairs there was as much room as down. With partitions and windows, what a house would there be! Sarah looked at the row of stanchions before the allotted space for cows, and reflected that she would have her front entry there.

At six o'clock the stove was up in the harness room, the kettle was boiling, and the table set for tea. It looked almost as home-like as the abandoned house across the yard had ever done. The young hired man milked, and Sarah directed him calmly to bring the milk to the new barn. He came gaping, dropping little blots of foam from the brimming pails on the grass. Before the next morning he had spread the story of Adoniram Penn's wife moving into the new barn all over the little village. Men assembled in the store and talked it over, women with shawls over their heads scuttled into each other's houses before their work was done. Any deviation from the ordinary course of life in this quiet town was enough to stop all progress in it. Everybody paused to look at the staid, independent figure on the side track. There was a difference of opinion with regard to her. Some held her to be insane; some, of a lawless and rebellious spirit.

Friday the minister went to see her. It was in the forenoon, and she was at the barn door shelling peas for dinner. She looked up and returned his salutation with dignity, then she went on with her work. She did not invite him in. The saintly expression of her face remained fixed, but there was an angry flush over it.

The minister stood awkwardly before her, and talked. She handled the peas as if they were bullets. At last she looked up, and her eyes showed the spirit that her meek front had covered for a lifetime.

"There ain't no use talkin', Mr. Hersey," said she. "I've thought it all over an' over, an' I believe I'm doin' what's right. I've made it the subject of prayer, an' it's betwixt me an' the Lord an' Adoniram. There ain't no call for nobody else to worry about it."

"Well, of course, if you have brought it to the Lord in prayer, and feel satisfied that you are doing right, Mrs. Penn," said the minister, helplessly. His thin gray-bearded face was pathetic. He was a sickly man; his youthful confidence had cooled; he had to scourge himself up to some of his pastoral duties as relentlessly as a Catholic ascetic, and then he was prostrated by the smart.

"I think it's right jest as much as I think it was right for our forefathers to come over here from the old country 'cause they didn't have what belonged to 'em," said Mrs. Penn. She arose. The barn threshold might have been Plymouth Rock from her bearing. "I don't doubt you mean well, Mr. Hersey," said she, "but there are things people hadn't ought to interfere with. I've been a member of the church for over forty years. I've got my own mind an' my own feet, an' I'm goin' to think my own thoughts an' go my own way, an' nobody but the Lord is goin' to dictate to me unless I've a mind to have him. Won't you come in an' set down? How is Mis' Hersey?"

"She is well, I thank you," replied the minister. He added some more perplexed apologetic remarks; then he retreated.

He could expound the intricacies of every character-study in the Scriptures, he was competent to grasp the Pilgrim Fathers and all historical innovators, but Sarah Penn was beyond him. He could deal with primal cases, but parallel ones worsted him. But, after all, although it was aside from his providence, he wondered more how Adoniram Penn would deal with his wife than how the Lord would. Everybody shared the wonder. When Adoniram's four new cows arrived,

Sarah ordered three to be put in the old barn, the other in the house shed where the cooking-stove had stood. That added to the excitement. It was whispered that all four cows were domiciled in the house.

Towards sunset on Saturday, when Adoniram was expected home, there was a knot of men in the road near the new barn. The hired man had milked, but he still hung around the premises. Sarah Penn had supper all ready. There were brown-bread and baked beans and a custard pie; it was the supper that Adoniram loved on a Saturday night. She had on a clean calico, and she bore herself imperturbably. Nanny and Sammy kept close at her heels. Their eyes were large, and Nanny was full of nervous tremors. Still there was to them more pleasant excitement than anything else. An inborn confidence in their mother over their father asserted itself.

Sammy looked out of the harness-room window. "There he is," he announced, in an awed whisper. He and Nanny peeped around the casing. Mrs. Penn kept on about her work. The children watched Adoniram leave the new horse standing in the drive while he went to the house door. It was fastened. Then he went around to the shed. That door was seldom locked, even when the family was away. The thought how her father would be confronted by the cow flashed upon Nanny. There was a hysterical sob in her throat. Adoniram emerged from the shed and stood looking about in a dazed fashion. His lips moved; he was saying something, but they could not hear what it was. The hired man was peeping around a corner of the old barn, but nobody saw him.

Adoniram took the new horse by the bridle and led him across the yard to the new barn. Nanny and Sammy slunk close to their mother. The barn doors rolled back, and there stood Adoniram, with the long mild face of the Great Canadian farm horse looking over his shoulder.

Nanny kept behind her mother, but Sammy stepped suddenly forward, and stood in front of her.

Adoniram stared at the group. "What on airth you all down here for?" said he. "What's the matter over to the house?"

"We've come here to live, father," said Sammy. His shrill voice quavered out bravely.

"What"—Adoniram sniffed—"what is it smells like cookin'?" said he. He stepped forward and looked in the open door of the harness-room. Then he turned to his wife. His old bristling face was pale and frightened. "What on airth does this mean, mother?" he gasped.

"You come in here, father," said Sarah. She led the way into the harness-room and shut the door. "Now, father," said she, "you needn't be scared. I ain't crazy. There ain't nothin' to be upset over. But we've come here to live, an' we're goin' to live here. We've got jest as good a right here as new horses an' cows. The house wasn't fit for us to live in any longer, an' I made up my mind I wa'n't goin' to stay there. I've done my duty by you forty year, an' I'm goin' to do it now; but I'm goin' to live here. You've got to put in some windows and partitions; an' you'll have to buy some furniture."

"Why, mother!" the old man gasped.

"You'd better take your coat off an' get washed—there's the wash basin—an' then we'll have supper."

"Why, mother!"

Sammy went past the window, leading the new horse to the old barn. The old man saw him, and shook his head speechlessly. He tried to take off his coat, but his arms seemed to lack the power. His wife helped him. She poured some water into the tin basin, and put in a piece of soap. She got the comb and brush, and smoothed his thin gray hair after he had washed. Then she put the beans, hot bread, and tea on the table. Sammy came in, and the family drew up. Adoniram sat looking dazedly at his plate, and they waited.

"Ain't you goin' to ask a blessin', father?" said Sarah.

And the old man bent his head and mumbled.

All through the meal he stopped eating at intervals, and stared furtively at his wife; but he ate well. The home food tasted good to him, and his old frame was too sturdily healthy to be affected by his mind. But after supper he went out, and sat down on the step of the smaller door at the right of the barn, through which he had meant his Jerseys to pass in stately file, but which Sarah designed for her front house door, and he leaned his head on his hands.

After the supper dishes were cleared away and the milk-pans washed, Sarah went out to him. The twilight was deepening. There was a clear green glow in the sky. Before them stretched the smooth level of field; in the distance was a cluster of hay-stacks like the huts of a village; the air was very cool and calm and sweet. The landscape might have been an ideal one of peace.

Sarah bent over and touched her husband on one of his thin, sinewy shoulders. "Father!"

The old man's shoulders heaved: he was weeping.

"Why, don't do so, father," said Sarah.

"I'll—put up the—partitions, an' —everything you—want, mother."

Sarah put her apron up to her face; she was overcome by her own triumph.

Adoniram was like a fortress whose walls had no active resistance, and went down the instant the right besieging tools were used. "Why, mother," he said, hoarsely, "I hadn't no idee you was so set on't as all this comes to."

Considerations

After the earliest pioneer hardships were past, a few capable female writers enlivened the scene of early American fiction: Sarah Orne Jewett (1849–1909), Kate Chopin (1851–1904), and Mary E. Wilkins Freeman (1852–1930). Mary Freeman was born of Puritan Salem parentage and lived less than half her life away from her birthplace. She probably read little compared to many authors, and her output was relatively small. However, her work offers a memorable commentary on early American rural life.

For such an early fiction writer, Mrs. Freeman is surprisingly competent at some of the most highly regarded modern techniques. The sharp clear details of her characters are shown more through their own actions and dialogue than through description. The story progresses along a single line toward the denouement and close, each new facet of the daughter's frailty or the father's insensitivity forging another link in the chain of events that makes the outcome seem inevitable. Neither of the main characters is overdrawn: the father is more unnoticing than cruel, the mother more dutiful than spineless.

The accent in this story is on human relationships—especially the feelings of a woman in that time and place and what she thought was expected of her. The Sarah of this story is a woman of integrity who works hard for her family, and keeps her word even if her husband does not. Is she in any sense an early proponent of women's liberation? Does she question the superiority of the male? When she does revolt, what does she revolt against or for? The motivating force behind her action seems to be the desire for a better life for her daughter. Is such motivation simply a cliché today? Do people continue to believe that no sacrifice is too great to make for their children?

Perhaps the heroine's name, Sarah, was selected for its overtones of the Biblical Sarah—a woman who emerged from her shell late in life to give birth to a child who would continue the lineage leading to Christ. Generally, as Robert Graves put it, "man does, woman is." Occasionally, however, woman acts as well.

Does Sarah feel that she has won a battle when she changes the housing arrangements? Does she exhibit a sense of triumph? What do you think her and her husband's relationship will be like in the future?

The Pins

Guy de Maupassant

"Ah, my friend, women are such vicious animals!"

"Why do you say that?"

"Because they've played an abominable trick on me."

"On you?"

"Yes."

"Women, or a woman?"

"Two women."

"Both at once?"

"Yes."

"What was the trick?"

The two young men were sitting at one of the outside tables of a big café on the boulevard, drinking liqueurs mixed with water, those apéritifs that look like infusions made with all the different hues of a box of water colors.

They were about the same age: between twenty-five and thirty. One was blond, the other dark. They had the semi-elegance of outside brokers, of men who go to the stock market and drawing rooms, are frequent visitors everywhere, live everywhere, love everywhere. The dark-haired one said:

"I believe I've told you about my affair with a woman I met on the beach at Dieppe, the wife of a head clerk in a government office."

"Yes."

"Well, you know how it is . . . I already had a mistress in Paris, and I loved her very much. She was an old friend, a good friend—a habit, in short, and I was attached to her."

"And to your habit too?"

"Yes, to both. And she has a very likable husband. I'm fond of him too. He's a good, warmhearted man, a real friend! My life was centered around their house. But . . ."

"But what?"

"But they can't leave Paris, so I found myself womanless in Dieppe."

"Why did you go there?"

"For a change of air. You can't stay on the boulevard all the time."

"Yes, and then?"

"And then one day on the beach I met the woman I told you about."

"The head clerk's wife?"

"Yes. She was terribly bored. Her husband came only on Sundays, and he's horrible. I understand her very well. So we laughed and danced together."

"And everything else?"

"Yes, later. Anyway, we met, we liked each other, I told her so, she made me repeat it so she could understand better, and she didn't put up any obstacles when I decided to make our friendship closer."

"Did you love her?"

"Yes, a little; she's very nice."

"And the other one?"

"She was in Paris! For six weeks things went very well, and we were still on the best of terms with each other when we came back here. Do you know how to break off with a woman when she's given you no reason at all to complain of her?"

"Of course."

"How do you do it?"

"I drop her."

"But how do you go about dropping her?"

"I stop going to her house."

"But what if she comes to yours?"

"I . . . I'm not at home."

"What if she comes back?"

"I tell her I'm indisposed."

"What if she takes care of you?"

"I . . . play some sort of dirty trick on her."

"What if she accepts it?"

"I write anonymous letters to her husband to make sure he keeps a close watch on her on days when she expects to see me."

"That's serious! I have no resistance. I don't know how to break off. I collect women. There are some I see no more than once a year, others every ten months, others every three, others whenever they feel like going out to dinner in a cabaret. Those I've already spaced out don't bother me, but I often have trouble when I try to space out a new one."

"Go on with your story."

"Well, the clerk's wife was still full of fiery passion, and she'd given me no cause for complaint, as I've already said. Since her husband is in his office all day, she began coming to see me unexpectedly. Twice she almost ran into my habit."

"Good God!"

"Yes. So I put them both on a fixed schedule, to avoid confusion. Monday and Saturday for the old one, Tuesday, Thursday and Sunday for the new one."

"Why the preference for the new one?"

"She's younger."

"That only gave you two days a week to rest."

"That's enough for me."

"Congratulations!"

"But then the most ridiculous and annoying thing in the world happened to me. Things had been going perfectly for four months; my mind was completely at rest and I was really very happy when suddenly, last Monday, everything fell apart.

"I was waiting for my habit at her usual time, a quarter past one, smoking a good cigar.

"I was daydreaming, thoroughly satisfied with myself, when I realized that she was late. I was surprised because she'd always been very punctual. But I thought she'd only been delayed. Half an hour went by, then an hour, then an hour and a half, and I finally decided she wasn't coming at all for some reason or other: a bad headache, perhaps, or an unwelcome visitor. It's annoying to go on waiting uselessly like that, and it makes me very nervous. When I was sure she wasn't coming, I went out. Not knowing what else to do, I went to her house.

"I found her reading a novel.

" 'Well?' I said to her.

"She answered calmly, 'I couldn't come. I was busy.'

" 'Busy with what?'

"'With . . . various things.'

"'What kind of things?'

"'A boring visit.'

"I assumed she didn't want to tell me the real reason, and since she was still very calm I didn't worry about it. I expected to make up for lost time with the other one the next day.

"On Tuesday I was . . . excited, and very much in love, in anticipation, with the clerk's wife. I was surprised that she hadn't come earlier than the time we'd agreed on. I kept watching the clock, and following the minute hand impatiently.

"I saw it pass one-fifteen, then one-thirty, then two o'clock . . . I couldn't stay still, I walked back and forth in my bedroom. First I'd put my forehead against the window, then I'd put my ear to the door to listen for her coming up the stairs.

"Two-thirty, then three o'clock! I picked up my hat and hurried to her house. She was reading, my friend, reading a novel!

"'Well?' I said to her anxiously.

"She answered, as calmly as my habit, 'I couldn't come. I was busy.'

"'Busy with what?'

"'With . . . various things.'

"'What kind of things?'

"'A boring visit.'

"Naturally I assumed immediately that they both knew everything; but she seemed so placid, so serene, that I finally rejected my suspicion and convinced myself it was only a strange coincidence, because I couldn't imagine she could be so deceptive. After an hour of friendly talk—with at least twenty interruptions when her little girl came into the room—I had to leave. I was very annoyed.

"And the next day . . ."

"It was the same thing?"

"Yes . . . and the day after that. And it went on for three weeks like that, with no explanation, no clue to the reason for their odd behavior, although I suspected the secret behind it."

"They knew everything?"

"Of course. But how? I suffered all sorts of torments before I knew."

"How did you finally find out?"

"By letters. They both wrote to me on the same day, in the same words, to tell me they were through with me forever."

"And what else did they say?"

"I'll tell you . . . As you know, women always have an army of pins on them. I'm familiar with hairpins and I'm careful about them, I keep an eye out for them, but the others are much more treacherous, those damned little black-headed pins. They all look alike to us, fools that we are, but women can distinguish them very easily, as easily as we can distinguish a horse from a dog.

"It turned out that one day the clerk's wife had left one of those revealing little pins stuck in the curtain beside my mirror. My habit immediately spotted its little black head, no bigger than a flea. She pulled it out without saying anything and stuck one of her own pins in the same place. It was black too, but differently shaped.

"The next day, when the clerk's wife reached out her hand to take back her pin, she noticed the substitution and became suspicious. She stuck two pins in the curtain, with one crossed over the other.

"My habit answered this telegraphic signal with three black pinheads in a row.

"Once they'd begun this exchange, they went on communicating, without saying anything, just to keep track of each other. Then my habit became bolder: she wrapped a pin in a little piece of thin paper on which she'd written: 'General Delivery, Boulevard Malesherbes. C.D.'

"Then they wrote to each other. I was lost. As you can imagine, they didn't tell each other everything from the start. They went about it cautiously, with all sorts of ruses, and all the prudence that's required in such cases. But finally my habit had the courage to make an appointment with the clerk's wife.

"I don't know what they said to each other. I only know that I was the subject of their conversation. And there you are!"

"That's all?"

"Yes."

"They've both stopped seeing you?"

"No, I still see them as a friend; we haven't broken off completely."

"And have they seen each other again?"

"Yes; they've become close friends."

"Well, well . . . Doesn't that give you an idea?"

"No, what idea?"

"Don't be thickheaded: the idea of having them both stick their pins in your curtain at the same time."

Considerations

This story opens with the hyperbolic statement of an injured man: "women are such vicious animals." And with a bit of prompting from his friend, he then proceeds to support his claim. Is he upset because his pride has been hurt or because the sweet rewards of his own little game are no longer available? Considering how neatly and self-indulgently he had arranged his life, is he merely angry at the thought of having to go through all of the annoying preliminaries and tedious working out of understandings with new women?

We would never expect de Maupassant to tell us the usual story of a tricked man. As in so many other of his tightly constructed pieces, he proves to be a polished O. Henry, capping his comment on human frailties with an ending that is both surprising and ironic. (An acknowledged master of the French short story, de Maupassant wrote in two distinctly different veins. Besides stories ending with a twist, he wrote dark, brooding, dramatic tales full of ambiguity and obscurity.)

The final sentence lingers in our minds: "Don't be thickheaded: the idea of having them both stick their pins in your curtain at the same time." In what sense is it ironic? Is it intended to suggest what might actually happen in the future, or does it simply resemble the punch-line to a joke?

Pins play such a large part in this story that it is natural to wonder if they represent something more than metal objects. They could be symbols of female tidiness or vanity, of sharpness, of teasing, of anticipation, or of that which holds things together. Did de Maupassant intend them to call forth these associations? Or are they meant to be no more than what in reality they are—pins?

What view of male-female relationships is presented in this story? What is the man's attitude toward women? How does the author characterize the women in the story?

Enemies

Anton Chekov

About ten o'clock of a dark September evening the Zemstvo doctor Kirilov's only son, six-year-old Andrey, died of diphtheria. As the doctor's wife dropped on to her knees before the dead child's cot and the first paroxysm of despair took hold of her, the bell rang sharply in the hall.

When the diphtheria came all the servants were sent away from the house, that very morning. Kirilov himself went to the door, just as he was, in his shirt-sleeves with his waistcoat unbuttoned, without wiping his wet face or hands, which had been burnt with carbolic acid. It was dark in the hall, and of the person who entered could be distinguished only his middle height, a white scarf and a big, extraordinarily pale face, so pale that it seemed as though its appearance made the hall brighter . . . .

"Is the doctor in?" the visitor asked abruptly.

"I'm at home," answered Kirilov. "What do you want?"

"Oh, you're the doctor? I'm so glad!" The visitor was overjoyed and began to seek for the doctor's hand in the darkness. He found it and squeezed it hard in his own. "I'm very . . . very glad! We were introduced. . . . I am Aboguin . . . had the pleasure of meeting you this summer at Mr. Gnouchev's. I am very glad to have found you at home. . . . For God's sake, don't say you won't come with me immediately. . . . My wife has been taken dangerously ill . . . I have the carriage with me. . . ."

From the visitor's voice and movements it was evident that he had been in a state of violent agitation. Exactly as though he had been frightened by a fire or a mad dog, he could hardly restrain his hurried breathing, and he spoke quickly in a trembling voice. In his speech there sounded a note of real sincerity, of childish fright. Like all men who are frightened and dazed, he spoke in short, abrupt phrases and uttered many superfluous, quite unnecessary, words.

"I was afraid I shouldn't find you at home," he continued. "While I was coming to you I suffered terribly. . . . Dress yourself and let us go, for God's sake. . . . It happened like this, Papchinsky came to me—Alexander Siemionovich, you know him. . . . We were chatting. . . . Then we sat down to tea. Suddenly my wife cries out, presses her hands to her heart, and falls back in her chair. We carried her off to her bed and . . . and I rubbed her forehead with salvolatile, and splashed her with water. . . . She lies like a corpse. . . . I'm afraid that her heart's failed. . . . Let us go. . . . Her father too died of heart-failure."

Kirilov listened in silence as though

he did not understand the Russian language.

When Aboguin once more mentioned Papchinsky and his wife's father, and once more began to seek for the doctor's hand in the darkness, the doctor shook his head and said, drawling each word listlessly:

"Excuse me, but I can't go. . . . Five minutes ago my . . . son died."

"Is that true?" Aboguin whispered, stepping back. "My God, what an awful moment to come! It's a terribly fated day . . . terribly! What a coincidence . . . and it might have been on purpose!"

Aboguin took hold of the door handle and dropped his head in meditation. Evidently he was hesitating, not knowing whether to go away, or to ask the doctor once more.

"Listen," he said eagerly, seizing Kirilov by the sleeve. "I fully understand your state! God knows I'm ashamed to try to hold your attention at such a moment, but what can I do? Think yourself—who can I go to? There isn't another doctor here besides you. For heaven's sake come. I'm not asking for myself. It's not I that's ill!"

Silence began. Kirilov turned his back to Aboguin, stood still for a while and slowly went out of the hall into the drawing-room. To judge by his uncertain, machine-like movement, and by the attentiveness with which he arranged the hanging shade on the unlighted lamp in the drawing-room and consulted a thick book which lay on the table—at such a moment he had neither purpose nor